"The sexiest series
I've ever read."
—Carly Phillips

USA TODAY BESTSELLING
AUTHOR OF SLOW RIDE

ERIN
McCARTHY

D0058914

JACKED
A FAST TRACK NOVEL
UP

**BERKLEY
SENSATION**

$7.99 U.S.
$8.99 CAN

ISBN 978-0-425-25080-8

5 0 7 9 9

S ▷ EAN

continued . . .

FLAT-OUT SEXY

"Readers won't be able to resist McCarthy's sweetly sexy and sentimental tale of true love at the track."   —*Booklist*

"A steamy romance . . . Fast-paced and red-hot."
—*Publishers Weekly*

"This is one smart, sassy, steamy, and flat-out sexy read . . . A fast and fun ride."   —*RT Book Reviews*

"A new series that sizzles both on and off the field."
—*Romance Junkies*

"The action starts on page one and doesn't stop."
—*Romance Reviews Today*

"A runaway winner!"   —*Fallen Angel Reviews*

PRAISE FOR ERIN McCARTHY'S
OTHER NOVELS
HEIRESS FOR HIRE

"*Heiress for Hire* is a must read."   —*Romance Junkies*

"Characters you will care about, a story that will make you laugh and cry, and a book you won't soon forget."
—*The Romance Reader* (5 hearts)

"An alluring tale."   —*A Romance Review* (5 roses)

"An enjoyable story about finding love in unexpected places, don't miss *Heiress for Hire*."
—*Romance Reviews Today*

"Priceless!"   —*RT Book Reviews* (4½ stars, Top Pick)

A DATE WITH THE OTHER SIDE

JACKED UP

UP

erin mccarthy

BERKLEY SENSATION, NEW YORK

THE BERKLEY PUBLISHING GROUP
Published by the Penguin Group
Penguin Group (USA) Inc.
375 Hudson Street, New York, New York 10014, USA

Penguin Group (Canada), 90 Eglinton Avenue East, Suite 700, Toronto, Ontario M4P 2Y3, Canada
(a division of Pearson Penguin Canada Inc.) • Penguin Books Ltd., 80 Strand, London WC2R 0RL,
England • Penguin Group Ireland, 25 St. Stephen's Green, Dublin 2, Ireland (a division of Penguin
Books Ltd.) • Penguin Group (Australia), 250 Camberwell Road, Camberwell, Victoria 3124, Australia
(a division of Pearson Australia Group Pty. Ltd.) • Penguin Books India Pvt. Ltd., 11 Community
Centre, Panchsheel Park, New Delhi—110 017, India • Penguin Group (NZ), 67 Apollo Drive,
Rosedale, Auckland 0632, New Zealand (a division of Pearson New Zealand Ltd.) • Penguin Books
(South Africa) (Pty.) Ltd., 24 Sturdee Avenue, Rosebank, Johannesburg 2196, South Africa

Penguin Books Ltd., Registered Offices: 80 Strand, London WC2R 0RL, England

This is a work of fiction. Names, characters, places, and incidents either are the product of the author's
imagination or are used fictitiously, and any resemblance to actual persons, living or dead, business
establishments, events, or locales is entirely coincidental. The publisher does not have any control over
and does not assume any responsibility for author or third-party websites or their content.

JACKED UP

A Berkley Sensation Book / published by arrangement with the author

PUBLISHING HISTORY
Berkley Sensation mass-market edition / June 2012

Copyright © 2012 by Erin McCarthy.
Excerpt from teaser by Erin McCarthy copyright © 2012 by Erin McCarthy.
Cover art by Craig White.
Cover design by Rita Frangie.
Interior text design by Kristin del Rosario.

ISBN: 978-0-425-25080-8

BERKLEY SENSATION®
Berkley Sensation Books are published by The Berkley Publishing Group,
a division of Penguin Group (USA) Inc.,
375 Hudson Street, New York, New York 10014.
BERKLEY SENSATION® is a registered trademark of Penguin Group (USA) Inc.
The "B" design is a trademark of Penguin Group (USA) Inc.

PRINTED IN THE UNITED STATES OF AMERICA

10 9 8 7 6 5 4 3 2 1

ALWAYS LEARNING   **PEARSON**

JACKED UP

CHAPTER
ONE

NOLAN Ford wasn't listening to Eve Monroe as she chewed him out. It wasn't that he was trying to be disrespectful, but Lord, the woman could start an argument in an empty house.

Besides, the top button on her blouse was straining, and each time she lifted her arm and waved it around, he held his breath, waiting for it to pop. He'd had something of a crush on Eve for years, always aware when she was around the track or the garage, stomping around in her heels and severe office clothes. She thought no one noticed that she was a woman, and seemed to work damn hard to make sure it stayed that way, but Nolan had always noticed.

Eve was hot. Full on, smokin', jalapeño pepper hot. From that lustrous deep brown hair with a hint of red, to her gold-flecked eyes, down past an amazing chest, to slim legs and a perky behind, she was all that and a bag of chips, in his opinion.

"I mean, seriously, I don't care what kind of underwear you wear, just wear some!" she said, making a sound of frustration. "I mean really, let's show a little decorum."

Nolan fought the urge to grin. She looked so serious when talking about his underwear. Or lack thereof. But he knew if he so much as curved the corner of his mouth up, her head would blow off her shoulders. Eve was not happy about the little incident during the race the other day. "Well, ma'am, it's hot in those crew suits. Some particular parts need air circulation."

She drew in a deep breath, obviously struggling for control, but it only made her blouse pull tighter. Nolan stared in fascination as the button slipped halfway through the hole. If that thing gave, he was going to see her bra. He wasn't sure he was capable of not getting a hard-on if that happened.

And since he wasn't wearing any underwear today either, she would probably notice.

"Stick a bag of frozen peas in your pants. Just wear them." Her hands went up to rake her hair back off her head. "Don't pretend you don't understand that this is a big deal. You have been in the business for years. Sponsors want a friendly, wholesome image for the sport their name is attached to. As do the team owners, and the powers that be in stock car racing. When a jackman goes over the wall and rips his suit, the whole world doesn't need to see his back end."

Nolan had to agree with that. He certainly hadn't intended to tear the seat of his pants going over the wall into pit road when Evan's car had stopped for a tire change. Or for his ass to end up on YouTube. But it had. So what were you going to do about it? That was his philosophy in life—don't sweat the small stuff. Or bare butts.

"I do understand, Eve. I'm proud to be a member of Evan's crew and I take my job seriously. It was an accident. I believe they even have a term for that—wardrobe malfunction."

She started talking. He stopped listening again. As her arms waved, the button gave up the good fight and parted ways with the hole it had been in. Her blouse sprang apart. He was assaulted with the sight of lots of pale creamy flesh bursting out of a hot pink bra, the cleavage high and perky. It was a gorgeous surprise, all that breast she'd been hiding under her crisp tailored shirts.

But then that was what he thought of Eve in general—that she was hiding a whole lot of woman under the attitude. It was a thought that had intrigued him more than once as he'd seen her typing furiously on her smartphone, clipboard tucked under her arm. What would it be like to see every inch of her naked body, to get her to totally come undone . . .

"That's just an excuse," she was saying. "Wardrobe malfunction. Give me a break. Are you even listening to me?"

Nolan nodded. "They do happen, you know," he drawled, really savoring the moment of triumph. Forcing his eyes off her chest, he let his grin win out. "You seem to have one happening right now."

He pointed to her blouse, wide open and catching the breeze.

She glanced down and turned as pink as the lace bra she was wearing.

"I think they call that tit for tat," he told her.

Her eyes narrowed.

A wise man would have run.

But he was more the type of guy to play chicken with a rattlesnake, so he stood his ground.

Her hand covered her cleavage. "That better have just happened, or I will erase your birth certificate."

Why did he have the feeling that was no idle threat? "Didn't you feel the breeze?" he asked. "At least I knew my pants ripped. There just wasn't anything I could do about it."

Eve buttoned her shirt again. "Don't be a smart-ass. I'm not in the mood."

He wondered what she was in the mood for. He could pretty much guarantee it wouldn't be him asking her out or, even better, taking a kiss. Which he found himself really wanting to do.

"The point is, shit happens and you can't do anything about it. No point in getting all worked up." He chanced a glance back down at her blouse. "That's not going to hold, you know. Your hole is compromised." Which sounded kinda dirty now that he thought about it.

God, his mind was just looping around sex today. It had been a while, and he had always been intrigued by Eve. She was just so uptight. There had to be moments in her life when she totally let go, and he had a feeling that would be the bedroom. Or maybe that was just wishful thinking.

"Excuse me? Are you trying to piss me off?" Her voice rose so high that several other heads in the garage swung their way, clearly curious.

"Well, no, not really." Nolan hooked his thumbs in the pockets of his jeans and gave her a smile. "I was hoping you'd reward my gallantry. There are some men who would have let you walk around with your assets on display and not said a word."

She fussed with the button, which was slipping again. "I'm going to reward you with a can of whoop ass, is what I'm going to do."

Nolan fought the urge to laugh. He tried, he really did. But she looked so damned indignant, her bra peeking out from behind her hand, her words so damned ridiculous, that he couldn't help it. A laugh escaped. He tried to cover it with a cough, but she wasn't buying it.

He didn't mean to laugh. It wasn't nice to laugh when someone was clearly upset, but if she only knew how stinking adorable she was, she'd see where he was coming from.

It was clear she didn't feel adorable when she clenched her fist tighter around her shirt. "Do you think that's funny? Do you think it will be funny when I fire you?"

If he thought she had that kind of authority, Nolan might be a little concerned. But as PR rep, she didn't. "I don't think there's a mandatory underwear clause in my contract. But we can check it together if you like. Over a beer would be great."

He'd like to see her on a bar stool, next to him, away from all the prying eyes of the garage. She wouldn't go for it, he knew that. She was out of his league with a capital L, but it didn't hurt to try.

Though given the expression spreading across her face, it just *might* hurt.

Eve couldn't believe he was serious. Was he really just standing there smiling at her, all sexy and nonchalant, mocking her concerns? She hated when men laughed at her. Despised, loathed, detested it. It was a throwback to growing up with two brothers who had made it their life's mission to annoy her. Well, primarily Evan. Elec had been easier to deal with, but nonetheless, she hated being teased. Really, really hated it.

She was trying to do her job, something no one ever seemed to respect.

Clearly Mr. Naked Butt was yet another one of those.

"How about I bust a beer bottle over your head?" Okay, so that wasn't the most professional thing in the world to say, but if she didn't release some of her rage, her head was liable to explode right off her shoulders.

"I don't think I would enjoy that."

His casual attitude made her nuts. Why wasn't he getting upset? Why wasn't he embarrassed? Pulling out her phone, she punched a few buttons. "Look at this."

Just seeing the video still clip on her phone made her blood pressure increase. She hated her job, she really did. Every day it was like navigating a mine field of morons. It was an industry of ego and big money, an intricate web of drivers, team owners, and sponsors. No one understood or cared how much pressure she was under being responsible for her brothers' public images.

Nolan moved in alongside of her and dutifully stared down at the screen with her. She was tempted to give commentary as the video started, but he had been there and the announcer at the race could be heard loud and clear.

"So Evan Monroe has chosen to pit, which we expected. After that last caution flag came up, we heard him on the radio with his crew chief."

There was a view of Evan's car along with a half-dozen others pulling into pit road. It was all normal race day activity. It was lap 275 out of 500, and no one was anxious yet, they were all just strategizing and jockeying for position on the track. The camera zoomed in on Evan's car.

"It looked to me like there was a bit of a drag on Evan Monroe's car, and we thought we heard mention of debris."

That's when it all went horribly wrong. Eve fought the urge to wince as Evan's crew went over the wall.

"But we see his crew going out now for the usual fuel and tire change. Doesn't seem to be any concern about debris now, whatever it was."

Then the announcer couldn't swallow his guffaw. "Woo-hoo, good grief, did you see that?"

Yes, she had seen it. It was right in front of her, the camera zooming in on it. As Nolan went over the wall, his jumpsuit ripped at the seat. He didn't even pause but went straight to the front right tire and started pumping his jack. Eve cleared her throat at the sudden realization of just how dirty that descriptive sounded.

The motion of working the jack to lift the car had Nolan bending over. Which had his butt clearly displayed through the tear in his pants.

"It looks like Evan Monroe's jackman has had a bit of an accident with his uniform out there. I commend the man for doing his job under adverse conditions but I think I see a penalty in his future. That's not exactly a family-friendly view."

No, it wasn't a family-friendly view to say the least. It was a whole lot of tight, sexy butt, the muscles in his thigh and rear flexing as he worked the jack. Eve swallowed hard, suddenly aware of how perilously close to her Nolan Ford was while his buns moved around on her phone.

"See?" she told him, needing to exert a bit of control in the situation. Unfortunately, her voice wavered just enough to make her cheeks flush with heat. She hoped he was looking at her phone and not her.

"I see. I was there, you know. Like I said, I felt the breeze. But what was I supposed to do?"

There was the rub. She wasn't really sure what he was supposed to have done at that particular moment. But she just knew that staring at his naked backside wasn't providing her with any answers.

"If I had stopped to duct-tape my pants together, we either would have lost a huge amount of time or Evan would have ended up with no tires on that pit stop. That would have been disastrous. You know that."

She did know that. One or two seconds slower in a pit stop could alter the course of the race. Not taking fresh tires could drop you back twenty spots. He was right and she knew it, but that didn't make the result any less horrible. It was a lose-lose situation that she wasn't sure how to fix and it was giving her a headache.

Finally she snapped, "You're supposed to wear underwear."

"They're constricting."

He was leaning even closer to her now, and Eve was desperate to shift away from him, but determined not to give him the satisfaction of thinking she was nervous or had backed down. She wasn't sure why she was having the reaction she was other than the fact that it had been approximately one thousand years since she had last had sex and there was something casually hot about Nolan Ford.

Plus there was no denying he looked good not wearing underwear. At least from the back. She nudged him with her elbow, but kept her view on her phone.

"Oh, so you have that much to constrict?" Sarcasm was her best defense against the discomfort she was feeling. It was a trick she had perfected throughout her life.

He gave a low, sexy laugh. "Who wants to know?"

There was no way to really answer that without it sounding like she was actually interested in the size of his penis. Damn. She'd walked right into that one, which was annoying as hell.

"No one."

"I think maybe you do or you wouldn't have asked."

She wanted to sigh. She wanted to rub her temples. She wanted to run away to a remote Pacific island where demigods would worship her.

Evan always insisted she created her own stress. But how could she have created a scenario where one of his crew members flashed his butt on camera? She had the ability to complicate things, she'd own that, but this was not her doing.

The video had stopped playing so she closed the screen and put her phone in her pocket, moving away from him. "Just. Wear. Underwear."

"That's fun to wear?" He grinned at her.

Eve blinked, debating how much jail time she would get for reaching over and ripping his face off.

"No sarcastic response? I'm disappointed."

He had no idea the control she was exerting at the moment. "I'm afraid if I open my mouth I'll start screaming and never stop."

Whatever his response would have been was prevented by her brother's car chief yelling from Evan's car, "Hey Eve, you done hollering at him? Clock's a-tickin' while you're a-bitchin'."

That pretty much summed up the utter lack of respect she got. She wasn't talking to Nolan for shits and grins. She was doing her job. Did no one understand that?

She didn't bother to answer Jim.

"Pay your fine on time," she told Nolan in a cold voice, turning on her heel, hand still holding together her gaping blouse. She felt . . . defeated. Tired. Overwhelmed.

In the past eighteen months she had navigated two pregnancy scandals her brothers had been embroiled in, the loss of a major corporate sponsor, Evan's spontaneous marriage and breakup and then reunion with the first female driver to compete in the Cup series, and being fired and rehired herself.

She just wanted to be done.

But there was no done.

Because what was she going to do?

She ground to a halt when Nolan unexpectedly touched her elbow. Whirling around, she demanded, "What?"

"Hey, sorry for the headache this is causing. It truly was an accident. Let me buy you a cold one to make it up to you."

So he could irritate her some more? "No thank you."

"Don't want to be seen with a lowly jackman, huh?" But he didn't look like he believed that. In fact, he looked like he was amused by her.

Eve didn't know what to do with that. No one found her funny. No one found her company enjoyable even. It was unnerving. "I don't want to be seen with a jackass. 'Ass' being the operative word."

"I double dog dare ya," he said, his eyebrows lifting as he stood there looking a whole lot of sexy. "Just one beer."

Damn it. She could never turn down a double dog dare. Even though it always got her in trouble. Three broken bones. Two speeding tickets. A black eye. And a tattoo on her inner thigh she'd just as soon forget.

But she couldn't resist and she knew it. Someone threw down the gauntlet and she had to pick it up.

"I can't tonight, I have plans with my sisters-in-law."

"Tomorrow then."

That would be better. She'd have time to throw away this blouse and steel herself against his annoying sexiness. "Fine. You're buying."

"Of course I am. That's the whole point. To apologize for the stress I've caused you."

He sounded sincere. He looked sincere. Eve was suspicious. Most men would have walked away from her with their hands tossed up, not invited her for a drink. She didn't really understand Nolan's reaction. Flummoxed, she wasn't sure what to say.

Jim saved her. "Ford, get over here. Seriously, enough arguing with the battle-ax."

Battle-ax. Nice. That was something every woman wanted to be called.

"I'm coming, Jim. Give me two minutes or less." Nolan quieted his voice and leaned closer. "What's your number? I'll give you a call and we'll make some plans without Jim breathing down our necks."

Eve never gave out her number. But she gave it to Nolan. Though she found herself pulling her phone out of her pocket and fiddling with it, unable to look him in the eye. He made her feel like . . . a woman.

Not a lot of men did that, sadly enough.

His eyes were that impossible green that made you think he was wearing contact lenses. But there were no telltale lines or floating lenses, just mossy green eyes that were raking over her when she found the courage to look up.

She relaxed her arm, abandoning the death hold on her gaping shirt.

His phone was at his ear and they were locked in a strange, sensual stare down that she didn't understand.

Eve's phone vibrated in her hand and she started at the unexpected sensation, even though he was obviously calling her.

"I take it this is you?" she asked, grateful for the interruption of a weird moment. She didn't do weird moments.

He nodded. "Now you have my number, too."

For what? She felt like asking, but she didn't. "Great. Let's contact the media with that important piece of news."

She expected him to roll his eyes or zing her with a comeback.

He just said, "That's your department, not mine. Talk to you later, sweetness."

Then with one last glance at her chest, he went back to work.

Eve went back to being unnerved.

And as she left the garage, she found herself watching that video of his tight butt yet one more time.

*   *   *

"YOU got any skin left after a verbal lashing from the battle-ax?" Jim asked Nolan as he went back to Evan's car, up on blocks.

"I feel pretty intact." In fact, he felt great. Intrigued. Aroused. Excited about seeing Eve the next night. "Don't see why you call her a battle-ax. She's harmless."

It was fairly obvious to him that Eve's whole problem was poor stress management. She had a tough job and she bottled up all that tension instead of releasing it. But she was all bark and no bite.

"As harmless as a shark is to a minnow."

Nolan studied the calluses on his hands, thick and yellow from hundreds of hours spent training in the gym and at the track. He wasn't about to let Jim dissuade him based on a whole lot of nothing. He suspected no one on this team really knew Eve particularly well. "Actually, I don't think a minnow would be in any danger from a shark. They're too small for a shark to bother with them. And they're in freshwater, not the ocean."

"Okay, Professor Smart-Ass. Still don't change the fact that the woman is a nag. No wonder she doesn't date. No man can get a word in edgewise."

Nolan shrugged. "She apparently does in fact date. I just asked her out and she said yes."

Jim and three of his other coworkers stopped their work on Evan's car entirely and just gawked at him. Nolan grinned. "What? You all have known me to ask women out before. Don't look so shocked."

"You date women who bake cookies and shit," Jim told him. "Not hard-asses like Eve."

Except that Nolan had a feeling she was anything but. There was no telling if she baked cookies or not. Which was why he had asked her out. "I'm just curious about her, that's all."

Rhett, who was Evan's gas man, and just happened to

be Nolan's kid brother, whistled low. "Make sure you wear a protective cup, bro, that's all I'm saying. She's a ball buster."

"And your bosses' sister. And in a way a coworker. Think that one through long and hard. They always say, don't shit where you eat," Jim said, shaking his head as he cracked his hairy knuckles.

That expression was one of Nolan's personal pet peeves. "I hate that saying. Shitting and dating are not the same thing. It's associating relationships with something negative and I don't dig that."

Jim was a big guy with a cute wife, a pack of kids, and the unwavering conviction that he was always right. "It's going to be like falling into a barrel of titties and coming up sucking your own thumb. Bad luck, trust me."

The image of Eve's breasts bursting out of her blouse popped into Nolan's head, a delicious carrot dangling in front of him. "Oh, I'm willing to chance it."

Sometimes you just had to play out the fantasy and see where it went.

Playing chicken with a rattlesnake. Yep. That was him.

CHAPTER
TWO

"WHY do you keep fussing with your blouse?"

Eve dropped her hand in frustration and looked at her sister-in-law Tamara, who was giving her a curious look. "Damn. I'm doing it without thinking because earlier today my button popped."

She hadn't had time to go home and change before meeting Tamara and Evan's wife, Kendall, at a Mexican restaurant that served margaritas the size of a toilet bowl. When she had walked in, Eve had been surprised to see Suzanne Jefferson, Imogen Wilson, and Tuesday Jones there as well. It had apparently blossomed into a full-on girls' night out. Of five women who were either married or engaged.

Leaving her the token single woman.

Fabulous.

"The best solution for that is to just leave it unbuttoned,"

Suzanne told her with a wink. She took a loud suck on her straw. "God, this tastes good. I realize there's no alcohol in it because I'm nursing still, but just the idea that I'm having what could potentially be an adult drink makes me very happy."

"How's the baby?" Kendall asked her.

Eve stared at her own margarita, not nearly so thrilled with it. She could have a drink any night she wanted. She was single, childless, able to spend all her free time exactly as she wanted. Which usually meant going for a run, eating a premade salad, and falling asleep on the couch watching *Deadliest Catch*, her laptop clutched against her chest as she worked until the last second before her eyes slipped shut.

She was lonely. Stressed. Bored. As she watched her brothers settle down into family life, she was even a bit envious.

Pumping her straw up and down vigorously in her drink, she fought the urge to sigh. It wasn't like she had a *bad* life. It was just getting old, damn quick.

"The baby is amazing. I love that little squirt more than I can describe. But he's seven weeks old, and this is the first time I have left him for more than five minutes, so I actually don't want to talk about him. He's with my husband, and if I think about that too hard, I might burst into tears. Ryder is a great father but he hasn't spent any time alone with Track. I'm always there."

"It's a challenging task parenting a child when your husband is gone every week for several days." Imogen pushed her glasses up her nose, her dark brown hair sleek and shiny in a way that Eve had to admit she envied. "That's something we all have had or will have to contend with. Well, except Eve."

Except Eve. There it was. Not that she could deny it. "No, I think I would rather gouge my own eyes out than marry a driver. No offense to any of you, but I've spent my whole life around the track, and I don't want to marry it."

"I don't know. I think I've married the man, not the sport," Suzanne said.

"But can you really separate the two?" Tamara asked. "I swore I'd never marry a driver again after I lost Pete. And it was damn hard raising kids alone after he died, but I'll tell you, it wasn't easy when he was alive either. He was barely home."

"But isn't Eve essentially married to the track herself? She is just as immersed in the sport as us, if not more so." Imogen lifted her drink up, the giant glass comical set against her elegant face. "I would almost think it would be difficult at this point to find someone outside of racing, because one, you spend all your time both personal and professional, involved in racing. And two, who could possibly understand your unique lifestyle if they're not involved in the sport?"

That was a nice verbal baseball bat to the head. Eve shoved her drink away, stomach suddenly sour. "Well, that's good to know. If I don't marry a driver and no one else will have me, that leaves me, what—sponsors, owners, PR reps, and crew members to choose from? Most of whom are married? So my dating pool is the size of a raindrop."

"I didn't say no one else would have you. What I was saying is that dating for women in stock car racing is unique. Rather like dating is for women in law enforcement."

"I'm not a cop. I'm just a PR rep. I think the real problem when it comes to dating is that I have no free time." Actually, Eve had no idea what the problem was. She just knew that she hadn't been on a date since the previous winter and hadn't had sex in way longer than should be legal.

"Eve does work an awful lot," Tamara said. "Which is why I worry. I don't want her most meaningful relationship to be with her cell phone."

If her brother's wife only knew how accurate that was. Her phone was currently sitting on the tabletop instead of tucked away in her purse because she didn't want to miss any important calls. "My phone is kind of a needy boyfriend, I have to admit."

"Balance can be hard," Tuesday said. "I have the opposite problem. I have flexible hours and Diesel works at home on his own schedule so lately, since I moved in with him, neither one of us have been particularly productive."

"More like reproductive," Suzanne said with a grin.

"No! No reproduction. Not yet. We're not ready to be parents. At least I'm not." Tuesday raised her diet soft drink in a toast. "Here's to balance. Happiness. Orgasms."

"Amen, sister!" Suzanne lifted her virgin margarita.

Eve did the same with her Cuervo Gold. She would definitely drink to orgasms. And anything that turned the topic of conversation away from her lack of a social life and slim pickings for a potential mate.

As all glasses went up, Eve's phone rang. She glanced at the screen. It was Nolan Ford. She hesitated. Part of her wanted to answer it. Part of her wanted to stay as far away from Nolan as she possibly could. He made her far too aware of her own body, and that wasn't good when she was talking about a member of her brother's pit crew.

"Who is that?" Suzanne asked. "Is it business or social?"

It figured that someone would call her out on it. "Um, it's business, for the most part. There's a jackman who had a little uniform issue."

"Oh, my God, that was awesomely hilarious," Tuesday said. "Nolan Ford's fine behind just splayed out while he pumped that jack . . . those are the days I live for in blogging."

"Yeah, same here. Not." Eve rolled her eyes. "I had to go tell him to wear underwear. This is the insanity of my job. I tell grown men they need to wear underwear."

"Have you seen his arms? And we all saw his ass." Tuesday said. "He is in top shape. That job demands it. He lifts a three-ton car. I say let him skip the underwear if he wants to."

Eve crossed her legs. "And I say I can't imagine your fiancé would appreciate that."

"It's called appreciation of the male form. I have no intention of touching, but I can look. You, on the other hand, you can touch."

"I don't want to touch Nolan Ford." Which was such a lie she was shocked her nose didn't leap out two feet.

"Who actually called you?" Suzanne asked, leaning over to try to see Eve's phone.

"Do you have an interest in Nolan?" Kendall asked.

They were coming at her like a swarm of bees, question after uncomfortable question. Eve felt herself panicking, felt anger surging. They meant well, she knew that, but she didn't have any answers.

"I don't know! All I know is that my job sucks and I'm pissed off all the time and I haven't had sex in a long time." Eve took a gulp of her drink, her mouth suddenly hot. "And then Nolan splits his pants and I yell at him and instead of giving me attitude, he says he'll buy me a beer. I mean, what is that? He double dog dared me so of course I had to say yes. I couldn't turn down a dare. But why do I feel like I have a fever around him?"

There was a moment of stunned silence as they all gawked at her around the table.

"Oh, sweetie," Tamara said.

Which made Eve feel like a complete loser. She wasn't asking for sympathy. She wanted explanations.

Tuesday just nodded. "From one control freak to another, hey, I get it. But maybe you shouldn't analyze your reaction. Maybe you should take him up on his offer of a beer."

"I agree," Suzanne said, twisting her blond hair into a bun, her diamond ring flashing in the light. "Sometimes the best things come out of spontaneity. Like my baby." She laughed.

"I don't know how to be spontaneous." Eve was pretty sure it would actually hurt.

"Well, if that was Nolan, call him back. That's an excellent place to start," Imogen said.

"To what purpose?"

"To letting go of the irritation and stress this whole incident has caused you. Sitting next to Nolan and acknowledging that it was just an accident and you need to let it go," Tamara said.

Eve studied her sister-in-law's face. She liked Tamara. There was something calm and maternal about her, and Eve admired the relationship she had with Elec. There was no judgment on her face. Just concern and encouragement. It all sounded pretty damn rational.

"I need to let a lot of things go, don't I?" She did. She was a bundle of stress. She was tired. Lonely. Approaching her birthday in a couple of weeks.

Letting go of some control and some stress wouldn't be easy, but would probably be smart.

"Probably. But that's up to you."

Her phone rang again. It was Nolan. Again. "It's him."

No one said a word. If they had egged her on to answer it, she probably wouldn't have. But since they stayed silent, waiting for her to decide, she actually found herself picking up the phone.

"Hello?"

"Hey! It's Nolan. How are you?"

"Good, thanks. How are you?" She cleared her throat, suddenly aware of the desire to sound sexy. Good Lord. It was ridiculous.

"I'm glad you picked up. I had called you a few minutes ago suggesting the steakhouse to meet up tomorrow, but I changed my mind. Oktoberfest starts tomorrow and I was thinking we could go there instead. Should be fun."

"To a festival?" Eve frowned. That sounded like a date. Like a real, honest to God, we're a man and woman out on a date thing. Not just a let's have a beer and forget we saw each other's body parts. Not just a simple dare. She was about to say no, but then she saw all those expectant faces staring at her. They all looked so hopeful, five women poised to be happy for her.

There was something really amazing about having these women in her life. She hadn't always had a ton of girlfriends, so having friends who cared about her, it felt good. They would want her to go. Be spontaneous.

"Sure. Cool."

Now she'd done it. She had said yes. She was already regretting it as Suzanne fist pumped in the air in celebration.

"Great. If you text me your address, I'll pick you up around seven."

Oh, no. There would be no picking up. Nope. Not happening. "I have to work until about six fifty-nine so I'll just meet you there. Just tell me where."

"Okay. I'll text you the details and I'll see you then. Have a good night, Eve."

"Great. Thanks. Bye." She hung up the phone, cheeks suddenly burning, anxiety levels increasing. "I feel like I'm twelve when I talk to him. God, this is so bad."

"Where are you going?" Kendall asked.

"To Oktoberfest. I hate those things. All those people walking around. Fried food. Why would I agree to do that?"

There was laughter. And knowing glances. But no one answered.

Because they all knew she knew the answer to her own question.

Damn it. She had a crush on Nolan Ford and his tight butt.

NOLAN eyed the parking lot and the time on his cell phone. He was fairly certain Eve was going to stand him up. He was surprised she had even agreed to go for a beer with him. She only had because he'd dared her to do it. He had figured asking her to hang out with him at Oktoberfest would be met with a big old hell no. But she had said yes.

He wasn't even sure why he had asked her. But she was a nut he'd like to crack. His mama had always said out of the nine kids she'd had, he was the most curious, and it was possible it had gotten him into trouble a time or two.

Tonight it was going to get him stood up.

But if Eve didn't show, he'd go drink a stein of beer, eat a bratwurst, and call it a night. Nothing ventured, nothing gained.

Only it seemed he wasn't being stood up. He smiled when he saw Eve moving across the parking lot toward him. Not only was she on time to the minute, she was dressed in a way he never could have imagined, but definitely appreciated. In the few years he'd been around the track, he had only ever seen Eve wearing business outfits—suits, blouses, fancy shoes. For some reason, he had kind of thought she'd be wearing a more casual version of uptight. But she was dressed in jeans and running shoes, with a hooded sweatshirt that was practically swallowing her.

She looked more approachable this way. Huggable.

"This place was impossible to find," she said by way of greeting. "Whoever is on their PR team needs to put better signage off the interstate."

Yeah, she wasn't wearing a suit, but she might as well be. She was scanning the ticket booth. "They're going to lose their major sponsors for next year's event if they don't do a better job of pimping out the festival."

Nolan shook his head, amused. "We found it. That's all you need to be concerned about."

She frowned. "It was just an observation, not a concern."

"It was you coming to the fair in work mode, and that's no good. You need to shut that off now and again."

"You don't know anything about what I need."

He knew he'd irritated her, but hell, it needed to be pointed out. She was a workaholic. But he wasn't about to let her stomp off angry with him. He intended to have fun. "I know you need a bratwurst."

"Excuse me?"

Now she just looked outraged and Nolan thought she was adorable. He was going to have trouble resisting the urge to kiss her because she had just about the best lips he'd ever seen. They were plump and pink and shiny. Eve didn't wear a lot of makeup and he liked that.

Mostly what she wore were expressions of annoyance.

"You know, like a hot dog. Dinner. With a beer. It's Oktoberfest."

The look she gave him was suspicious, like she was trying to find the loophole in what he was saying, the trick. "I want a funnel cake," she said with great dignity, her hands in the pockets of her sweatshirt.

"Well, let's go then."

When they approached the ticket booth, he said, "Two please."

And Eve corrected him. "Just one. I'm paying for my own."

He turned from the ticket clerk to Eve. "Why? I invited you. It's my treat."

"But then I'm indebted to you." She was pulling her wallet out of her bag, which was across her body like a satchel.

"For a five-dollar ticket? That doesn't make any sense. It's not like I offered you a kidney."

"But then we have to do everything your way and on your schedule."

Nolan went ahead and paid for the two tickets. "Two," he told the clerk firmly. Then he told Eve, "You don't have a very high opinion of me. I think I would appreciate it if you got to know me a little bit before you put that kind of attitude on me." He wasn't annoyed. He just found it a little sad that such a small gesture had her back up. He thought maybe she thought too much.

That seemed to stymie her. She just shoved her wallet back into her bag and said, "Thanks. And it wasn't personal. It's just I know people. All I do is deal with people."

"Doesn't everybody?" he asked mildly, handing her a ticket.

She made a face at him. She made a lot of faces. Clearly he was going through some kind of phase because for some reason he thought the expressions she pulled were adorable.

It wasn't like he didn't date. He did. He'd been doing an online dating service and he'd had a handful of women he'd met over the last year, one lasting several months before petering out. Yet none had given him that feeling he was looking for. That kicked in the gut intensity. That wanting to grin every split second he was with a woman.

Not that he expected that would be the outcome of any time spent with Eve, but she did amuse him. It made no sense, but she did.

"If I had my way, I'd live on my own private island." Eve handed her ticket to the gate clerk and pushed through the turnstile. "Just me, myself, and I."

"Then you'd miss Oktoberfest." He followed her through the turnstile. "And that would be a damn shame."

She snorted, but she did reward him with a smile. "You're Suzy Sunshine, aren't you?"

"Nope. I don't look good in yellow. But sure, I like to look on the bright side. Makes life much more enjoyable." It was a simple philosophy and one that had always worked for him. He had a family he loved, a job that was a dream come true, and enough money to have some fun now and again. A little less now that he had to pay a fine for showing his backside, but enough to get by.

The only thing he was missing was a good woman. And he figured the right one would come along when she was supposed to.

For now, he was getting a beer with Eve Monroe. How was that for an interesting turn of events?

"I'd wear head-to-toe yellow every day if it made my life more enjoyable. But for now I'll settle for funnel cake."

"What's so unenjoyable about your life?" From his perspective, her life seemed just fine to him. She had a close-knit family. A job that he imagined paid the bills and then some. A hot body. Maybe she had hemorrhoids and that's why she was so tense.

The thought made him smile before he could stop himself. It was hard to imagine Eve had any physical imperfections under those concealing clothes she always wore.

"That makes you smile? Thinking my life is not enjoyable?" She held her hand out. "Give me ten bucks."

That caught him off guard, but he automatically dug into his back pocket. "For what?"

"A funnel cake. I changed my mind about you paying. If you're going to laugh at me, I'm going to eat lard on your dime."

He laughed. "I'm not laughing at you."

"You look like you're laughing to me. And I don't think you want to laugh at me. Just ask my brothers."

He didn't need to ask her brothers. He could well imagine. Not to mention, he came from a big family so he had seen his share of sibling squabbles. "You know what would be nice?" he asked her, slapping a ten-dollar bill into her hand. "Would be if you laughed with me."

"Are you going to tell a joke?"

"No."

"Then why would I laugh?"

The kicker was she was serious. Nolan just looked into her brown eyes for a minute, trying to puzzle her out. She stared back. He stared. She didn't blink. He didn't blink. There were no answers in those eyes. There was just a competitive gleam sparking as he realized they were suddenly locked into an unintentional no-blinking contest.

"What are we doing?" he murmured. It was hard to talk when you were trying not to blink.

"I don't know." She was muttering, too.

Her eyes got wider, and he was amazed at how at ease she seemed. None of her facial muscles moved. She looked like she could pull a ten-minute stint in this spontaneous staring contest.

But his nose was itchy and he wanted to pull the plug. He knew the perfect way to get her. "I'm going to kiss you." He wasn't really going to, but he knew she would react.

Though he would really like to kiss her.

She squawked and drew back away from him. Then almost immediately, she realized her mistake. "Oh, you're a rat."

"Maybe. But you have my ten bucks."

Her mouth moved. Her nose wrinkled.

"You know you want to laugh. Come on," he teased. "Everybody's doing it."

"You're a dork." She pressed her lips together hard and didn't give in.

"Apparently a dorky rat. Now will you go get a damn funnel cake and quit worrying about *everything*."

"I don't know what you're talking about." She spun on her heel, tossing her hair back in his face.

It was tempting to smack her on the ass, but he didn't know her well enough to do that. So he just watched her ass, nicely curved in those jeans.

That would do for now.

EVE closed her fist around the ten-dollar bill Nolan had given her and fought the urge to sigh. She was being a bit bitchy. She could feel it. He was trying to be nice, encouraging her to have fun. Whatever reason he had invited her, obviously he wanted to hang out and have a good time. Yet she could feel the tension in her, like she felt the majority of her time lately. It felt like hands reaching out and squeezing her, so that she tightened all her muscles and gritted her teeth.

She hadn't always been like this.

But every year that went by, she got a little more rigid. She wanted to stop it, wanted to reverse it, and enjoy her life.

But she worried.

She couldn't be the only person who worried.

She worried a lot. About losing sponsors. About her brothers losing points in the chase for the Cup. About losing money. About losing face. About choking alone in her condo and dying. About the cellulite she'd just found on her left ass cheek. About the migration of her body hair past the bikini line and onto her thighs. About not being married. Or even dating anyone. About not having children. About wanting to have children and not knowing if she could or not. About the risk of cancer from using her cell phone. About her parents dying.

She worried.

It wasn't good.

But she didn't know how to stop it.

Maybe Nolan was right. Maybe she just needed to laugh a little.

Or have sex. She had been shocked at her ridiculous reaction to his threat to kiss her. If she were even remotely spontaneous, she would have let him. But she had been so freaked out by the thought she did want him to kiss her, she had recoiled in a total overreaction.

"A funnel cake, please." Eve glanced at the price. Three bucks. "Actually make that two." It seemed only nice to order one for Nolan. If he didn't want it, she'd eat it. It was that kind of night.

When she turned, two paper plates in her hand, he was right behind her. "Ack!" She jumped and powdered sugar flew up in her face. "You scared the shit out of me."

"You scare easily." He smiled and took the plates from her. "Let me carry these. You want to sit for a spell? There's a band playing in the gazebo."

"Sure." She eyed the band, which seemed to involve large men in tiny shorts with tubas, but she wasn't going to worry about it.

That was her new motto. If it wasn't work, she wasn't going to worry about it. Work or if it was about anyone's health. Plus cellulite. Those three she could fear and rightly so. But other than that, she wasn't going to worry.

Nolan found them a seat at a picnic table and he straddled it, one leg on either side, so he was facing her. Eve sat correctly, unwilling to spread her legs like that just a foot away from him. The band was playing a rousing song that sounded to her untrained ear like it fit right in at Oktoberfest.

He tore a piece off his funnel cake and chewed it. "I need a beer," he said, powdered sugar puffing out of his lips.

Damn, he was cute. Tuesday had been right, too. He was wearing a long sleeve Henley shirt, but that didn't prevent her from seeing all that rippled muscle he had. "Is that your way of asking me to go get you one?"

Nolan frowned. "No. Why would I expect you to go get it? It was just an observation that I would like a beer. Which I was about to follow up with 'I'm going to get one, do you want one, too?'"

"Oh." Why had she assumed that? "Sure. Thank you."

As he got up to hit the beer stand, Eve shoved a piece of her funnel cake in her mouth. Why was he even here with her? She didn't even want to be around herself so why the hell would he?

Don't worry.

Have fun.

She could do this.

Taking a deep breath, she watched the band. They were having fun. They were older men wearing bad outfits, and yet they were bouncing around, tapping their feet to their music, smiling at the fairly sparse crowd. One of them, who looked about ninety and like his tuba weighed more than he did, caught her eye and winked. Amused, Eve smiled back at him and waved.

"Flirting with the band?" Nolan asked, setting a gigantic beer down in front of her.

"Yep." She stuck her finger on her plate and got the pad covered in powdered sugar, then popped it into her mouth and sucked. Her eyes drifted shut. "Man, that's good shit."

He laughed. "Take it easy there. We don't want you to have to detox tomorrow."

"Why does sugar taste so good?" It was a rhetorical question, one she didn't expect him to have an answer to. But she would have thought he'd say something along the lines of, "To torture us," because that would be her answer.

"To make life pleasurable."

Eve paused with her finger halfway back to the plate. Wow. It really was a mind-set. He was a glass half full kind of person and she was . . . what? The glass is going to break before you can even pour kind of person.

Yikes. That wasn't how she wanted to be.

"I am getting a lot of pleasure from this right now." She licked her finger again, slowly, savoring.

His eyes darkened and his smile relaxed. "I can see that," he said, his voice husky.

Eve froze, recognizing that look, that tone of voice. Uh-oh. She had turned him on. It was the finger licking. Most men found that hot. It was probably an oral envy thing. She wasn't sure how to react.

Her body seemed to be sure. Her nipples had instantly hardened and she felt a growing warmth between her legs.

But the rest of her didn't know how to handle it. So she carefully removed her finger like she wasn't aware of any sudden flood of pheromones into the air around them. "So, you've been a jackman with Evan for three years. You like it?"

It was a stupid, generic question, but it was the first thing that popped into her head.

He didn't answer for a second, just took a long swallow of his beer, eyeing her. She couldn't read his expression.

"I love it. It's the only job I can imagine doing. I consider myself very lucky to be on a team. We're working some kinks out this season, getting back on track. Pun intended."

She was going to ignore the pun. "Yeah, it's definitely been a rough ride." She could just pun him right back. "But our deodorant sponsor is sticking around for the long haul, and Evan's driving better than he has in a while. You guys on the crew are doing a great job, too."

"Thanks." He raised his beer. "Here's to a big finish."

She could drink to that. "God, I hope so." Eve lifted her glass and took a big sip. Over the season, Evan had been steadily climbing the ranks, but his poor start had hurt him. Eve wanted him to crack the top 15 to keep his sponsors happy and to prevent him from retiring. He'd been making noises that maybe it was time for him to step away from the wheel, and that was the last thing Eve wanted. She knew he would regret it, and she knew that she would feel like she had failed. Before the decade was done, she wanted one or both of her brothers to win a championship title.

"You're doing it again."

"Doing what?" she asked.

"Wrinkling your forehead. Frowning. You do that whenever you talk about your job."

God, she was. She wanted to deny it, but there was no point. "It's a habit."

"So you don't love your job? Or it just stresses you out?"

"Both." Eve crammed another piece of funnel cake in her mouth, chewing hard. "I actually kind of hate it."

"So why do you do it then?"

Because her family was counting on her. Because it was important not to fail. Because what else was she going to do?

"Everyone has to have a job."

"But you don't have to do one you hate. You have an education. A family that supports you. Why don't you do something else?"

Well, he made it sound easy. It wasn't that simple. And he had a lot of nerve just dismissing all of that other stuff, which he knew nothing about, and just casually saying, yeah, just change careers.

Pfft. Eve opened her mouth to blast him.

Instead, the tuba blared out a resounding note that had her jumping on the bench. "Holy crap."

Nolan laughed. But then he said, "Hey, don't get upset. I'm not trying to tell you your business. But it just seems a shame to me that you're not happy. Don't you think you deserve to be doing a job you can enjoy?"

Eve wanted to stay angry, but Nolan made it hard. He was . . . reasonable. She didn't deal with reasonable people very often. She dealt with egos and money and stubbornness.

For the first time in she wasn't sure when, she answered completely truthfully, in a way she couldn't with her family. "Yes, I think I deserve to be happy. But I don't know how to get out. And I don't know where to go. Racing is all I know."

She wasn't sure why she spoke the simple truth, but she was tired of being flippant and defensive. "Though I don't know why I'm telling you this. I don't even know you."

"Maybe that's why you can tell me. Or maybe it's because I asked."

There was a disturbing thought. Had no one ever asked her before? And what was wrong with her? Her whole life was focused on a career she didn't like, and yet here she was wasting a beautiful fall night with a hot guy complaining. She waved her hand. "Enough of my lameness. We're here to have fun, right?"

"That was my plan."

"Then let's do it." Determined to be something other

than a wet blanket, Eve took another sip of her beer and swung her head back to the band. She could relax, damn it.

The skinny man who had waved to her earlier was gesturing to get her attention. He was calling her over to him. Eve looked around to make sure it was really her he was gesturing to.

"I think your boyfriend is trying to get your attention," Nolan told her, tipping his head in tuba man's direction.

"I'm not sure why or what he wants." There were five guys in the band and they were bouncing around as best they could at their age, with the accordion player sweeping back and forth across the gazebo floor in front of the others. Several small children were dancing in front of the band, looking totally adorable doing wild spins and silly kicks that would drag a smile out of Satan himself.

"He wants you to dance."

Yeah, she was starting to get that impression, given the way he was pointing to the kids then to her. "I don't think so."

"Why not?"

"Um, because I would be the only adult out there and this isn't club music. You can't dance to it solo unless you're three."

"I'll dance with you."

Was he serious? He looked serious. Eve eyed the crowd around them. There were only a few people in the area, probably the parents of the hip-wiggling preschoolers. Once upon a time she had liked to dance. When she had been about the same age as the little brunette out there who kept lifting her dress up over her head. Now that was living. Just lift your dress if you wanted to get down and don't worry what anyone thought.

"You want to polka?"

"Polka? I hardly know her."

Eve stared at Nolan blankly for a second. "What?" She repeated his words back in her head in the fake random Italian accent he had used. Understanding dawned and she could not believe he had just been so absolutely corny. "Oh my God. Poke her. I hardly know her. Are you kidding me?"

He grinned. "Come on, it was funny."

"Dork." The joke one hundred percent was not funny. Well, maybe it was a little funny. But mostly what was cracking her up was him. He was laughing and that made her laugh.

"Wait until you see me dance. You'll take that back."

"Are you an aficionado?"

"A what-o?"

Eve laughed again. She wasn't sure why she found him so entertaining, but she did.

He stood up. "I'm anything you want me to be, babe."

"Can you be peanut butter fudge ripple ice cream?" Eve reluctantly left the bench. He was going to dare her to dance if she didn't so she might as well save them both the hassle and just go ahead and do it in the first place.

"How do you know I'm not?" He took her hand and drew her to the dance floor, walking backward.

There was no explanation for why she was letting him touch her in any way. It wasn't like holding hands given he was just leading her, but still, this wasn't a date. Or hell, maybe it was. Neither one of them had mentioned the reason he had offered to buy her a beer in the first place, which was his missing underwear. Underwear he probably wasn't wearing now either. Eve looked down at his crotch before she even realized what she was doing.

"You're peanut butter fudge ripple?"

He burst out laughing. "Well, not down *there*." His eyes were twinkling. "Though some of the same principles of eating ice cream do apply to it."

Oh, Lord, how had she fallen into that well? Now all she could think about was undoing his jeans and drawing his thick long penis into her mouth, licking it like an ice cream cone. That sounded delicious.

Damn, this was all her fault. She had looked at his crotch. But she wasn't going to take that path into Dirtyville with him. Not yet. "Keep your mind out of the gutter."

"You're the one who looked at my crotch."

"I thought I saw movement."

"Maybe you did."

Ho, boy. Now he'd done it. She was not going to look again. She wasn't. Even though now she was seriously curious as to whether he had an erection or not. Holding her hand couldn't possibly be erection-worthy.

He was still pulling her, only he had stopped walking. It took her a step or two to realize, and when she finally stopped moving, she was very close to him. His eyes were dark and dancing.

"We're going to polka and that is all," she told him firmly, though she wouldn't swear to it that she couldn't be persuaded to consider other things.

"Really?" The hand that was holding hers enclosed her skin more firmly. The other went to her waist. "Because I was kind of hoping to steal a kiss."

"Why would you do that?" she asked him truthfully. As much as she wanted him, and as obvious as the desire in his eyes was, she found it confusing. He didn't know her, and the only time they'd really interacted was when she had berated him for his wardrobe malfunction. It didn't exactly make her the kind of woman men wanted to steal kisses at the fair from.

She'd never been that girl. She'd been a tomboy who had used threats to get her first kiss at the age of twelve.

Which was a pretty sour thought.

"Because you're beautiful."

So Nolan was one of those—a guy who liked to pour on the flattery, slept with a woman, then lost interest. The urge to roll her eyes was intense. "I'm average. But thank you."

"You're not average. You are beautiful, whether you see it or not. I've been watching you for three years and I can tell you straight out, you are gorgeous. Hot."

That was almost impossible for Eve to believe. She had never mastered eye makeup or the art of accessorizing. Most days she figured she looked like her brothers in a pencil skirt. But there was no denying the way Nolan was staring at her now, as he fit his body in alongside hers. He wanted her.

So maybe part of her new philosophy of letting go was that she needed to learn to trust people. If they said it and it appeared to be so, stop doubting it.

Just roll with it.

"Maybe we can try that kiss later, fudge ripple. Just to see how you taste," she said, her voice low.

His hand tightened on her waist and he opened his mouth to respond.

"But first, show me these moves you're talking about."

She pulled him into the tightest form she could, listened for the music, and took off to the right.

CHAPTER
THREE

NOLAN'S mother was fond of saying that dance was the vertical expression of a horizontal desire, usually in reference to grinding couples at family wedding receptions, but clearly she hadn't meant a polka.

There was no way to be sexy doing the polka. With all the jumping and running and bouncing, Nolan felt more like a kid on a pogo stick than a man on a date with a woman who was like lighter fluid to his charcoal. When she had looked him in the eye and said she wanted to see how he tasted, he had almost looked down at his crotch to see the flames he was sure had to be shooting out from his jeans. She was sexy with a capital S.

Yet she didn't seem to think she was, which amazed him.

She also didn't seem particularly happy in her life, so he was glad that this insanity they were engaging in seemed to be amusing her. Without their discussing it, she had taken the lead in the dance and was spinning him around in circles on the makeshift dance floor in front of the gazebo. Since he had no clue how to polka, he was fine with following.

The thing was, she didn't seem to know how to polka either. She was definitely making it up as she went, which could explain why they kept running into each other.

"Go left!" she screamed, breathless and laughing.

"My left or your left?" he asked, confused as hell.

As they went in opposite directions, they lost their grip on each other. Nolan ending up almost plowing down a kid and Eve wound up spinning off into a bush.

"I guess your left," he said with a grin as he pulled her out of the foliage.

She was laughing, her hair falling in her eyes. For the first time, he noticed she had dimples that appeared when she laughed, making her even more adorable.

"Whoops. Sorry. My bad."

The band was winding up their number. "Thank you! Thank you!" the accordion player yelled as Eve and Nolan and the rest of the audience clapped. "And thank you to our dancers."

A little girl who had been traipsing around stopped, looked out at the crowd, and curtsied. No self-esteem issues there, which was nice to see.

Then Eve blew him away by giving her own little curtsy, though hers was directed at the band.

"Sassy," he told her. "I think you should go on tour with them."

"Should that be my new career? Polka band groupie. I don't think the cash flow would be as high as you'd think it would be though."

"You're probably right." They reached the picnic table

where their funnel cake was coagulating. He took a sip of his beer. "Warm. Time for a new one."

"I'll drink mine warm." She took her own sip then shrugged. "It's not warm. It's just not ice cold. Though I'm warm from all that dancing."

And lo and behold, she set her beer back down on the table and peeled off her sweatshirt. Underneath she was wearing a black tank top. That was it. Nothing but a stretchy shirt that clung to her breasts. Lord have mercy on his horny soul.

"Whew, that's better."

Oh, it was better and it was worse all at the same time.

She didn't seem to notice that his tongue was hanging to his knees because she just continued their conversation.

"I learned to drink warm beer in college. I was too broke to let a little thing like room temperature beer stop me. No wasting the suds."

"So you went to college? Where at?"

"Clemson. First one in my family to graduate from college."

She sounded proud of that fact, as she should be. "How about Evan and Elec? They go to Clemson, too?"

"Nah. There was no reason to go to college when they were already both driving in the truck series by eighteen. But I was supposed to learn a skill. How about you?"

"I didn't go to college. With nine kids, there was no money for that and I wasn't ambitious enough to pay for it myself." College had sounded like fun actually, but he wasn't that big on learning in a classroom. It hadn't been the right choice for him. He liked to get his hands dirty in the real world.

"You have *eight* siblings?" She sounded amazed and horrified.

Nolan pitched his beer in the nearest trash can and

gestured to start walking. As they strolled to the beer tent, he told her, "Yep. Seven sisters, one brother. Some of the girls paid their way through school and went off in different directions with their careers. I went to vocational school to be a mechanic and eventually got lucky enough to get on a pit crew. My little brother, Rhett, is the gas can man for the team."

"Does that bother you, working with him?"

"No, it's the greatest thing ever. I was thrilled for him when he got on the team. He's a good guy, if a bit of a horn dog."

"With a name like Rhett, he's justified." Eve drained her beer. "Is it a family name?"

Hardly. Nolan laughed. "Hell no. He got saddled with the name just like you're imagining, because my mom was all hot for Rhett Butler in *Gone with the Wind*. She couldn't name me Rhett because I was her first son and I'm named after my dad. But after a run of five girls in nine years, my dad told her she could name the last baby whatever the hell she wanted as long as she'd go get her tubes tied."

She laughed. "Charming. I'm sure that hasn't affected Rhett's self-esteem at all."

Nolan could have been offended on his parents' behalf, but the truth was, the story didn't sound all that great if you weren't one of the people involved. He knew his parents were just tweaking each other. Every one of their kids had been a conscious choice, he was sure of it. "Don't go feeling sorry for Rhett. My parents think the sun rises and sets with him. He's charming. Good looking. Lazy as shit but manages to get away with it. And he's a good guy, and I do enjoy working with him."

"You're one of those families that just digs each other's company, aren't you?"

"Absolutely." Nolan studied the choices at the beer

booth. He wanted something bigger this time. "My sisters are all amazing women. Well, my sister Jackie is a whiner, but we've learned to deal with it. My parents would die for each and every one of us. Just like your folks, I'm sure."

"My parents don't really get me."

"No one's parents get them. But they love you just the same." It was kind of a rule, it seemed. "Can I have the harvest ale in a stein?" Nolan asked the woman manning the beer booth.

"Sure thing, honey." She reached before her for a stein and eyed him. "You know they're doing a strongman contest every night of the festival. You should enter."

Huh. Not only was it flattering to have a woman old enough to be his grandmother suggesting the contest, but he found himself intrigued by the possibility of showing off in front of Eve. He was a guy. He wasn't above flashing his biceps if he thought it might help get the girl naked. "Yeah? What do you have to do?"

"Hold your full beer stein straight out at arm's length. Can't lower your arm at all. The last man left wins a hundred-dollar gift card to the BBQ joint down the road and a commemorative beer stein."

That sounded easy enough. "I do like my BBQ."

"Just head to the orange booth over there and they'll check out your beer, make sure it's regulation." She had the raspy voice of a lifelong smoker and jet-black hair that looked better on Cher than it did on her unfortunately.

Nolan paid her. "Thanks, hon. Appreciate it."

She winked at him. "No problem."

"Are you actually entering the contest?" Eve asked him, her sweatshirt over her arm, blocking his view of her breasts.

He shrugged. "I like barbeque. It sounds easy enough. I haul a thirty-five pound jack over the wall then crank up a three-ton car. I can hold a damn beer mug out for ten minutes."

"Don't get defensive. I wasn't suggesting you were anything other than big, strong, and manly. I just wasn't sure if you were being polite or you really wanted to do it."

"I'm not being defensive." He didn't think. Though he had to admit, he couldn't help wanting to impress her. That was just part of being a dude. They were born with a bragging gene. "But yes, I'd like to do it. Want to be my cheerleader?" He gave her what he hoped was a charming smile. He'd never quite had Rhett's skill with the ladies, but he did alright.

"I'd kind of rather swallow glass than be the chick standing on the sidelines cheering on a man, but I'll make an exception this one time."

Be still his heart. There was something every guy wanted to hear. "Oh, yeah? Thanks. How did I happen to earn this exception?"

"Because if you were a total douche bag like half the men I know, you'd have let me stroll around with my bra showing yesterday and you didn't. Plus you can't dance for shit, but you were willing to make an ass out of yourself with me, which I appreciate. So the least I can do is stand there while you go macho man."

She really needed to hold back on the flattery there. "Your generosity knows no bounds."

"That's sarcasm."

"Yep."

"Why?" She frowned, like she really didn't get it.

"Because you just insulted me about three different ways," he told her mildly. It didn't bother him so much as it puzzled him. There was more to Eve than met the eye. Something had happened to her to make her so quick to lash out, and he was more determined than ever to figure out what it was.

"I did? I didn't mean to." There was a pause when she seemed to be rewinding her words and replaying them. "Okay, so maybe telling you that you can't dance could be taken as an insult, but you have to know it's true."

Nolan raised an eyebrow at her. "Babe, you're not doing any better."

"The truth is the truth." Now she was just being stubborn, a quality she didn't seem to lack.

"Sure. Nothing wrong with the truth. Honesty is definitely a good policy, but it's your delivery. Gotta sprinkle a little sugar on that sour."

This was why she had the reputation of a battle-ax. But Nolan would swear she didn't really realize that she was potentially hurting people's feelings. She was just cocooned in her own discontent.

If she tore his face off right now, well, then maybe he'd be forced to admit he might be wrong. But she didn't, which satisfied him tremendously.

She looked troubled, a little sad. "A lot of days it seems my sugar canister is empty by about ten A.M. If I knew how to fix that I would." Her hand came up as if to stop him. "And don't go suggesting I need Xanax like Evan always does. I think antidepressants can be very helpful to some people, but I don't think I can call myself depressed. I'm just . . . bitchy. I was born this way."

That was a cop-out and they both knew it. It was in her eyes. "You're not bitchy. You're just stubborn. You've decided you're miserable and you'll be damned if anyone is going to talk you out of it."

He'd hit a nerve, that was clear.

Her eyes narrowed. "You're a jerk."

"Who speaks the truth."

"Your sugar seems to be missing, too."

"I said you're not bitchy. Sounds like a compliment to me."

"Go enter your damn strongman contest."

Nolan wanted to laugh, but he figured that wouldn't go over well with her. "I'll do that. You could enter too, you know. It's open to women."

"I'm a runner. My arms aren't my strongest asset."

Nolan pondered her assets, clearing his throat at the thought of her naked, long muscular legs wrapped around his waist. "No? What is?" Without thought, his gaze dropped to her breasts, filling out her clingy tank top.

She seemed to realize that he wasn't asking from an athletic standpoint because she made a sound and rolled her eyes. "Not my arms!"

Now he did laugh. "I can think of a thing . . . or two."

Eve turned on her heel and marched over to the entry tent. Nolan had no choice but to follow her. Five minutes later, the contest was under way and he was standing with three other guys holding his beer stein straight out. It wasn't hard. It didn't strain his biceps. But he had to admit it was awkward and a little boring.

Cheerleading didn't suit Eve. She tried. He had to give her credit. She fist pumped and yelled, "Go Nolan!" a few times in a voice that she tried to inject enthusiasm into but sounded as fake as it was.

Finally she strolled over to him and said, "Is your arm getting tired like that? That guy on the end is starting to shake."

"I'm fine." He was. This was nothing compared to the daily workouts he put himself through to keep in shape for the job.

"Hmm. You are a stud, I have to admit."

If she only knew how much of a stud he could be. The corner of his mouth turned up. "Thanks."

Eve had sauntered up very close to him. Nolan eyed her warily. This was the closest she had voluntarily gotten to him yet. "What are you doing?"

"If I kiss you, will you put the beer down so we can go do something else?" she asked, sounding more hopeful than seductive.

"No."

Her face went mulish. "Why not?"

"One. There's a lot of barbeque at stake. Two. I want you to kiss me because you want to, not because you're bargaining with your lips." End of story.

"Oh, Lord. Why do you always have to make sense?"

Why did she have to be so adorable? "It's a terrible flaw. I'm sorry."

Eve took a step back. "Do you mind if I go play the shooting gallery? The booth is right over there and I've been eyeing it. I'm a good shot."

"Now why does that not surprise me? Go for it."

"Because I'm not your average woman and we both know it. Don't be afraid though. I've never shot a person."

"I'm not afraid. I think it's hot." He did. He thought a whole lot of things about Eve were hot.

She looked equal parts astonished and intrigued. "You're nuts."

With that, she walked over to the carnival game and paid the attendant. Since he was just standing there, Nolan watched her. Eve fired off ten rounds, pinging the center of half a dozen of the standing targets, knocking them backward. She took them all down except for one. Impressive.

The attendant was wearing a grin Nolan could see from fifty feet away. He handed Eve a stuffed animal. She turned and gave it to a little girl who had been watching her. The child turned to her mother for permission, and when she got an okay nod, she took the fluffy white animal and squeezed it hard against her chest. Eve and the mother exchanged a few words and a laugh. Nolan wished he could hear their conversation.

Eve reached into her purse and pulled out more money. She played two more rounds, and this time, she hit all the targets, which was sexy as hell. Even sexier was that both times she gave away her prize to one of the kids standing around her in the growing crowd. He had known she had a kind heart, despite her blustering. Eve was a good woman and he really enjoyed watching her.

He did feel a little lonely standing all by himself with his arm out. The guy next to him was sweating profusely, his arm shaking. He didn't look up for a chat. The strong-man contest coordinator was staring at the three remaining contestants intently, her glasses slipping down her nose, her arms crossed against her enormous chest. Now there was a battle-ax. She was waiting for one of them to lower his arm, even for a split second, but it wasn't going to be him.

Now it wasn't even about the barbeque restaurant. It was the principle of the thing. At least he had Eve to watch. She won two more times, tossing a stuffed penguin to a little boy, then keeping the other white thing for herself. He thought it was a cat, but he wasn't sure. Figuring she must have dropped a wad of cash at this point, he wasn't surprised when she turned and strolled back toward him, her sweatshirt tied around her waist, purse across her body.

"Amazing job," he told her, meaning it sincerely. "You're a regular Annie Oakley. Remind me not to piss you off."

"And you're a strongman apparently. The guy next to you just caved."

Nolan turned. The man who had been shaking had quit the field. "Good job, man. This isn't as easy as it looks, is it?"

He shook his head and laughed, his face red. "Hell no. Though you don't look like you're struggling too much. Guess I don't hit the gym enough."

"I probably wouldn't if my job didn't depend on it."

"What do you do?"

"I'm a jackman for stock car driver Evan Monroe."

The guy's face lit up. "No way? Are you serious? That's so freakin' awesome!"

"It's a great job, I love it. This here's his sister."

"You're Evan and Elec Monroe's sister?" He stared at Eve like she was a goddess. "That's so cool."

Nolan expected she'd be annoyed, and he was already regretting having said something. But fans were fans and it was a cool job. He shared the guy's excitement. Eve impressed him.

She smiled and said, "I sure am. And their PR rep. If you want to give me your name and contact info, I'll send some autographed gear your way."

"Really? That would be sweet."

"It's the least I can do after you stood here holding a beer out for thirty minutes."

"Thanks!"

A couple of minutes later he was on his way, perfectly happy with the end result of the strongman contest. "That was nice of you," Nolan told Eve.

She shrugged. "That's what it's about—the fans. Without them, there's no sport, no money. I remember being a kid, that thrill you'd get when you got to meet your favorite driver. It's cool that I can do that for someone else now."

A thought hit Nolan, one he was surprised hadn't occurred to him before. Eve's father had been a driver. Her two brothers were. She was very competitive. He'd seen that already multiple times in the limited contact he'd had with her. Some of her unhappiness just might make sense. "Did you race as a kid?"

"Yep. I won the quarter midget championship at fourteen." She looked proud of that fact, as well she should.

That was no small feat. Nolan was impressed. "Damn, girl. That's quite a title. So what made you quit racing?"

There it was. Her expression changed, became guarded. A tinge of sarcasm crept into her voice. "Because girls don't drive professionally, don't you know?"

"Is that what your daddy told you?" The thought troubled Nolan. Facts were facts, and it was damn hard to break into pro-racing as a woman. But he hated to think her father might have squashed her dreams.

"No, my dad was all for me. But the rest of the world wasn't. You can only hear no so many times before you start to think they might have a point."

"So you did the practical thing and went to college." It was a decision that he was getting the feeling she had regretted every day in one way or another for the last ten-plus years.

"Yeah. I did. And now my sister-in-law Kendall is the first female driver in the Cup series."

A title he imagined she had always wanted for herself. His heart hurt just a little for the girl she'd been, and the woman she was——both disappointed, both betrayed by men. "I'm sorry, Eve. That is a tough pill to swallow."

She hurried to amend what she had said. "Kendall deserves it. And I love her."

"I'm sure she does. And I'm sure you do. Doesn't make it sting any less." With his free hand he reached out and stroked her cheek. Her skin was soft, her eyes vulnerable.

For a split second their gazes held. Nolan was shocked at both the heat and the tenderness he felt coursing through him when he looked at her. Lord, she was beautiful and sweet and so underestimated.

"You could still do it, you know. Drive."

His words shattered the moment. She stepped out of his touch and snorted. "Yeah, right. I'm past thirty and

I haven't driven in a dozen years. That ship has sailed, strongman."

Damn it. He hadn't meant to upset her. She looked tense again, and it was his fault for pushing a topic that brought her pain. But before he could say anything, she shoved the stuffed animal at him.

"Here. I won this for you."

Touched, he looked down. Then frowned. "A white kitten? Thanks. I think." What in the Sam Hill was he supposed to do with a plush animal? Growing up, his sisters had owned them by the tens of thousands it seemed, and he'd spent a hefty amount of time holding them for ransom and threatening to tear their eyes off and stuffing out if the girls didn't meet his demands. Somehow he didn't think that would have the same thrill now.

"I was going to give it to you with some incredibly inappropriate double entendre, but now I've realized that's not a good idea."

A double entendre involving a cat? Gee, what could that be? Nolan felt an erection immediately spring to life. "No? Why not?"

"Because telling you I'm giving you my pussy sends the wrong message."

Oh, shit, she'd said it. Nolan gave a strangled gasp. His jeans were suddenly so tight he felt light-headed. "Why is that the wrong message? I really like that message." He really, really liked that message. Like that was the best message he'd ever gotten in his entire life.

"Because it's a bad idea, and I'm not even sure you really want me that way."

He nodded so hard he almost gave himself whiplash. "Oh, I do. I really, absolutely do."

"Your beer stein is drooping," she said in alarm.

"I don't care." What he cared about was losing the stuffed cat and the beer and hauling her sweet ass right up close to him and kissing the daylights out of her. But the competitor in him instinctively raised the glass up to the appropriate level.

She sighed in relief. "After all this, I want that BBQ now. The last guy is about five seconds from losing."

Irrelevant. Didn't she see that? He wanted to get back to the part where she offered him her kitty.

Eve monitored Nolan's hand, her heart pounding. It had been a welcome distraction from the way he had been looking at her. For a second, she had thought he was going to kiss her, right there in front of the beer booth at the Oktoberfest.

"Just tell me the second I've won," he told her, still staring at her.

Nolan Ford confused the hell out of her. Eve wasn't a moron, she knew when a man wanted to get her naked, and she definitely got the impression Nolan fell in that category. She wanted to get naked for him. Hence the naughty little thoughts that had run through her head about offering him her pussy when she'd won the stuffed cat. But she didn't understand him, which was why she'd changed her mind, only then she'd gone and said it anyways. What did he really want from her? So far she hadn't even been particularly nice to him, yet she didn't get the impression he was turned off by that or that he was just looking at her as a one-night stand or a booty call. He seemed actually interested in getting to know her, and that weirded her out.

It also disturbed her that she was telling him things about herself. Legitimate, honest answers to his questions were coming out of her mouth without hesitation and that was so not her. It took a crowbar to pry her feelings out of her normally, and here she'd told him she had wanted to be a driver. It made no sense.

"I want you more than I want the barbeque."

Eve didn't even know what to say. Nolan wasn't saying it in a wheedling way. Or in a charming, playboy tone. It was just direct. Sincere. Maybe even a little heartfelt.

When she didn't understand something, it made her angry. Scared.

So she stepped back, away from the temptation of his body, but most of all, the temptation of what she saw in his green eyes.

Fumbling in her purse, she pulled out her phone. She held it up, wanting to capture the image of him holding the stein and the stuffed cat. And more to the point, needing to change the charged atmosphere in the air between them to something more lighthearted.

He caught on to what she was doing. His head went back and forth. "No. Hell no, you are not taking a picture of me right now. If I see that online I will—"

She took it. "Got it."

Glaring at her, he said, "Don't save that."

Then what would have been the point? Grinning, she saved it to her phone. "Just one more."

He dropped the cat onto the ground, just letting it fall out of his hands. "At the very least, let's leave the stuffed animal out of it. I can't explain that easily."

"Oh, come on." Eve held her camera up, moving back and forth, searching for the best angle. "You're about to win a strongman contest. No one is going to doubt your masculinity."

"I don't feel the need to chance it." He put his foot on the cat's back, like he was squashing it. "Just in case."

With the one arm up with a beer, the opposite foot on a ball of fluff, and a grimace on his face, it was a confusing, albeit hilarious picture. "That's it," she told him. "Make love to the camera. Work it, girl."

The expression on his face was priceless. Eve started laughing so hard her hand shook, making the image of him on the camera screen blurry.

"Eve. The minute I get to put this beer down, I'm going to tan your hide."

Now why did that both amuse her and send a jolt of heat to her inner thighs? Eve steadied her hand and got another shot off. She didn't doubt for one minute that he was going to come after the camera. It's what she would do.

"We have a winner!"

The woman with the glasses who had been monitoring the contest stepped in between Eve and Nolan and congratulated him. The other remaining contestant was bent over, massaging his arm muscles. Nolan looked impatient, but his arm was steady. The woman took his free hand and raised it up in the air in a fist pump. Eve clapped and cheered, admittedly proud of him. She was competitive by nature, so she understood his drive to win even something as simple as a contest at the fair. It was why she'd blown two twenties at the shooting gallery.

"Woo hoo! Go Nolan! Strongman, yeah!"

He turned his attention away from the woman and met her eye. He lowered the beer mug and excused himself from the judge.

"Oh, shit." He was coming for her phone to delete the pictures. Eve tried to shove it into her purse, but the latch was caught and she couldn't cram it inside fast enough. She started backing up, dropping her sweatshirt in the process. Leaning over, she snagged it and tried to haul ass, but Nolan was already in front of her, a devious gleam in his eye.

"Delete those pictures."

"No."

"Give me the phone."

"No."

He grabbed for it. She feinted to the left, dodging his reach.

"You're not putting those pictures online, Eve Monroe, or I will bust your behind."

He was grinning, so she couldn't take him particularly seriously, but she wasn't about to just hand the phone over to him either.

Nolan tried again and this time he got her arm. Eve shrieked, laughing, and tried to yank herself out of his grip. But of course, he was the strongman and she couldn't escape. So she punched him in the gut. Not hard. Not to hurt. Just to startle him. It worked. He let her go.

"I can't believe you just punched me! That's dirty pool, girl."

"Dirty pool would be pantsing you." She tried to stuff the phone into her front pocket, but Nolan got a hand on it, too.

She was shoving, he was pulling, they were laughing.

Then suddenly, as his hand slid down into her jeans pocket along with the phone, they both seemed to realize how he was touching her. His palm was alongside her thigh, perilously close to an area of her body that Eve seemed extra aware of when Nolan was around.

His eyes darkened. Her laugh died out.

There was a hand on her other thigh suddenly, his thumb caressing the front of her leg through the denim of her jeans. His head tilted. His mouth moved toward her.

Eve felt the most intense anticipation she'd ever experienced. It was like the moment was occurring in slow motion, her breathing loud and echoing in her own ears, his expression sexy and feral.

When his lips finally touched hers, she sighed into the kiss, opening her mouth fully for him. They moved together, the touch more raw than tender, more hot than sweet. His hands caressed across her thighs and Eve slipped her tongue in to tangle with his. She wasn't sure when she had done it, but at some point, her hand had lifted to his head, and she buried her fingers in his hair.

A deep wet ache throbbed inside her core and she was contemplating doing him behind the beer booth when he broke the kiss and stepped back.

His lips were shiny, his breathing ragged.

His erection huge.

Then he held her phone up in the air, swinging it back and forth. "I can play dirty pool, too, precious."

That took some balls of steel. Instead of being angry, Eve was impressed, the corner of her mouth turning up.

And for the first time ever, she thought it was possible she just might have met her match.

CHAPTER
FOUR

NOLAN was pleased to see Eve fighting back a smile. It had been a gamble, teasing with her. She might have gotten pissed that he'd stolen her phone while they were kissing and just left the fairgrounds altogether. But he'd wanted to tweak her back. She had punched him in the stomach, after all, and he was fairly certain that was the first time a girl other than one of his sisters had done that.

"Nicely played, Ford. You did distract me."

He'd distracted himself. That kiss had been off the charts. Eve had a volcano of passion inside her, and he didn't think it would take much for it to erupt. He definitely wanted to be the one around when it did.

"It wasn't easy. I almost forgot what I was doing when you started in with your tongue. We've got some chemistry between us, just like I suspected."

"Maybe. But you don't taste like fudge ripple."

"No?" Nolan figured this was going to be good. "What do I taste like?"

"Jackass."

Yep. That was good. He laughed. "I guess you'd know."

"What does that mean?"

"It means I'm about to delete these pictures." He hit the picture icon on her phone to bring up the shots.

"You're a sore loser."

"How am I a loser? I have the phone and I'm about to go collect my barbeque gift certificate. That sounds like a winner to me." He scrolled through the pictures. They weren't that awful actually. He only deleted the one where he was clutching the kitten and his eyes were closed. That one was awkward.

"You're no fun. I wasn't going to post those online."

"You swear to it?"

"Yes, I swear to it."

He gave her the phone back. "I only deleted one. The rest you can keep for your personal amusement when you want a good laugh at my expense."

Her jaw dropped. "You didn't delete them all?" She took the phone and checked for herself.

"No. I can be a good sport, and you gave your word you won't show them to anyone else." He wasn't uptight and he could take a joke.

"Oh. Wow." She looked genuinely surprised, like she wasn't used to people being reasonable. Which maybe she wasn't. "You da man."

Which made him laugh. "Yeah, I'm the man about to pick up my prize."

They headed toward the booth the judge had directed him to. "So Eve, you know I can't eat all that barbeque by myself. Would you care to join me for dinner sometime?" He liked spending time with her. She continued to intrigue him and he wanted to hang out with her.

"Are you asking me on a date?"

Apparently he needed to spell it out. "Yes."

"Do you really think it's a good idea for us to date? It's basically a conflict of interest. We work for the same company."

"I didn't give it much thought." He hadn't. Sure, Rhett and Jim had said something to him, but he didn't see why it mattered. They weren't on the pit crew together. And he'd yet to end a relationship with a woman and been unable to remain civil to her after. "You're frowning again. Stop worrying."

She was. That line in the middle of her forehead had reappeared.

"I can't help it. It would be a disaster if we were a disaster and it affected our work."

"It's one date for some ribs and maybe a pulled pork sandwich. Why would that be a disaster? And we are both mature adults who see each other at the track like once a month. I think we can handle it." He did. Putting his hands on her shoulders, he rocked her back and forth a little. "It's okay. Chill out. Have some fun. Hug a kitten." He handed her the stuffed cat she'd won for him.

Eve rolled her eyes, but she did smile at the same time. "God, okay, fine, whatever. Let's go out on a date. But if this goes horribly wrong I'm blaming it on you."

He wasn't about to point out that technically they were currently *on* a date. "I'll be the fall guy. That's fair. Not. But I'll take the blame."

"When are we doing this? I need to get it on my calendar."

Nolan pulled a face. She had no idea how to have fun. He was catching glimpses like when she danced or wrestled with him, but man, she was wound tight. It felt like he'd been given a personal mission to loosen her up. Which gave him an idea.

"I hadn't thought that far ahead," he told her truthfully. "But this weekend I'm competing in the demolition derby. You should come with me, drive a car in it."

Eve paused in the middle of pushing buttons on her phone, probably checking out her calendar. She gave him a look that showed precisely what she thought of that idea. "Now why would I do that? And how? I don't have a car."

So she was considering it. "You would do it because it's fun. Because knocking around on the track banging into people is a great stress reliever. Think about it—you get to smash up a car and no one's going to get pissed."

She seemed to be debating the idea. But then she shook her head. "Again, I don't have a car. And I don't drive anymore. It's a crazy idea."

"You can use my car and I'll drive Rhett's. He hasn't driven it in six months or more. And you drove for years, you can handle a derby. Come on, it'll be a blast. Hell, you may even win."

That got her. He could see the competitive fire spark to life in her eyes.

She snorted. "There's no way I'd win. But yeah, it might be fun. I'll think about it."

"Think about it fast, that's only three days from now."

Staring hard at him, she jammed her phone into her purse, then pulled her sweatshirt back on over her head. It was a stall tactic that he recognized clearly. If she decided to drive, she'd need a practice session behind the wheel, just to get the feel of the car, and he wasn't sure when they were going to squeeze that in if she didn't make a decision tonight. But he wasn't about to tell her that. If he put too much pressure on her, she'd just say no.

"Okay, fine, I'll do it. Only to prove to you that it's a bad idea."

"Well, as long as you're going in with the right attitude." Nolan slung his arm over Eve's shoulders and pulled her in close to him. "You want your own brat or do you just want a bite of mine?"

"What?" She looked up at him in confusion. "What the hell are you taking about?"

"I'm buying myself a bratwurst to eat. You want your own wiener or just a bite of mine?" He smiled at her. Two could play the double entendre game. It was only fair. He still hadn't fully recovered from that pussy comment. It was a game she was good at.

"I'll just take a big old bite out of yours, thanks." She gave him a challenging smile.

Yeah, she was good at this game. Nolan felt a stirring down south. A call to arms. He wanted to kiss Eve again while imagining her biting him.

But when he leaned forward to do just that, she took a step back. "On second thought, I'll take a rain check on the wiener. I'm going to head out for the night."

It took him a second to process what she was saying. "No wiener?"

"No wiener."

Disappointed, he tried to regroup. No wiener. That sucked. "That's a shame, but alright. I'll walk you to your car."

"No, you go ahead and collect your prize and get your bratwurst. My car is only a few spots from the gate, I'll be fine."

With any other woman, he would insist on walking her out. But his gut told him if he insisted, it would just piss Eve off. "Are you sure?"

"Positive."

She was already taking a few steps back. She was done and she was bolting. Best to let her go. "Alright, I'll call you tomorrow about the derby."

"Great. Enjoy your sauerkraut."

"Thanks. Night, Eve."

"Bye, strongman."

As he watched her go, his eyes automatically dropping down to check out her stellar curves, Nolan had a feeling his car might not be the only things getting smashed up this weekend.

His ego and his libido might be taking a beating as well.

But he was willing to risk the bruises.

Because if he won, well, he had a feeling the prize was going to be well worth it.

"YOU want to do what?" Elec stared at her in surprise.

Eve fought her annoyance, which was directly related to the fact that she was embarrassed, and took a deep breath. "I want to drive in the demolition derby. And I was wondering if I could borrow a car. I know you have a bunch of beaters laying around."

Elec had been amassing a car collection for years, and last time she'd counted, he had about seven or eight, most in storage since his house with Tammy only had a three-car garage. Some were vintage stock cars, some sports cars, and one or two were rescued from the scrap pile.

"I have a couple, yeah. Sure you can borrow one." Elec leaned back in the rocker on his front porch and made it tip off the floor. "So what made you want to do this all of a sudden?"

Eve had been over for dinner with Elec and Tammy and the kids, and now they were sitting on the porch in the crisp fall air in the dark. Only a porch light was illuminating their faces, which was good for this conversation. Eve was thoroughly embarrassed and not sure why.

Though there was no denying it was easier to talk to Elec than it was to Evan. She and Evan were too similar, too competitive. They both wanted the last word. Elec had never had a lot of words, period. When he had spoken when they were kids, she and Evan had drowned him out. But it had never seemed to bother him. He had a naturally content disposition. It was like there'd been no sass genes left by the time their mother had given birth to him.

So it didn't really surprise her that, outside of his career, he had chosen to marry a woman with children and a house, and settle down into a domestic routine. He had never been the party type, even when he'd been trying to live the playboy lifestyle.

Rocking on his porch looked natural for him, and Eve sometimes found herself a touch jealous. Not that she saw herself as domestic exactly, but Elec had his own family, people to come home to who were happy to see him. She had an empty condo that wasn't a home—it was just a place she owned and had had decorated.

"It's been pointed out to me," she told Elec, "that I am a little uptight."

He snorted, letting go so the rocker slammed back down to the porch. "Maybe."

"So having a way to let some steam off might be a good thing. Fun."

"I think that's a great idea. Seriously."

"You do?" Because she wasn't really sure it was all that brilliant, but she couldn't come up with a good reason to say no to Nolan without just sounding bratty.

"Yeah, I do. You always loved to drive. I'm sure you miss it. And you don't have to worry about wrecking the car—that's the point. No sponsors to please. Just slamming into people. Bumper cars for grown-ups."

"I always did love the bumper cars." She remembered the thrill of going full throttle at another kid's car and knocking him off course. Good times.

"Of course you did. You're one of the most competitive people I've ever met. And you're not competing. That's bound to make you antsy. You can't fight your nature, you know."

Was that what she was doing? Fighting who she was? Maybe he had a point. "Huh. Maybe you're right."

"When is the derby?"

"Sunday."

"Too bad. I'd come watch you if I wasn't racing myself."

"That's okay. I don't know if I can even do this. I don't think I want anyone watching me just yet."

"Cool." Elec took a sip of his beer. "So you dating anyone?"

She was instantly suspicious. Had he heard something around the garage? He and Evan's teams worked mere feet away from each other, and there was always gossip. Plus Tammy had been there for the margarita night when Nolan had called her. "Why?"

"Just making conversation." He put his hands up. "Geez Louise, don't tear my face off. My wife asks all the time why I don't know more about your life, so I'm trying to be a good brother and inquire."

"Oh." Her wariness dissipated. "There's nothing to know about my life. It's a boring life." With her heels, she made her own rocking chair zip back and forth vigorously, debating how much she should reveal. She did trust Elec not to mock her. "Tammy might have mentioned I had someone ask me out."

"She might have."

"Do you think it's stupid to date a pit crew member?"

"It's only stupid if he's stupid."

Eve brought her chair to a halt. "That's the only reason it would be stupid?"

"Best as I can figure, yep."

"I can think of a lot of reasons it would be stupid. Like bare minimum, a hundred. But no, he's not stupid."

"Does he have a name?"

"Nolan Ford." Saying it out loud gave her a weird tingling feeling in her nipples and her girl parts. Thank God it was dark because she had the sneaking suspicion that she was actually blushing. Something she never did outside of anger, and that red color on the cheeks wasn't called blushing. That was called pissed off.

But right now, talking about Nolan, she was blushing. Ridiculous. That's what that was.

"He's a good guy, from what I've seen. A hard worker. You should ask Evan more about him."

"Hell, no." Was Elec crazy? "Do you know how much shit Evan will give me?"

"I don't know. He's mellowed a bit."

"I went to Oktoberfest with his jackman. He'll never let me hear the end of it."

Elec's head swung in her direction. He looked astonished. "You went to Oktoberfest? You hate those things."

She did. Didn't she? It hadn't been so bad. It had actually been kind of fun. "I don't *hate* them. That's a strong word."

"I believe your exact words when Mom and Dad invited you last year were, 'I'd rather arm wrestle with a king cobra.'"

She didn't remember saying that, but it was entirely possible that she had. It sounded like words that would come out of her mouth. Having it pointed out to her, though, was entirely unnecessary. "I'm trying new things, okay? Geez, you'd think that was a crime."

"I'm all for you trying new things. In fact, I think if you could try a new attitude in general, we'd all be a whole lot happier."

Eve bristled. It felt like her whole life she was always

being criticized by her family. Nothing she did was ever good enough. She didn't want it to hurt, yet it always did. This was a particularly painful sting, given that it came from Elec and it was when she was trying to share personal tidbits with him.

But instead of yelling at him, or bottling it up until every muscle in her neck was sore like she normally did, she took a deep breath and said, "That hurts my feelings. I'm trying to tell you that I know I need to relax and you just got a dig in on me."

There was a long moment of silence where he gaped at her. Then he nodded. "You're right. I'm sorry, that was rude of me. I don't want to hurt your feelings."

"Okay. Thanks." They both rocked. She wasn't sure about him but she felt awkward. Talking about her feelings wasn't easy. Communicating without yelling was novel. Funny enough though, being rational about it definitely left her less stressed.

But nonetheless, she was still grateful that Tamara chose that moment to step out onto the porch.

"Brr," she said. "It's nippy out here. Do you want some coffee?"

"No, thanks. I'm fine." Eve hadn't noticed the cold. She was wearing a sweatshirt and she tended to be hot-blooded. It was ironic, but true.

"Hon?" Tamara asked Elec.

"I don't need coffee, I just need you cuddling up with me."

Tammy gave a flirty laugh and went over to him.

Gag. If they were going to get all lovey-dovey snoogie-wookums with each other, Eve was leaving.

Her sister-in-law dropped onto her brother's lap.

Yeah. Time to go. "Okay, on that note, I'm going home." She stood up.

Tammy and Elec finished their hello kiss. Like they hadn't kissed in the kitchen ten minutes earlier. Or right before dinner.

She was so jealous it was ridiculous.

"No, you don't need to leave," Tammy protested. "It's early still. The kids don't need to be in bed for another hour."

Which meant sixty minutes until boom-boom time. It was written all over their faces. Eve would prefer not to be around for any discreet fondling or other forms of foreplay that might occur in the meantime.

"I want to work out still tonight." Or imagine Nolan moving over top of her while she got cozy with her mechanical friend. "So from your sister who isn't getting any, I bid you good night."

"Sounds like that might be changing." Tammy winked at her.

Eve gave her a stare. "Who are you—Suzanne? Since when do you encourage people to sleep with men they've just started dating?"

Elec coughed into his hand, a grin splitting his face.

Tammy's face turned red, obvious even in the dim porch light. She hugged her arms around her midsection and gave a shrug. "I don't know . . ."

Oh, God. They had had sex on the first date. Too much information. She'd always known they'd moved fast in their relationship and she seemed to recall a moment of horror when she had realized her brother was shagging a racing widow, but she'd never known details really. She didn't want them now.

Nor did she want to share her own.

Which was why she was an idiot to have broached the subject in the first place.

"Never mind. Forget I mentioned sex or men or anything that has to do with the interaction between men and women. I'm going to say good night to Pete and Hunter, then I'm heading to the gym." Where she could sweat her way through thoughts of Nolan, then get home and sweat through some more.

"Let me get you the keys to the car and the code to the storage unit," Elec said, patting Tammy's behind so she would stand up.

"What car?"

"Eve's borrowing one of my cars for the demolition derby. She's driving on Sunday."

"Really?" Tammy's eyebrows shot up.

"Really."

Her smile lit up the whole damn porch. "That's awesome! I think that's such a good idea. Wow! What made you decide to do that?"

"I don't know. Someone suggested it."

"That's great. Elec, isn't that great?"

"It is. I think it's a damn good idea."

They were starting to freak her out. Eve backed up from their smiling faces and pulled open the door to the house.

If everyone thought this was such an amazingly wonderful idea, she was starting to wonder if in fact, it was a truly awful one.

"So, what are the rules of the derby? How does it differ from stock racing?" Tammy asked.

Eve had no clue what the rules were. She'd witnessed the demo derby at the county fair a few times, but there were very likely regulations about the car itself. "You smash each other until you're the last drivable car on the track."

She made a mental note to look up the rules online when she got home.

"You purposely *hit* each other?" Tammy sounded horrified.

"Yeah. Doesn't that sound like a perfect hobby for Eve?" Elec asked cheerfully. "Smashing things. Right up her alley."

It was his face that was going to get smashed if he didn't stop making her sound so bloodthirsty.

Of course, that would just prove his point.

Yeah. This was probably a bad idea.

"SO, you in?" Nolan asked Eve the next morning, lying in bed contemplating a shower, phone to his ear. He was surprised, but pleasantly so, that she had called him instead of the other way around.

"Well. I thought I was." She sounded a little breathless and there was a loud clank in the background. "But I asked Elec for a car and there's a bit of a problem."

Hauling himself to a sitting problem, he yawned. "I told you that Rhett's car is available. It's no problem."

"I'd rather use Elec's because the point is to wreck it. I can't wreck your brother's car. Then I'll owe him a car. But the problem is . . ." She paused to grunt like she was shoving something. "I just read the car specs required to race, and I don't think I have time to get this hunk of metal up to regulation."

"So let's haul it to the garage. Three mechanics will have it in shape in an hour."

Nolan glanced at his watch. It was early still, only 8 A.M. Of course, Eve was an early riser, but he was still feeling a little lazy and half-awake. Scratching his bare chest, he stretched, the morning sun streaking across his navy blue bedspread.

"I can't ask those guys to do that!"

"Why not?" She was Evan and Elec's sister. There wasn't a mechanic on that team who wouldn't be happy to spare her a few minutes if it was going to get them in good with the bosses.

"In case you haven't noticed, I'm not exactly Miss Congeniality. No one is going to be dying to do me a favor."

Nolan was about to protest then he recalled the battle-ax comment. She might have a point.

"Besides, I don't want anyone to know."

"Why not?"

"Because it's none of their fucking business, that's why."

Now he was awake. Nolan sat up straight, his line of scratching migrating south. He'd woken up with an erection, and funny enough, Eve's cursing didn't kill it. It made it harder. "What can I do to help you out? Whatever you need, cupcake."

The nickname seemed to catch her off guard. The noise in the background quieted down. "Cupcake? Come on, that's just ludicrous."

"I like it." He did. He knew she was sweet even if she didn't.

"Never mind. The thing is, I have a hauler I can borrow and I can drive the hauler myself, but I can't load the car on it alone."

He waited for the question that should follow, but she couldn't seem to bring herself to ask him so he just rolled with it. "Sure, I can help you. We need to get you entered and the car has to be there by Saturday at five P.M."

"And I need the chrome trim, the glass, the headlights, and taillights all removed." She sounded breathless again.

"Are your doors painted?" The front doors needed to be whitewashed so that the staff could paint her competitor number on them.

"No."

Nolan wished she would have just accepted his offer of Rhett's car. They were going to be hard-pressed to get all that done by inspection time. But he understood why she was saying she didn't want to do that—she would owe Rhett a car. No one but the winner drove away from a derby, and it wasn't likely she'd win her first time out.

Frankly, it must be killing her to ask for help, and Nolan was pleased she trusted him enough to come to him. "Well, it's Friday. We can knock this out in a couple of hours today if you have some time. We can haul it to my parents' house. They have ten acres, plenty of gravel to park it and work on it."

There was a pause where he figured she was debating accepting that much help from him. Maybe the idea of meeting his parents unnerved her as well. But Nolan had figured how to deal with Eve for the most part. He just lounged in bed and waited, neither coaxing nor pushing. She'd decide what she wanted to do and that was that.

In the meantime, he relaxed against his pillows, eyes half-closed, his hand lightly stroking over his erection. This was a good way to wake up. The sunlight, a soft bed, the sound of Eve breathing over the phone. It obviously would be way better if she were actually in bed with him, naked, and not talking about the demo derby, but he could only hope someday soon she would be. In the meantime, he had a good imagination.

"I guess that would work. What are you doing right now?"

"Uh." Somehow he didn't think she'd want the truth. "I'm still in bed."

"Really?" An intrigued tone entered her voice. "Are you . . . never mind."

Nolan fought the urge to groan. His hand tightened on his cock. "Naked? Yes, as a matter of fact I am."

"That's not what I was going to ask!"

She was such a fibber. "No? Then what?"

"I was going to ask if you were busy, but then that seemed like a dumb question."

He didn't believe her, but he was willing to let it go. He was willing to let his erection go for now, too. Dropping his hand, he said, "Give me directions to where you're at. I can be there in twenty minutes."

"How do you know you can be there in twenty minutes? You don't know where I am."

Nolan laughed. "You got me there, cupcake."

"Stop calling me cupcake. It's sexist."

"Okay, muffin."

"Now that's *really* sexist."

He'd called her muffin, not muff. There was nothing sexist about baked goods as far as he could figure. But he knew better than to argue with her.

"Peaches?" Nolan threw back his covers and forced himself to stand. "Angel? Dollbaby? Hot stuff?"

"How about no nickname? How about you call me Eve? That works."

"Anyone can call you Eve."

"And what makes you so special that you can call me something else?"

Nolan paused in the act of rooting around in a drawer for his jeans. Ouch.

"I'm sorry," she said quickly. "I didn't mean that to sound as rude as it did. I was just giving you a hard time."

It took a lot to annoy him. He was annoyed. "I seem to recall you calling me strongman and peanut butter fudge ripple. More than once."

"You have a point. Okay, call me cupcake. It's only fair."

That was a major concession for her.

"And I am sorry. And I appreciate you helping me."

Those were catastrophic concessions. His anger deflated. "It's all good, Eve. I'll see you in *twenty* minutes."

She laughed. Which was what he wanted. Getting Eve to laugh felt like an achievement worthy of recognition.

"You're a stubborn man."

"That's the pot calling the kettle black."

"Except I'm not a man."

"I noticed. Oh, trust me, I noticed."

The erection was back, full force.

"We're going to end up having sex after the demolition derby, aren't we?" she asked, her voice husky.

Nolan loved that she just threw it all out there. Eve was definitely honest.

Working together, competing, banging cars, the adrenaline rush, and a post-derby beer . . . yeah, she had the right of it.

"I can pretty much guarantee it."

CHAPTER
FIVE

EVE had grown up around cars and haulers and had been allowed to drive on her parents' property by the time she was ten years old. It was no big deal to be behind the wheel of a hauler, and she wouldn't have cared less what anyone else thought. So why was she nervous pulling into Nolan's parents' gravel driveway?

Because Nolan Ford didn't criticize or mock her.

And she didn't seem to irritate him.

So for that very backward, messed-up reason, she was nervous around him. Whereas with everyone else, she knew what she was capable of and didn't give a rat's ass what they thought, with Nolan she wanted to show him she could do it.

It was so stupid it needed a whole new word for it.

So as she followed him up the long drive, nothing but

grass and corn growing as far as the eye could see, she vowed to get her shit together.

A brick ranch house sprung up out of nowhere. It was tidy and sprawling, but it still didn't look big enough to house nine kids. Nolan's arm popped out of the window of his truck and gestured for her to park to the left. There was a big gravel turnaround in front of the garage, a barn a few hundred feet from that.

As she turned the truck off, she saw the front door open and a man who looked an awful lot like her own father come strolling out. He was around six foot tall, still in good shape, hair almost completely gray. Behind him came Rhett, who Eve knew, but had never really made the connection was Nolan's brother. Rhett was the kind of guy who walked with swagger, who joked and teased and charmed.

The kind of guy Eve took great pleasure in slamming down into the dirt when he hit on her.

Nothing like Nolan.

Well, maybe a little like Nolan in that he was attractive and had green eyes. But Rhett's arms weren't as buff, and you always got the impression he wasn't telling you the full story. Nolan was pretty much the you got what you saw kind of guy. She dug that about him.

Oh, hell, who was she kidding? She just dug him.

They were going to have sex after the demo derby. He said he'd guarantee it. It was going to be hard to drive with that kind of anticipation.

She probably shouldn't have just thrown it out there like that. It probably made her look easy. But she said what she was thinking and that was exactly the thought that had been running through her head. Too late to take it back now.

Hopping down out of the truck, she swiped her hair out of her eyes.

"Eve, this is my dad, Nolan Ford Senior. Dad, meet Eve Monroe."

"It's nice to meet you," she said, sticking her hand out for a shake. "Thanks for letting me work on the car here. You have a nice property."

"My pleasure." He shook her hand firmly, which she appreciated. It was no wimpy you're a girl so I'll hold back shake. "We've got the room, might as well use it. Now that all the kids except for this loser"—he pointed to Rhett—"are out of the house, we have more land than we know what to do with."

"Gee, thanks, Dad. Way to make a guy feel good about himself." Not that Rhett looked the least bit concerned, really. He was grinning. "Eve, good to see you."

"Yeah, you, too. Nolan says you've driven in the demo derby before. Got any tips for a newbie?"

"Yeah. Hit hard."

Well, duh. "I'll remember that."

"No, seriously, hit first. They'll be gunning for you because you're a chick. And if anyone catches wind of who you are, they'll really be after you."

"Who am I?" she asked, even though she knew what he meant. The thought made her want to sigh.

"The Monroe family is racing royalty. Your father, your brothers . . . there's some serious record holding going on there. The other guys will want to take a piece of you just to have a story."

That pretty much summed up her life. Her dad and her brothers were the stars . . . she was the one everyone wanted to take a swipe at. She was the easy mark. The nondriver. The girl. Man, that pissed her off.

"I'll give them a story alright. When I tear off their bumpers and shove them up their asses. Metaphorically speaking, of course."

The three of them laughed. Nolan Senior rubbed his

chin. "Girl, I'm glad I'm not out there as your competition. I have a feeling you're going to be a power to contend with."

"I *am* driving against her," Nolan said, his hands in his sweatshirt pouch. "But you won't rip off my bumper, will you, cupcake?"

"Oh, actually yours is first," she assured him. "I'm taking you out right away because I don't need you distracting me."

Nolan Senior and Rhett seemed to find that riotously funny.

She was just being honest.

"You think you can take me out, huh?"

"Oh, I know I can."

"Then why am I helping you with your car? Not that I really think you can beat me."

But he did. It was written all over his face, and Eve found that incredibly flattering. "Because you're a nice guy, that's why. You're very thoughtful."

It was true. She was finding Nolan to be easy to be around for a lot of reasons, and that was definitely top of the list.

"Aw, how sweet," Rhett said. "Too bad she doesn't really know you yet."

Nolan glared at his brother. "Rhett, why don't you go looking for Scarlett in the house and mind your own business?"

Embarrassment had forced Nolan to take a low blow and mock his brother's name. Eve knew where this was going. She'd seen it between her brothers from time to time but mostly between herself and Evan.

"Shut up, dick."

Yeah, that was usually the way it went.

"Are you kidding me?" Nolan Senior asked. "You all

are going to stand here and name-call in front of this poor girl? I'm embarrassed for you both."

"Don't worry about me. Remember, I have brothers." Actually, she was usually the one name-calling.

"Yeah, well, that still doesn't make it right." Nolan's dad pointed to the car. "Boys, just get the poor girl's car down and do what needs to be done."

Eve wasn't sure she liked the label "poor girl" any more than "cupcake."

"Yes, sir!" Rhett saluted his father.

Nolan looked like he wanted to grumble. Eve figured he wanted to say that he was planning on it already, but stopped himself. Or maybe that's just what Eve would have wanted to say in those circumstances.

Instead of saying anything, Nolan just leaned over and gave her a quick kiss before taking the hauler keys out of her hand and heading over to help his brother.

Uh . . .

Eve stood there for a second, cheeks burning as she caught Nolan Senior's eye. Were they at that point? Kissing in front of a parent? They'd barely kissed without any parents present. One of Nolan's dad's eyebrows went up in question. She just gave him a sheepish look and went to join his sons.

She was in over her head. No question about it.

That became even more evident ten minutes later when she broke a taillight prying the plastic cover off. "Shit." She wasn't cut out to be a mechanic. Her skills lay in driving and telling drivers what to do.

"What's the matter?" Nolan asked her, peeling the chrome trim off the side of the car.

"I broke the taillight."

"Why did you take the cover off?"

"To remove it. You said to remove all glass."

"Isn't the cover plastic?"

Eve paused, her boot crunching a piece of glass in the gravel. Shit. "So you're saying I didn't have to remove it?"

"I reckon not."

"Ugh." Despite it being a cool day, Eve was sweating. She'd already painted the doors while Rhett and Nolan had removed the windows. Now Rhett was under the car running a gas pipe and she was starting to become very conscious of how much time she was spending. Both hers and theirs. Running the derby was supposed to be fun, spontaneous.

She wasn't having fun.

Why that was surprising her, she didn't know. Eve suddenly felt like crying. Why was it so goddamn hard for her to relax and enjoy herself? She had literally forgotten how.

Nolan, who was so damn intuitive it was downright scary, abandoned his chrome removal project and came over to her.

"Hey." He put his hands on her shoulders. "Don't sweat this. It's no big deal. We're going to be done in ten." He glanced at his cell phone. "We've only been out here for an hour and fifteen. Just a drop in the bucket of time."

She stared at him, wondering yet again why he was bothering with her. If she were him, she wouldn't. He wasn't a hugely tall guy and it didn't strain her neck to look up at him, searching for answers in his eyes. There weren't any there. All she could see was a confidence in what he was saying.

"I feel bad that I'm wasting your time."

"This was my idea, remember?"

"Yeah, but I asked you to help me with my car. Well, Elec's car."

"And I said yes, because I wanted to help. Easy as that. Don't go making it all complicated."

She was practical, not complicated.

"I swear, cupcake, when you get to heaven you're going to ask to see the upstairs. You complicate things."

Eve clamped down on a laugh. Okay, Nolan had moments where he was just funny, no doubt about it. "That's ridiculous," she told him with great dignity. "I would do no such thing. Mainly because it will be hard to do that from my place down south."

Heaven and hell weren't things she thought about all that often, but she figured it was more than likely she wasn't going to need a coat where she was going.

"In hell?" Nolan smiled. "What makes you think that's where you'll be? Are you a naughty girl, Eve Monroe?"

"Probably mean more so than naughty," she told him in all honesty.

Nolan had leaned in closer to her and Eve licked her lips. He was going to kiss her again, that was obvious. The air between them had changed as their bodies had shifted toward each other and their words had become flirtatious. It was a strange mystery how easily that happened to her around him. One minute she was normal, the next she was very aware of her breathing and her body, now with tightened nipples and a deep aching between her thighs.

Nolan kissed the side of her mouth, sliding up to her ear. "I don't think I agree with that. I don't think there's a mean bone in your body. I think you are naughty, though, and I want to see it," he murmured.

Eve shivered. If anyone else had said that to her, she would have rolled her eyes and walked away. She might have racked his testicles first, or threatened to anyway, and then turned her back on him, but she definitely would have left, muttering how he was an idiot.

But for some insane reason, hearing those words from Nolan just turned her on. She wanted to do naughty, dirty things to him, with him, under him, over him . . .

"You have no idea just how naughty I can be."

Nolan let out an exhalation of air then shifted his head so his mouth was on hers. It was a hot, intense kiss that had Eve digging her fingers into the fabric of his sweatshirt for a grip. The man could kiss. He took her lips perfectly, leaving her tingling and hungry for more.

His leg came between her thighs and his hands gripped the waistband of her jeans. It took only a few seconds to go from a teasing kiss to a passionate springboard to sex. Eve wanted to touch Nolan and she slid her hands downward. She wanted him to touch her just as much and he answered her silent plea by cupping her breast, while his tongue met hers in a hot tangle.

She was past his waist and honing in on his erection, wanting to stroke and grip it, when something hit her leg. Off balance, she shifted to the right, losing her contact with Nolan, the kiss interrupted.

Nolan groaned in disappointment, his hands raking into his hair.

Movement below them forced Eve's eyes downward and she realized what she had felt bumping her was Rhett sliding out from under the car on his back. He was grinning up at them, right between their legs.

"Oops, sorry."

"Seriously, man?" Nolan asked him. "I want to kill you right now."

"How was I supposed to know you were sucking face? I can't hear jack under the car." Rhett sat up. "But the good news is, the tank's in."

Eve wasn't sure she could speak yet. She was still panting. What the hell? She had completely lost control. Normally she wouldn't have dreamed of making out with his brother so close by and his parents probably looking out the kitchen window at them. It was not like her at all to forget about her surroundings. To forget about her responsibilities. To forget about everything but the man kissing her.

"Screw the tank," Nolan grumbled.

"I don't think that's what you really want to screw." Rhett bounded to his feet and gave Eve a grin and a wink. "Sorry, Eve. But if I were you, I'd make him wait anyway. It'll be good for him."

Eve sort of wanted to punch Rhett, but at the same time, she knew she should be grateful to him. It wasn't so much that she felt like she needed to make Nolan wait or play some kind of game with him. But she shouldn't be nailing him in his parents' driveway. That just wasn't Emily Post.

She couldn't claim she was a big expert on etiquette, but she did think having sex in front of the parents crossed a certain line, and the way she'd been feeling, it had been a real possibility.

She was not going to touch that comment. "I don't know what you're talking about," she told Rhett. "Thanks for doing the tank and pipe. If you're done, I think I'll take the car for a test drive."

Rhett was standing between her and Nolan, in what she suspected was an intentional move to piss his brother off. She recognized the signs. So instead of allowing their conflict to escalate, she figured she'd just separate them. It was what her mother always did, and the truth was, she didn't want to be a source of tension between them. Nolan was always telling her to chill, so she figured she could do the same for him. There would be opportunities to make out that didn't involve his brother lying at her feet.

"Nolan, want to race me?"

That got the reaction she was hoping for. He grinned at her and said, "Oh, hell, yeah, I will race you."

Eve hadn't been behind the wheel in years, and now

that the possibility was in front of her, she had to admit she was looking forward to it. "Can we drag in your parents' driveway?"

He shrugged. "Sure. It's long enough. We've always gone off-road, too, but we don't want to risk killing your engine before the derby." He clapped his hands together. "This is going to be fun."

"I'm warning you, Eve, he cheats," Rhett said, smiling at her again as he wiped his hands on a rag.

"Do you think you can stop being a jerk for five minutes? God, I feel like we're teenagers again."

"We weren't teenagers at the same time," Rhett pointed out. "I'm eight years younger than you."

By this point, Eve very possibly would have hit her brother. But Nolan just looked amused. Even when he grumbled at Rhett, he didn't really sound angry.

In response to Rhett's comment, he just laughed. "You've got a point, bro. Even more reason you shouldn't be so disrespectful to your elders." He gave Rhett a nudge and Eve a grin. "Eve would never talk to me like that."

That was reason for all of them to laugh. But to give Rhett credit, he didn't guffaw. He just shook his head and said, "Alright, I'm going in for a shower. I don't want to be around for whatever is about to happen. I'm of an innocent and delicate nature."

"That's the biggest load of bullshit I've heard in a while. But thanks for your help. Appreciate it."

"Yeah, thanks, Rhett." Eve pulled the keys out of her pocket. A sudden rush of adrenaline pumped through her at the thought of racing. She had always loved it. The speed. The strategizing. The triumph as she drew past an opponent. She'd loved it all and she realized how much she had missed it.

In the years since she'd quit, she had ignored the feelings, shoved them in a box and kept the lid on. When she was at the track, she thought in very clinical, professional terms. She never stood and watched a race with the eye of a spectator or with the thrill of a driver. She saw it with business eyes.

Not nearly as entertaining.

Happier and lighter than she had felt in ages, Eve reached out and gave Nolan a smacking kiss on the lips. "Start your engine, strongman."

NOLAN was starting to think that his passing crush on Eve Monroe had increased. A lot. It was the only explanation for why seeing her smile made him feel like a kid with one fist full of candy and the other full of fireworks.

"Let me get my keys and it's on, girl." Nolan wondered if he could snag another kiss, but figured maybe he should wait for her to come to him again. He really had enjoyed it when she'd taken the initiative because it showed him she'd let down her guard, something he just knew she didn't do very often.

"Now I'm 'girl'?" She put her hands on her hips. "We really need to have a talk about this nickname crap. After I kick your butt racing I'm going to make you write 'Her name is Eve' a hundred times."

"You don't scare me."

"Well, I should. I scare everyone else." She tossed her keys in the air.

It wasn't often that Nolan brought a woman to his parents' house. It had probably been a few years since he had. Yet he liked Eve standing in the driveway, her derby-ready car behind her, the late harvest corn in the field behind that. She was just wearing jeans and a sweatshirt again. It seemed to be her out-of-work uniform and he liked that. She didn't wear a lot of makeup either, and he had no trouble picturing her as a rough-and-tumble tomboy, wrestling with her brothers and getting into trouble. Some men might not find that sexy, but he did. He didn't want a high-maintenance woman whose every conversation revolved around clothes, gossip, and her latest diet.

He liked a woman who could wear heels when the occasion called for them, but play in the dirt the rest of the day.

Like Eve.

"I guess I'm just not like everyone else."

She studied him, like she was debating a wisecrack or not. It was a look Nolan was already familiar with. Finally, she just shook her head. "No, you're not. And you're nuts."

"Come on inside for a second so I can grab my keys and hit the garage door opener." His dad had told him his mom was in the shower, but Nolan figured she had to be done by then and he kind of wanted her to meet Eve, even if it was just for a minute.

"Sure."

When they went in the back door into the kitchen, Eve asked, "Should I take off my shoes?"

"Oh, Lord," his mother said, at the counter slicing a tomato for a sandwich she was assembling. "Don't worry about it. After nine kids, this floor has seen better days. When I win the lottery I'm replacing it."

It was one of his mother's favorite statements. There were a lot of things she intended to do when she won the lottery, except she never bothered to play it.

"Hey, Momma." He kissed her cheek and swiped a tomato. "This is Eve Monroe. Eve, this is my mother, Sandy Ford."

Nolan had seen Eve irritated. Uncomfortable. Antagonistic. But he'd never seen her shy.

At the moment, she was looking just that.

"Hi, Mrs. Ford, it's a pleasure to meet you. Thanks for letting me work on my car in your driveway."

His mother waved the knife in the air. "Oh, sure thing,

honey. The boys are always taking things apart in this driveway. Tractor parts, car parts . . . they're scattered all over. It's nice to meet you, too. You're Evan's sister?"

"Yes. Elec's, too, obviously."

"She is their PR rep," he told his mother. "She's like the person between the drivers and the fans and the drivers and the sponsors."

"So you deal with all the pain in the butt stuff and everyone else gets all the glory, huh?"

His mother was good at cutting to the chase.

Eve grinned. "Yeah. That about sums it up."

"I guess not everyone is born to be a show-off. Hopefully your brothers appreciate you."

"Sometimes. But that's okay. Because I don't always appreciate them."

"It's hard that way with family. You take them for granted." His mother finished making her sandwich. "Are y'all hungry? Do you want a sandwich?"

"No, thank you," Eve said. "I ate a late breakfast."

Nolan would have liked to have said yes, but he could wait a little while. He didn't want to pass up a chance to race Eve. "I'm fine, too, thanks. We're going to test out Eve's car."

He'd left the keys to his car on the wooden key rack that had been hanging by the back door for as long as he could remember. Its lettering stating the obvious—KEYS— was almost completely worn off.

"Have fun. Your sisters are bringing the grandbabies by this afternoon, so cease and desist when you see the mini-van pull up. It's not safe."

"What time?"

"About an hour."

They weren't going to be drag racing for an hour. Nolan wanted to be kissing by then. "Okay, no problem." He wasn't sure which sisters his mother meant. Five of them had kids and they all lived fairly close by. Only his sister Rachel had moved away. She'd gone to college in Atlanta, then had migrated all the way out to California, which his dad seemed to think meant she had suffered brain fever. In his eyes, only crazy folk wanted to live in a state that might fall into the ocean.

Nolan snagged another tomato slice and popped it in his mouth. Eve made a face at him. "What? You don't like tomatoes?"

"No."

"Tomatoes are perfect. How could you not like tomatoes?"

"They're slimy. And seedy. And the rind is chewy. They're a guaranteed gag."

"Tell me how you really feel."

"I always will." She opened the kitchen door. "Now quit avoiding your butt-beating. Thanks again, Mrs. Ford."

"Call me Sandy, honey. And don't show my son any mercy out there."

Eve laughed.

"Gee, thanks, Mom. I appreciate the support."

"I just think the best driver should win, that's all."

That was going to be him. If he could stop staring at Eve's butt long enough to focus on driving, that is.

As he pulled his car out of the garage, Nolan automatically checked his brakes and his engine. Everything felt good. He pulled up next to Eve.

"We need a flagger," she yelled out her window at him.

Damn, she looked hot behind the wheel. She was surrounded by that hunk of metal, windows out, doors a sloppy white, her hair pulled up in a ponytail. It was beyond sexy and he had to remind himself to focus again.

"Nah. Fingers up, on three."

She nodded and they both brought their hands up. "One, two, three . . ."

Eve managed to hit the gas a split second before he did, which made him grin. Cupcake had some good reflexes. Then he concentrated on the straightaway. They had agreed to go to the end of the drive, turn in the field, her right, him left, then back to the garage. It was a bit narrow with two cars and they were kicking up a bit of dust, but that was what made it fun. He nudged ahead of her, but to her credit, she held within two feet of him. But he was going to smoke her on the turn. She didn't know the feel of the drive the way he did, and she hadn't been racing in years. The turn was going to kill her speed.

Or not.

Damn.

Nolan came out of the turn hard and hit the gas, amazed to see that Eve had only lost another foot on him, but not nearly what he had expected. "Hell yeah!" he yelled, even though she couldn't possibly hear him. He was impressed. Turned on. Adrenaline pumping.

As he put the gas pedal to the floor, gravel spinning out behind him, Eve narrowed the gap between them. Shit, she might actually tie with him. Nolan went from impressed to concerned she might beat him. He lost the grin and focused on holding a straight line, making sure he avoided her drag. His car wasn't running as well as he'd like, but then again, he'd built it for the derby, for short bursts of acceleration, not a full-out race.

But so had Eve's.

They were coming in on the garage and neither one of them was slowing down. He realized that because he had assumed he would outpace her by fifty feet or more, the winner would be obvious and they wouldn't need a finish line. But they were neck and neck and the only finish line they'd stated was the garage. Which meant they were both riding up on it hard and fast, unwilling to be the one to brake first.

Eve had guts, he had to give her that.

Or they were both just stubborn.

Which he already knew she was.

He should brake. Any second now.

But he knew his car, knew the road, knew precisely how much time he had before he would hit the door.

She braked a split second before he did, coming down hard, tires spinning, her brakes squealing, his eyes focused on the rapidly approaching aluminum door. They both slammed to a stop just a hair's breath before impact, his body continuing forward until the seat belt jerked him back. Glancing over, he made sure Eve was okay. She was grinning as she killed her engine.

Yep. She was okay. More than okay.

"Holy shit," she called over to him. "That was freakin' awesome!"

"Baby, you were on fire!" he told her, grinning from ear to ear as he climbed out of his car. He leaned around the front of his car and measured the distance between his fender and the door. It was two inches, tops. He held up his fingers to show her, still grinning. Damn, it was fun to be around her.

She was climbing out of her car and she climbed right out onto the hood of her car, then his. Leaning over, she studied the difference between the two. "Dude, we are dead tied."

"That's because we were both stupid enough to ride up the ass of the garage door. That was driving, cupcake!"

Eve stood there, one foot on her hood, one on his, and laughed. She looked sexy as hell, windblown and happy, freer than he had ever seen her. The sun rose behind her, the sky blue and stuffed with clouds, a perfect fall day, a perfect woman.

God, he was in trouble.

But if this was trouble, it felt pretty darn good.

The kitchen door opened and his mother's head popped out. "Next time wear a helmet, for Chrissake!" she screamed. "I don't need any more gray hairs, Nolan Junior!" The door slammed shut again.

He laughed.

Eve looked sheepish. "Oops. I'm not making a good impression on your mother."

"She just likes to make her point loudly. You kind of have to when you're the mother of nine. Don't worry, she'll hold it against me, not you." He wasn't worried about his mother. He wasn't worried about anything.

He jumped up on the hood next to her.

"Hey! You'll bang up my car," she protested, backing up, smiling slyly.

She knew what he was going to do. She knew he was going to kiss her and she wanted it just as much as he did. And she wasn't even remotely worried about her car, he'd bet the farm on it.

"You're standing on it! What's the difference if I stand on it?"

"You're bigger than me."

He was stalking her on the hood as she backed up in a circle. "I'm not that much bigger."

"You calling me fat?" She backed up again, giggling.

"No. You calling me fat?"

"No. I'm calling you bigger than me. Muscular."

He liked the sound of that. "So stop moving and let me wrap my muscles around you."

"I don't even want to think about how dirty *that* sounds." She took a light jump backward and moved from her car to his.

"That doesn't sound dirty. It sounds weird if you even try to make it dirty." He put one foot onto the hood of his car. "Why are you running away? Do you have more pictures of me on your phone that I should delete? Did you catch me picking my nose?"

She laughed. "While going a hundred miles an hour? If we could do either one of those things we'd be freaks."

"I could probably pick my nose while driving. But I didn't. I actually don't ever pick my nose. So you don't need to run." Nolan was finding their whole exchange highly entertaining. They had descended into the ridiculous.

"I'm running because it's fun to make you chase."

He laughed. Her honesty cracked him up. He also knew just how to make her stop backing away. "Tease."

She came to a grounding halt. "I am not. I'm never a tease. That's for ditzy girls who suck lollipops."

"What?" Nolan laughed even louder. "Lollipops? Are you for real?"

"Yes. I am not a tease," she said adamantly.

"I was just giving you a hard time, you know. But Lord, now I know to never offer you a lollipop. You'll take my head off."

"Have you noticed I stopped moving?" Eve held her arms out.

Yeah, she was no tease. She wasn't necessarily a flirt either. But she was sexy as hell.

"I noticed. My muscles are coming for you. Just a warning."

"About time."

Nolan closed the space between them, wanting a kiss like the desert wants a rainstorm. The car rocked as he stalked.

As he reached out for her, Eve ducked to the right and jumped back onto her hood, her breathless laughter ringing in the air.

He should have seen that coming. "Dude, I can't believe I fell for that."

"Like taking candy from a baby."

Oh, she was so going to get it. Nolan jumped with a big leap so that he landed within inches of her. The car shook and she lost her balance.

"Ah!" she said, grabbing on to him to keep from falling.

"Now you're just all grabbing on me. Make up your mind, cupcake."

"You're an idiot," she said with a giggle, her eyes shining.

Man, he thought she was beautiful.

He wanted his lips on her in the worst way possible.

A horn blasted in the driveway behind them and Eve jumped again, almost going down a second time.

Shit. He turned, already knowing what he was going to see.

Minivan, six o'clock.

The car was barely brought to a stop when the side doors were sliding open and a pack of kids spilled out.

Nolan sighed. That was unfortunate. He couldn't exactly make out with Eve now.

"Uncle Nolan, why are you standing on that car?"

"Who is that lady?"

"Is she your girlfriend?"

"Do you kiss her?"

"Can I drive your car since I'm ten now?"

The questions came fast and furious from so many little mouths that Nolan couldn't tell which question belonged to which kid.

He jumped down off the car and offered a hand to Eve. He leaned in close to her and whispered, "We need to run. They can suck the life out of you in three minutes or less."

She smacked his arm.

"Ooohh, she hit you."

Eve's eyes widened.

"Told you." He grinned at her and turned to face the masses.

"All questions will be answered at the end of the program. Gran has cookies in the kitchen but you'd better hurry before Pops eats them all."

They scattered like roaches when the lights came on, trying to get to the kitchen door first. Nolan counted six of them and noted they were his two oldest sisters' kids. When the dust settled, he saw both women were eyeing him curiously.

"Hi," Jeannie said, sticking her hand out to Eve. "I'm Jeannie, Nolan's sister."

"Eve. Nice to meet you."

"I'm Sammy. Nolan's oldest sister."

"So what were you two doing?" Jeannie asked.

Eve was smiling, but it was a little strained. He figured she hadn't bargained on encountering ten-plus Fords in one afternoon outing. There were always a lot of them around. It came with the territory, but he did not want to scare her off.

"We're getting our cars ready to race in the derby tomorrow. But we're leaving now before your rugrats crawl all over Eve and ask her more inappropriate questions."

"Oh, it's fine," Eve protested. "We don't have to leave. I like kids."

"Jeannie's and Sammy's offspring aren't kids—they're piranhas. They devour everything in their path, including your sanity." Nolan was kidding. Sort of. He loved to play with his nieces and nephews, and act as their climbing tree. But they asked a lot of questions and he was nervous about how Eve might react to that.

"Are you a kid hater?" she asked him, her forehead wrinkling. "Because I don't do kid haters."

He wasn't sure if she meant that to have a double meaning or not, but he was certainly taking it that way.

"Oh, geez," Jeannie said, looking like she suddenly felt very sorry for him. "We can vouch for Nolan. He adores kids." Then she looked like she wasn't sure that was the right thing to say. She made a face and his sisters both trucked off toward the house.

Nolan barely noticed. He was focused on Eve. He wanted to nip this in the bud before he was denied the right to nip her bud. "I'm not a kid hater. I was joking. It's called kidding around." He put his hands on her shoulders. "Sometimes I do that."

Eve let Nolan rock her gently forward and back as she focused on his green eyes. She was feeling off-kilter. There were children and sisters and parents and she wasn't even sure how she had ended up here. A week ago she'd barely known Nolan Ford's name. Now his nephews wanted to know if he kissed her, and his sisters were studying her like she was a circus curiosity.

She didn't like meeting new people without wearing heels. In her career, that was how she gained her sense of power, feeling like she had the upper hand. She strolled around in power heels, her phone in her hand. But in jeans and a sweatshirt, caught nearly making out on the hood of a car with Nolan, she felt awkward.

It didn't seem in character that Nolan wouldn't like kids, but she was feeling like she didn't quite have a handle on the situation. It was jamming her ability to read him. But now, locking gazes with him, she both saw the truth and lost her nervousness. Nolan was such an easygoing guy. Of course he would like kids. And he liked her, and was concerned about her comfort level and was offering her a way out.

Which was thoughtful.

Which seemed to be the adjective that always popped up when she thought about him.

Plus hot. That was another good word for him.

"Sometimes I say that I'm going to rip your face off and I haven't really done that either," she told him. "So yeah, I get the concept."

He snorted. "You're a piece of work."

"Better than a piece of shit."

Then she remembered that he wasn't one of her brothers and it had been pointed out to her in the past that men didn't always appreciate her sense of humor. Like every man she'd dated in the last decade.

But Nolan laughed. He laughed with his mouth. He laughed with his eyes. He laughed with her, his hands slipping down from her shoulders to clasp hers.

Oh, God, they were holding hands. She was past thirty years old and she was pretty sure she hadn't felt this much like a giddy schoolgirl since she was a schoolgirl. Even then she'd never been giddy.

"Do you really want to leave or were you just trying to give me a choice?" she asked him, because she didn't like not really knowing what a person's true intention was. She dug clarity all the time.

Tuesday had pointed out she was a control freak.

She could admit that. But it didn't mean she was going to change it.

"I was trying to give you a choice. I'm fine either way. I wasn't sure if you had the time blocked today to hang out or if you needed to get to work. Or if a whole houseful of strangers was not in your plans. I'm flexible." He lifted his arm and flexed his muscle.

Eve rolled her eyes. "What is this, charades?" But she appreciated that he was being . . . thoughtful. Damn, there it was again.

She decided it was time to go home. She'd shaken things up enough for the day.

She had driven a car for the first time in years. Really driven it. Opened that sucker up and pushed the engine. When she and Nolan had been neck and neck toward the finish line, she had felt an exhilaration she hadn't experienced in she couldn't remember when.

Taking it right to the edge of when she could brake, trusting her instincts, proving herself right, had been a fantastic high.

Then joking around with Nolan, meeting his family.

It was a lot of stimulation.

She didn't want to bolt, but she definitely thought it was time to go home. "I think I should go and get some work time before the weekend. Should I take my car back tonight or can I leave it here until the morning?"

"I'll have Rhett drive your hauler to the track. Just meet us there about four, okay?"

"Sure. Thanks." Eve felt like she should kiss him. She wanted to kiss him. Yet she hesitated and wound up giving him a hasty awkward hug before getting the hell out of there.

When she got home, she threw on her sweats and went for a run, pounding the pavement with hard, angry movements, unsure what was going on in her life. Unsure why she was reacting the way she was to Nolan.

Unsure why it was so easy to laugh with him.

As the sweat started to accumulate on the back of her neck and under her bra, Eve pushed harder, her mind slowing, clearing.

Running was her savior. Before, when she'd been competing as a teen, driving had been a way to focus. It had settled her scattered and frantic mind. Once that was gone, she'd found running. When her feet pounded and her arms pumped, the only thing she could hear was her own breathing.

She tried to reach that state of nothing, but it eluded her tonight.

Even though she was going fast enough to feel the burn in her calves, Eve still saw Nolan in front of her.

How annoying was that.

Maybe she should have ripped his face off when she'd had the chance, then he wouldn't be disturbing her run like a sexy jack-in-the-box.

Left foot.

There was him flexing his biceps.

Right foot.

There he was jumping on the hood of her car.

After two miles, she gave up, went home, and took a shower.

Then opened her nightstand drawer, pulled out her special friend, and let Nolan dance in front of her all he wanted.

And when she reached climax, she murmured his name, feeling like an absolute and utter dork as she did it.

But she did it anyway.

CHAPTER
SIX

NOLAN was playing Rock Band with his niece draped across his back and shoulders when his mother came up and stood next to him, a kitchen towel in her hand. "Did you need something, Momma?"

He was playing guitar and it took a bit of concentration. His nephew Ford was on drums and his niece Asher was singing her six-year-old heart out to Def Leppard. Or an approximation of singing anyway. Her reading skills were sketchy and she seemed to be interpreting the lyrics at will, but that only made it all the more entertaining.

"I just wanted to ask you what exactly you're doing with the Monroe girl."

Oh, Lord. Nolan passed the guitar back over his shoulder to Jessa. "Take my spot, baby doll. I'm going to help Gran in the kitchen."

Jessa conked him on the head accidentally with the guitar when she took it, but otherwise the exchange was seamless and Nolan stood up.

"That Monroe girl has a name, Momma. It's Eve."

"Don't sass me."

"How is that sassing you?" Suddenly Asher's screeching was getting on his nerves. He started toward the kitchen.

"Where are you going?"

"I want a cookie."

"Nolan Junior, I'm talking to you."

"Let's chat in the kitchen. It's noisy in here."

His mother looked bewildered. She was used to constant noise. She'd spent the last forty years with children hollering all around her. But Nolan was used to living alone now and his head was hurting. Eve had left in a hurry. Without kissing him. She had hugged him like they were platonic friends.

Was that how she saw him?

It was a puzzle that had him a tad worried.

He didn't like to worry.

Now his mother wanted to talk to him. Never a good sign.

There were still cookies on the cooling rack and he snagged one. Snickerdoodle. "What I'm doing with Eve is dating her. It's brand-new though, so it's of a delicate nature." He actually thought she was of a delicate nature, despite her obvious tough side. That hard exterior was hiding a vulnerable inside.

"She's your bosses' sister."

"Technically Carl is my boss. Evan is sort of like my manager."

The look she gave him said she wasn't buying it. But it was the truth. "Momma, don't worry. I'm not doing anything stupid. I would never jeopardize my job."

"Have you really thought this through? You know you have a tendency to rush into relationships."

"What? I do not." He did not. Maybe in high school, but all teenagers did that.

"Carrie Wheeling."

"Momma, that was tenth grade."

"Lauren what's her name, the redhead. You knew her for two days and you were out at Walmart shopping for a diamond."

Way to embarrass the hell out of him. "I was twenty-one. I was very passionate at that age."

"Langely. And Nicole."

He shrugged, popping the rest of the cookie in his mouth. "Those were both really good relationships, you know."

"They lasted about a minute."

It was a year, easily for both, but he wasn't going to argue with her. She needed to say her piece.

"Do you know why they burned out?"

Talk about a rhetorical question. "Why?"

"Because you rushed into a serious relationship with a woman who you wanted to help. To fix."

He needed another cookie for this. Nolan filled his mouth so he wouldn't tell his mother exactly what a load of bullshit he thought that was.

"I think you're a good man for wanting to help, but you can't fix someone else. You can't take in a stray dog without realizing it will bite you at one point."

Now she was comparing his former girlfriends to dogs. Time to extract himself from this conversation.

"I'm thirty-three years old. My love life is my own and for the most part I've been happy with it. So don't stress. It's all good." He peeled himself off the counter he'd been leaning on and kissed his mother on the top of her head. "Thanks for caring."

She gave him a suspicious look. "I just want to know what's wrong with her. There's always something wrong with the girls you bring home."

Nolan laughed. "There's nothing wrong with her. She doesn't have an eating disorder, or drink too much. She doesn't have daddy issues and she's not OCD." Though as the words came out of his mouth, he realized he didn't one hundred percent know any of those things. It wasn't like he spent that much time with Eve.

"She doesn't seem happy, that's for sure."

That gave him pause. "You didn't see her laughing when we were dragging. I make her laugh."

His mother's finger came up. "See? There it is. You're trying to make her happy. Fix her. Bad idea, Junior."

"I respectfully disagree. We're just getting to know each other. I'm not repeating any patterns." He didn't really believe he had any patterns. "I repeat, it's all good."

But her words nagged at him.

He ended up eating half a dozen cookies and bombing out at Rock Band before saying good-bye and heading home.

When he lay in bed later that night, he tossed and turned, his mind unable to escape the image of Eve laughing, her amber-colored eyes sparkling in the crisp autumn air.

Maybe introducing her to his family so soon had been a mistake.

But racing her? Kissing her?

He didn't regret either for one minute.

Something that felt so damn good was never a mistake.

He punched his pillow, hot and restless.

When the images of Carrie, Lauren, Langely, and Nicole filled his head, like an assembly line of all his failed relationships, he groaned.

It wasn't bad to be thirty-three and never married. It meant he was waiting for the right woman.

So how was that rushing into things?

Giving up on sleep, Nolan got out of bed and trotted into his kitchen barefoot for a glass of orange juice. His apartment was poky and dark with a motley assortment of cast-off furniture from relatives. But now as he squinted against the bright light of the refrigerator, pulling out the carton of OJ, he wondered about Eve, growing up with money.

Living in a big old house as a kid and probably in a ritzy condo as an adult.

Did things like that matter to her? His apartment was small but clean. For the most part.

He drank straight out of the carton, because he lived alone, and hey, he could do that.

Everyone kept insisting it was stupid to date his bosses' sister.

Were they right?

He slapped the carton of juice back on the shelf. Now he was worrying about stupid shit the way she did.

If it worked out, it worked out. If it didn't, it didn't.

In the meantime, he was just looking to enjoy Eve's company.

End of story.

EVE was in a foul mood by the time she got to the track on Saturday. She hadn't slept more than an hour. She'd been up and down all night, her muscles sore from pushing too hard during her run, her head pounding from lack of sleep and stress, and her nerves jangling over the upcoming derby.

She did not want to make an ass out of herself.

Dragging with Nolan in the driveway had been one thing, but this was in front of thousands of people. People who were looking to judge her and find her lacking. Hell, media might even be there and find it an entertaining story. This had never been her style of competition. It was a different skill set to race at high speed around the turns than to purposefully crash into other vehicles.

As she entered the pit area, helmet under her arm, she felt irrationally angry with Nolan. This was his fault. All this stress she was feeling wouldn't exist if he hadn't suggested she do something as stupid as enter the derby on about a minute's notice. She wanted to stomp. She wanted to quit. But she wasn't a quitter.

Or was she?

She had walked away from competitive racing after all.

The thought just made her angrier.

It took a lot of effort to greet Nolan with any sort of civility. "Hey," she said when she walked up to him and Rhett, both cars off the haulers and ready for inspection.

For the first time since she'd met him, Nolan didn't have a smile for her. He barely glanced at her as he filled out paperwork. "Hey. You need to sign these release forms and hand them in."

He shoved some paper at her. Still not looking at her.

What the hell did she do to deserve that?

Then she berated herself. What did she expect? Him to greet her with a big old smooch and words of encouragement?

Actually, yes.

She was already used to that with Nolan. Five days and she'd never known him to be anything but eager to see her.

This must be his game face before competition.

His game face sucked and she hated it.

Of course her game face was on, too, and it was a bitchy one, so she had no room to talk.

Which also annoyed her.

"I can do that. Do you have a pen?"

"I'm using this one. Don't you have one in your purse? All women have one in their purse."

Eve had come to the track alone. Her phone was in her back pocket and her change purse with her ID was in the pouch of her sweatshirt. She didn't have a purse. In fact, she rarely carried a purse. She either streamlined like today or she had a gigantic bag that held promo items and other miscellaneous items along with her wallet, but she would call that a satchel, not a purse. None of which mattered in the slightest other than she didn't like being lumped in the "chick" category, and excuse me, was his tone surly? She was not in the mood for surly.

"If I had one in my freakin' purse, I wouldn't be asking you for one, would I?"

He raised his hand in an imitation of a cat swipe. "Pull the claws back. It's just a pen."

Eve blinked. He so did not just say that.

She reached out and yanked the pen from his hand. "What is your problem?" Without waiting for an answer, she started filling out the form.

Name. Eve Pissed-Off Monroe.

Expecting Nolan to make a comment, she held the pen tightly. But he didn't. She did hear Rhett ask him, "Are you okay, man? You look rough."

"I didn't sleep much last night."

She paused, wanting to look up, but restraining herself. So Nolan hadn't slept well either? Did that mean anything?

Probably all it meant was that explained why he wasn't as chipper as he usually was. It couldn't possibly mean that he had been thinking about her the way she'd been thinking about him. Eve's cheeks burned as she stared down at the paper, remembering how she had touched herself, imagining it was him, sliding his fingers deep down inside her while he kissed her jaw, her neck, her nipple.

"You sure you want to do this?"

Eve wasn't sure about anything. Well, actually, she was sure about wanting to have sex with him. But she realized Rhett was asking Nolan, not her.

"Of course I'm going to do it."

Which was exactly what she would say if anyone asked her. There was no way she was backing out now, despite the potential for humiliation. She had something to prove. To herself. To Nolan. To every man out there who had looked at her as a kid and a teenager and told her girls don't drive. To her family, who thought she didn't know how to have fun.

She was going to make fun her bitch.

"Ready for inspection?" Nolan said.

She realized he was talking to her so she looked up. It shocked her how tired he actually looked. There were dark circles under his eyes and his shoulders drooped. A wave of sympathy washed over her. "I guess I'm ready. Are you okay? I heard you say you didn't sleep much."

He shrugged. "I'll live. And I'm guessing you had the same problem." His finger brushed under her eye, sending a shiver up her spine. "We have matching luggage."

Not what she wanted to hear. It was true, but she didn't need him to tell her she looked like crap.

"My dreams of besting you kept me from a deep sleep."

His eyebrows rose. "Oh, yeah? Good luck with that, rookie."

"Don't underestimate me." A part of her realized she was baiting him, but she couldn't seem to stop herself. Evan always told her she was itching for a fight, and she had a feeling that was what she was doing here.

But Nolan wouldn't rise to her challenge. Or irrational poking, however you wanted to label it.

"I wasn't planning on it."

"Good." Deflated, she went back to her paperwork.

She was in the middle of writing an "r" when the pen was whisked out of her grasp.

"You done with that?" he asked her with a grin.

So much for not rising to her bait. Eve wanted to laugh. She wanted to beat him with her clipboard.

And mostly she wanted to kiss him, to feel him rocking his body against hers, thick hot erection pressing against her.

It made no sense, but there it was. She could be in the worst mood possible and he could manage to make her smile. And horny.

"You better watch it, Ford. Your ass is grass and I'm the lawn mower."

That made him grin. "You sound like my grandfather."

"Were you scared of him as a kid?"

"Yes."

"Good. Be scared of me, too."

Nolan turned up the twang in his country voice. "I ain't afraid of you. I ain't afraid of nothin'."

The urge to kiss him returned. She was going to combat that. God only knew who was watching them. She wasn't ready to deal with anyone asking her about her relationship with Nolan. Not that it was a relationship. But she didn't want anyone asking her about whatever it was.

"I'm walking away from you," she told him. "Because you're a dork."

He let out a crack of laughter before he reined it in. "See you on the track when I take you out."

"You wish." Eve suddenly realized that some people might consider their exchange witty banter. Or people might say they sounded like a couple of middle schoolers at the roller rink arguing over whether to join the couples skate or not.

She was hoping the truth was somewhere actually in the middle.

Her experience with dating wasn't excessive. Or even average. So she truthfully didn't know what she was doing when it came to men. All she knew was she was who she was and she wasn't going to change for a man. She wasn't going to start simpering and tempering her opinions for a penis. She was pretty sure that would actually kill her if she even tried.

"I wish a lot of things," he told her. "I usually get them."

She studied him for a second, knowing full well he was flirting. But that wasn't the kind of flirting that sat well with her. Teasing or not, she didn't want to be something he got because she was a challenge. Another accomplishment to boost his ego that he wouldn't be denied his choice.

It didn't seem to her that Nolan would be that kind of guy, but what did she really know about him? Why did she think she knew if he would smile or frown or brag or be modest?

She didn't know him.

At all.

And for a woman who liked to be in control, that annoyed her. A lot.

"I'm not that easy," she told him and walked away.

Eve resisted the urge to turn around but she felt his eyes on her. On her butt. Or maybe that was wishful thinking.

That worrying thing? It was back.

She busted out an expletive that would make a sailor's hair curl.

Did sailors have hair?

So many damn things to worry about.

She was going to have a heart attack without ever having seen Nolan naked.

And that was a crying shame.

* * *

NOLAN sat behind the wheel waiting for the flag, trying to channel his irritation into the derby. He didn't like feeling annoyed. He rarely was. But something about Eve Monroe had him feeling like his skin was too tight. He hadn't decided if that was good or bad.

Maybe it was the lack of a good night's sleep. Which had also been because of Eve, but he was feeling off. Irritable. Not good.

Edgy. That's how he felt. Like he was on the verge of something.

When the flag waved to start the competition, he was ready. With more determination than the thrill he usually had. Usually he enjoyed the derby—that's why he did it. But today, he felt like he was on a mission to destroy every car around him.

He couldn't see Eve yet. Her car had been painted with a big number 1 on the doors. No one ever got the number 1, but when the crew had been assigning numbers, some smart-ass had seen Eve was the only woman in the competition and given her the number 69. She'd had a little chat with the man in charge, and after he looked like he wanted to caress his balls to make sure they were still there, the number 1 had gone on her car.

It had made Nolan grin. No one was going to mess with Eve.

What didn't make him grin was that he had no idea what was really going on in that head of hers. Sometimes she flirted. She kissed him passionately. She implied they were heading to a mutual naked state. But other times, she seemed more friendly than flirty. Today she'd been downright annoyed with him, and he had no clue what he'd done.

The question was did he want to go around feeling like

that? It seemed like a whole lot of complicated and he wasn't big on that.

He slammed into the car on his right, sending it hurtling back into the wall. Yeah, that felt good.

A car nailed him from behind. Glancing back, he saw the driver and recognized that slender neck and caramel hair sliding out of that helmet. Eve was gunning for him.

She could hit him from behind all she wanted. It wouldn't take him out. It would just propel him into the cars in front of him, several of which were turned sideways. When he went straight into them, they scattered like bowling pins. One hit the wall, one went into the infield, another just stalled on the track. He raised his hand and did a fist pump to show Eve she'd helped him out. He had a sneaking suspicion that had not been her intention.

Nolan liked the sound of the track. He could vaguely hear the crowd, but mostly it was the roar of the engine, the clash of metal, and the spinning of tires in the mud. It smelled like gasoline, exhaust fumes, and hay, a combination that reminded him of childhood. He'd been playing at the derby for years, and he'd gotten Rhett into it when he'd turned eighteen. He considered it a good way to let off steam, and to have the challenge of strategizing where to go and who to hit and how hard.

It was like a real live-action video game and he enjoyed it.

They were running in a qualifying heat. Top two drivers of the four heats went on to the final derby the weekend after next. It was dumb luck that he and Eve were even competing against each other. If he didn't know better, he'd think she had paid off the judges to arrange it that way. The only reason he didn't think she had was because she hadn't had time. Otherwise, he had an inkling she would pay to nail him and his car as hard as she could.

Which made him think of sex again. Bad timing. He forced his thoughts back to the task at hand.

When he turned his car slightly to maneuver around the stalled number 43, there was plenty of time to see Eve drive past him into the hole in traffic he'd been planning to use, flipping him off.

Flipping him off. How unsportsmanlike was that? She wouldn't do that to anyone else out there. Punk.

That girl needed to learn some manners and he figured he was just the man to teach her.

EVE almost let out a squawk when she saw the look on Nolan's face. She'd been messing with him, pulling past him and giving him the bird. It had been an impulse and not a particularly smart one. Why on the rare occasions she chose to be spontaneous was it always a mistake? She hadn't factored in that game face on Nolan probably meant he wouldn't be in the mood for her teasing. Even with his helmet, she could see the intensity on his face.

"Oh, shit," she said to no one in particular. At this point, she felt like the field of eight was half cleared. The traffic of moving cars was thinning, but there were stalled-out cars in various positions on the track, creating an obstacle course of junkers. Her own car had a blown front end tire, making driving through the mud tricky.

Hitting her gas, she skirted a Camaro, or what was left of a Camaro, and skidded sideways, wanting to hit another car with her bumper. She was definitely enjoying herself. The quick decisions, the adrenaline, the teeth-rattling impact of hits were all exciting. Fun.

It was like racing at Nolan's parents' house. She felt alive. Giddy. Not stressed or tired, just exhilarated. When she got high like that, she tended to use hand gestures, hence the flipping Nolan off. It had seemed like good clean fun. Now he was after her, nudging her backside like she had been doing to him. It just made her want to laugh.

The truth was, she didn't one hundred percent know what she was doing behind the wheel, and her strategy was sketchy at best, yet she was still having fun. That was liberating.

When she tried to wiggle into a spot between two cars for protection, her plan backfired and she ended up taking a full-impact hit on her front end, while Nolan took her back end. She needed to tell him to stay away from her rear for future reference.

She knew that was it. She stalled, her engine sputtering, half of her bumper dragging in the dirt. Her hood had crumpled and her visibility was poor, but she managed to limp a few feet before it was over. Just for grins, she tried to get the engine to turn, but it had officially quit the race. Glancing around, she saw that there were only two cars still moving on the track, one of them Nolan's. She hadn't done a bad job for her first time out.

She couldn't really blame Nolan for taking her out. She'd tried to do it first. It was the way the game worked. But she was definitely going to grumble about it.

No one could beat her when it came to grumbling.

CHAPTER
SEVEN

NOLAN finished a very respectable second, but as he climbed out of his car, he still didn't feel right. He felt caged. Wound tight. Unsure of how to proceed with Eve.

He was never unsure when it came to women. He trusted his gut. He listened to the words and the physical cues they were giving him. It wasn't complicated.

Why the hell was Eve so complicated?

Or maybe it was his mother's words rolling around in his head, telling him he rushed into things.

So while he wanted desperately to follow up on their earlier flirt and invite Eve over to his place for a night of wine and sex, hold the wine, he was kind of thinking maybe he shouldn't.

He climbed through his windshield and stood on the hood of his car, giving a gesture of victory to the crowd when they called his name. His finish meant he would be going on to the next round in two weeks, but Eve wouldn't. He wondered if she was pissed about that fact, or pissed about the fact that the announcer kept referring to her as "the girl" while they were competing.

But she didn't look pissed about anything as she climbed out of her car, onto the hood, then leaped to the dirt. Her helmet was already off and she was grinning.

When the announcer said, "Let's hear it for our girl out there, Eve Monroe, of the legendary racing family," she just waved to the cheering crowd.

Nolan's car was still drivable, so he took it off the track, then bit his fingernails, wondering if he should find Eve or not.

Instead his brother found him. "Good run, bro." Rhett slapped him on the back.

"Thanks. I still don't understand why you weren't out there." The derby had been a long-standing favorite pastime of Rhett's until six months earlier, then suddenly he had decided he didn't want to do it anymore. Just like that. But that was Rhett. He was into something, then he wasn't.

"My talents are better used elsewhere."

Nolan snorted. "As what, a male stripper?"

"Maybe."

That was a tone of voice he didn't like. Nolan eyeballed his brother. "You'd better fucking be kidding."

"What if I was a stripper, so what? It's my life." Rhett was pouting, decimating a pinecone lying on the ground with his boot heel.

Oh, Lord. Nolan rubbed his temples. The lack of sleep was catching up with him. He was tired. "You sound like a sixteen-year-old brat. And if you're a stripper, I hope it pays well because Mom is going to throw your ass out into the street."

"Maybe that wouldn't be such a bad thing," he muttered.

Before Nolan could respond to that out of left field comment, Rhett was looking around him.

"Hey, Eve," Rhett said with a nod.

Nolan whirled around to see her approaching them. She always walked with purpose and she was doing that now.

"Hey, Rhett, how's it going?"

"Good, good. I'll catch up with y'all later. I'm going to buy some fries before they close the grandstand down."

Nolan stared after his brother for a second. "Something's bugging him, but I guess if he wanted to share, he would."

Speaking out loud wasn't necessarily a conscious decision, so he was startled when Eve responded.

"Maybe you should ask him what's bothering him."

Prying with Rhett was never a good strategy. He knew that from experience. "I'm sure it's nothing more than the fact that he got stuck with that name."

"I think you're jealous of that name."

Hardly. "I'm happy with the one I got, thanks." Nolan smiled at Eve. "So not bad out there for a first-timer."

"Thanks. Congrats to you, too." She smiled at him.

There was a pause where they just stared at each other, smiling, and Nolan decided Rhett wasn't the only one acting sixteen. So he moved in closer to Eve, raising his eyebrows up so she would clearly get his intent.

She shook her head, backing up a step. "Don't you dare kiss me in this infield with a whole grandstand of people watching."

"No one's looking." He ran his finger down her arm. "Come on. Give me some sugar."

He thought she would. That she'd realize that no one was the least bit concerned with what they were doing.

But she put her hand out. "Stop. No. By the way, you know your hit is the one that took me out. I think you should apologize for that."

Feeling the sting of rejection, Nolan scoffed. "No way. It's the way the game works. I can't play favorites out there. Especially when you won't even kiss me."

"So if I give you sexual favors, you'll skirt me on the track? That's misogynistic."

That made him mad. That went beyond teasing. It was just insulting. "Eve. I'm going to pretend you didn't just say that."

Her face took on a mulish quality.

Yeah, this was not going to be the night of passion he had envisioned a day or two earlier. "Look, I'm going to go get some fried cheese. And maybe some fried Kool-Aid. Washed down with a beer. You want to join me or do you want to stay here and argue with yourself?"

Her eyes narrowed. Her jaw was set. She said, "You know, my first instinct is to tell you to go fuck yourself."

That sounded about right for her.

"My second instinct is to turn around and walk away without giving you the time of day."

Well, she'd already blown that one.

"Then my third and final thought is that maybe a beer wouldn't be so bad."

Her begrudging attitude was so flattering. "At least it would give you a companion to needle."

"Do I do that? Needle you?"

She looked sincere. Troubled.

Nolan didn't want to hurt her feelings. Or piss her off. But there was some truth to it and he wasn't into lying or sugarcoating. If he had a flaw, he'd want it pointed out to him. "Sometimes," he told her. "And sometimes it's probably not necessary, but guess what? I can take it."

And he kissed her. Just a light quick barely there blink

and you miss it kiss. But it was the period on his sentence. "Now let's get some fried cheese."

Ten minutes later they were sitting on the wreck that was Eve's car, feet dangling into the hole where a windshield normally went. Sitting on the roof, it was a little chilly, and he'd seen Eve shiver a time or two, but he liked it. The heat in summer could be brutal, and he was ready for sweatshirts and blankets and air that filled his lungs cleanly and sweetly.

He was eating a pulled pork sandwich and the fried cheese he'd been craving all day. Eve was licking an ice-cream cone. Some of his earlier tension had eased. "So you bummed out you didn't win?"

"Nah. I didn't expect to win. I just didn't want to be last." She grinned. "Okay, so I wanted to finish in the top four, I'm not gonna lie."

"And you did, so there you go. Didn't it feel good to nail other cars and have it be legal?" In stock racing, contact happened, but there were disqualifications if you took someone out intentionally, and the risk of injury was greater if you hit someone at those speeds. In the derby that was the point.

"Hell, yeah. It did."

Nolan slung his arm around her. "Did you catch the derby bug?"

"I don't know." She kicked her legs back and forth. "We'll see, I guess. Can't wait to see Elec's face when his car shows back up. It has more than a ding." She patted the roof. "But the engine wasn't bad for a six-cylinder."

"Do you think you'll make it to watch the finals in two weeks? I know how much you love to act as cheerleader." He wasn't going to think too hard on the fact that he really wanted her there, rooting for him.

She snorted. "Yeah, right. I'm not sure. I try to go on the road for the race at least once every third week and

I'm obviously missing tomorrow. But then next weekend I'm going to Vegas for the race, so after that is debatable still."

It was hard for him to indulge his hobby given his own work schedule. As it stood, he was flying out in a few hours on a red-eye for the race in Dover the next day. Fortunately, it wasn't a long distance. The following weekend the race was in Atlanta, so again he was close enough he could get there quickly. The weekend the race was in Vegas, Nolan was going to go early, when Evan did, and make up for some of his missed time. He had to cram in a lot of workouts, too, on his own to make sure he didn't slow down the rest of the crew.

He loved his job but right now he was seriously wishing he didn't have to leave so soon. "My flight for Dover is in four hours."

"You're flying out tonight? I thought you said we were having sex tonight. I think you even said there was a guarantee."

Leave it to Eve to just state it boldly. He felt sheepish and horny. "Yeah, well, I think that was wishful thinking. I forgot I had this flight." Nolan watched the tip of Eve's tongue slide into that creamy ice cream yet again. He swallowed hard. "All I could think about was you."

She paused. "You're a charming bastard, I'll give you that." Then she sighed. "I understand. Work is work. I need a shower anyway."

He frowned. "You need a shower? Washing your hair is more important than sex with me?"

"Yes, I need a shower. I don't want to get naked and have your mouth between my legs when I've been sweating in polyester all day."

Oh, my God. He was sure his jaw was down about somewhere by her steering wheel.

"And how do I know if sex with you is any good, by the way? Washing my hair might be a better way to spend the night."

Now she just being sassy to be sassy.

"I'm going to wash your hair," he told her. "And your mouth. And your whole dang body."

"Promises, promises. I think your guarantee's about as worthless as this car right now." She kicked the frame with her boot.

Nolan wanted to laugh. She was so asking for it.

Without giving her a chance to block, he went in for a kiss. Screw the imaginary audience. He wanted his mouth on hers.

God, she felt good. Her lips were sweet from the ice cream and a little sticky, and they tasted perfect. She had this moment, when he kissed her, when she sighed and gave in to her passion, to him. He loved it when she did that. It was a sound, a sigh, he could get addicted to. It was also the sound equal to a match striking. When her fire lit, his did the same, and he nudged her down onto the roof of the car.

Hovering over Eve, he let his hand drift over her thigh, skirting her end zone and rising to the waist of her jeans. For the first time, he allowed himself to slip under the cotton of her shirt and touch her bare skin. She was smooth and warm and he wanted more, more, more. His erection grew thicker, his tongue went deeper, and his breath went ragged.

He was on the verge of lifting her shirt up so he could see her breasts, taste her nipples, but he stopped himself. They were still in public. But he wanted to take Eve to bed and lick her from head to foot and he didn't want to wait. Looking down at her, he took in her glassy eyes, her disheveled hair, the creamy patch of skin glowing in the lamplight. And the ice-cream cone she was still clutching, half the scoop plopped on the roof, the other half running down her arm.

Leaning over, he licked from her elbow to her wrist, catching the sweet trail. "Mmm."

She sucked in her breath. Her chest was rising and falling rapidly. "I could have used a napkin," she told him.

"Shh." He kissed her again, knowing that he didn't want to leave. He didn't want to go to Dover. But he couldn't not go. But there was another option. "Come to Dover with me."

"What?" She sat up so fast and unexpectedly that they bumped foreheads. "What do you mean?" Rubbing her head, she looked at him, aghast, like he had suggested something horrible.

"Come to Dover." The minute the words were out of his mouth, he liked the idea a whole lot. It was perfect. "We can fly in together, get a few hours of sleep, head to the track. Then afterwards we can burn up the sheets."

There was almost a panic on her face. "How can I get on a flight this late? And how can I explain why I'm there when I said I wasn't going to be there?"

The high he'd been on, the feeling that they were connecting, started to deflate. "Why would anyone think twice about you being there?"

"I don't have time to pack."

Annoyed suddenly, Nolan put his mouth around her remaining ice cream and sucked it all into his mouth. The cold stung his teeth and hurt his head. It was the distraction he needed.

"Hey, that was mine."

"You weren't eating it." He stared down at her, trying to read her thoughts. Was it that she didn't want to be with him? Or was it just too spontaneous?

"Okay," he told her. He wasn't going to beg. Or pressure her. Or let her think that he was being a jerk about it. "Like you said, I understand. Work is work. Maybe this isn't the time to mix it with pleasure."

She frowned. "Yeah. Okay." Taking a bite of her soggy-looking cone, she lay on her back again and chewed. "My phone is vibrating in my pocket. I really want to ignore it."

But she wouldn't. He knew she wouldn't. "I left my phone in my truck." He could ignore his for fairly large amounts of time and not feel the slightest bit guilty.

Making a sound of disgust, she shoved her hand into her pocket, the maneuver dragging her jeans low enough to almost give him a heart attack. She lifted the phone up over her head, squinting at the screen. "It's my dad. He wants to know if the rumor is true that I was stupid enough to run in a derby."

"There was nothing stupid about it."

"My dad will be mortified that I did this without practicing." Her arm went up over her eyes, like the track lights were blinding her. Or she was weary.

"You had fun. Stand your ground."

"Yeah. I did." She turned her head toward him. "Thanks."

The sincerity on her face made him feel good. Proud. "For what?"

"For suggesting I do this. It pushed me out of my comfort zone. Out of my rut. That's a good thing."

Yet going to Dover, where no one would be shocked to see her, was pushing just a little too hard apparently. Well, she'd taken a few steps to loosening up, and he was pleased that she had enjoyed herself. "I'm glad to hear that. I do think it's a good stress reliever."

Sex was, too. He was just saying.

Sex in a hotel with room service and a big fluffy bed.

But he'd already suggested it once. He wasn't going to suggest it again.

She lit the screen up on her cell phone again. "How much time do we have? Sex is a stress reliever, too. Five minutes in my backseat."

The woman drove him crazy. She had no idea. She grinned at him as he tried to swallow the truckload of saliva that had suddenly pooled in his mouth. Shifting to give his now enormous erection more room in his jeans, Nolan gave her a stern look. "Don't tempt me."

Laughing, Eve sat up, pushing her phone back in her pocket. "You wouldn't do that."

"How do you know?"

"Because there's no backseat in my car."

Nolan snorted. "Well, you got me there." Of course she had no backseat.

See what lust did to a man?

It made him stupid.

EVE tried not to eye-roll her father. "It's no big deal."

She was at her parents' house for dinner, the race on the TV in the family room and the TV in the kitchen. A hundred laps down and Elec was running tenth, Evan twenty-second. Her father's attention was mostly on the race, but enough on her to criticize her for entering the derby.

She was in the kitchen chopping tomatoes for her mother for the salad. Her father had wandered in during a commercial break to check on the status of dinner and to hound her.

"What do you mean, it's not a big deal? You just run off half-cocked and enter a demo derby? You trashed your brother's car. You didn't tell anyone what you were doing. You have no experience."

Pausing with her knife on the cutting board, she felt an even stronger urge to roll her eyes. "Half-cocked is a bit of an exaggeration. And I have experience behind the wheel. I know how to handle a car."

"Not in a derby. Not in ten years, girl. What were you thinking?"

Eve whacked the knife way harder than was necessary. She did not want to fight with her father.

"Elliot, leave her alone, for crying out loud," her mother said, checking on the lasagna in the oven.

The smell of cheese and marinara sauce drifted through the room. Normally it had a calming effect on Eve, but not today. She could feel the tension in her shoulders that the conversation was generating.

"You're not concerned about her safety?" he asked defensively.

"No. She was wearing a helmet and a seat belt. There's emergency staff present during the derby. Get a grip."

That was what Eve loved about her mother. She was laid back by necessity. With her husband racing for the first twenty years of her marriage and now both her sons, she had to learn not to sweat every spin out on the track.

"Yeah, listen to Mom. She always knows what she's talking about."

"I just don't get why you would just up and do that. It doesn't make any sense."

"Maybe I thought it would be fun." Done with the tomatoes, she looked up from the cutting board.

Her father looked dubious. "I've never known you to do anything just for fun."

He had her there. It had been a while. "Someone suggested it and I just decided to try it. I always loved driving."

"Who suggested it? Elec?"

Oh, Lord. Now her father was going to yell at her brother after he was done yelling at her. "No, it wasn't Elec. He just loaned me the car after I asked him for it. It was someone on Evan's pit crew." Then she realized that was a mistake.

"Who?"

"I'm not telling you. You are not going to go and give the poor guy shit when he just made a friendly suggestion." If she was going to screw things up with Nolan, she was going to do it all on her own, thank you very much. She didn't need her family to speed up the process.

"Eve Alexandra, don't you cuss in my kitchen."

She'd been swearing since she was twelve. Her mother kept correcting her and she still kept doing it. Neither one of them showed any signs of stopping. It was as familiar a rhythm as Sundays in this kitchen. Over the years her mother had remodeled the kitchen twice, ditching the dark country wood of the eighties for the stark white of the nineties to its current Brazilian cherry cabinets and unpolished granite with an apron sink. But it was still the house she'd grown up in, and she liked that. Details changed but never the big picture.

"Why would you say that?" her father asked. "I wasn't going to go talk to him, I was just curious."

"Curious, my foot. You were going to yell at him. And I don't want you to scare him off. He's a nice guy."

She didn't think she had revealed much in that statement, but her mother was a pro.

"Are you dating him?"

Shit. "I have been on a date with him." If she didn't make it clear, they would leap to conclusions.

"And he's a nice young man? I'm so glad you finally have a boyfriend."

Leap complete. "Mom, he's not my boyfriend."

"He better not be. I thought you said he was on Evan's crew." Her father looked aghast.

He didn't miss anything either. Eve set the knife down before she was tempted to slit her wrists.

"He is."

"I can think of a hundred reasons why that's a bad idea."

"Oh, look, commercials are over." Eve pointed to the TV nestled in a cabinet next to the fridge. "With Elec in the Chase, today is make or break." Diversionary tactic. It almost always worked.

Not this time. Her father glanced at the race, quickly assessed the current rankings, then returned his gaze to her. "I understand your need for male company."

Oh. My. God. Eve choked back a laugh. Was she going to get the birds and the bees talk from her father?

"Honey, I covered that with her when she was eleven." Her mother was cutting a loaf of soft Italian bread, her mouth turning up in a smile.

Eve did laugh, especially at the look of outrage on her father's face.

"I'm not talking about . . . *that*."

"You weren't talking about sex?" she asked, amused. "Because it certainly sounded like you were talking about sex. Mom, did it sound like Dad was talking about sex?"

Her mother grinned. "I definitely thought he was talking about sex."

"What is wrong with you two?" he grumbled. "I'm just trying to have a conversation about my concerns and you're taking it in the gutter."

"Oh, I think it was you who took it in the gutter," she said, thrilled with the way this chat was turning out. He had amused her right out of her irritation and he seemed to have forgotten his original point.

Unfortunately not for long. "There are other men you can date. Men who aren't a part of the equation of your brother's career and success."

"I don't see how me dating his jackman is going to affect Evan's career." Not that she hadn't had this same argument with herself. She just didn't like hearing the reality of it from someone else's lips.

"Jackman? You mean Nolan Ford? The idiot who had his ass splashed all over pit road?"

Uh-oh. She'd kind of managed to forget about that incident. Though now that her dad brought it up, it reminded her what a very nice ass Nolan had. She could have been digging her nails into that delicious hard behind of his if she had gone with him to Dover. But the very thought had freaked her out on all kinds of levels, and now instead of exchanging body fluids with Nolan, she was listening to her father lecture her like she was sixteen.

It would have been impulsive to go, no doubt.

But maybe that wasn't such a bad thing.

"That was an accident. You have to give him props for not letting it hinder his performance."

"Who doesn't wear underwear?" her dad asked. "Idiotic. There's no way you're dating him. No way. Out of the question."

Her jaw dropped. Was he serious? "What is this, the eighteenth century? You can't forbid me to date someone. I'm an adult. I have a career and my own condo."

"Elliot . . ." her mother said, her tone filled with warning.

"Evan dated Kendall and you didn't make a big deal out it."

"Evan didn't date Kendall. He went and eloped with her about thirty seconds after they hooked back up for the first time in ten years. I didn't have time to tell him how stupid it was."

"Well it seems to be working out just fine for them. It didn't damage either one of their careers in any way." Annoyed, she filched a piece of the sliced bread and tore off a bite. "If I were your son instead of your daughter, you would have never said that to me."

"The hell I wouldn't have."

"I guess you're right." Furious, Eve squeezed the bread in her hand, decimating both the slice and the bite she'd pulled off. "Because if I were your son, I'd be a driver, so I wouldn't be dating a jackman. But I'm your daughter, so I'm not a driver. I'm just a stupid PR rep who you don't think can date or drive in a demo derby without screwing them up."

Suddenly feeling like she was on the verge of tears, she threw the bread on the counter and stomped off, locking herself in the bathroom. She didn't do tears.

Staring at herself in the mirror, she willed them to retreat and they obeyed. She wasn't even sure why she was so upset. It made perfect sense for her dad to be warning her off Nolan. Hell, she'd warned herself off Nolan.

It hadn't worked.

She wanted to date him, stupid or not.

Part of her had desperately wanted to say yes to his suggestion to fly with her. But the pattern of overthinking was too engrained in her. She questioned everything. She did the safe thing, always.

Look what it had gotten her. A job she hated and a world of boredom and frustration.

What would have been the harm in taking a spontaneous trip?

As she stared at her reflection, eyes glassy from her would-be tears, she realized her hands were white-knuckled on the marble countertop of her parents' powder room. It was another room that had undergone a makeover, with a new vessel sink and recycled glass tiles. Her mother had good taste.

Eve wasn't sure what her own taste was. She wasn't even really sure who she was. What defined her? Career? Family? Both?

But was that her perception of her or really her?

She didn't know.

My God, she was how old and she'd never found herself?

Rolling her eyes at herself in the mirror, Eve let go of her death grip on the sink. She went back into the kitchen and tossed the salad.

As they were putting the food on the table, her father cleared his throat. "I didn't mean to suggest you don't make good choices. You're an intelligent woman, Eve, and I'm proud of you."

For a second, the tears threatened to make a break for it again. But she recovered.

"I know. Thanks, Dad."

"I do think it would be courteous to talk to Evan about dating his jackman," her mother said. "But Nolan seems like a hard worker, and if he makes you happy, I'm happy. Plus that cute butt doesn't hurt his cause."

Eve laughed. That's what she was talking about.

"Oh, Lord." Her father paused with a forkful of lasagna halfway to his mouth. "Do I need to feel jealous?"

"Of course not. I *love* you. I just happen to *like* his foxy backside. But pretend I never said it."

If people had to ever wonder where Eve got her boldness from, they only needed to look to her mother. It seemed to be genetic, though her mother couched hers with charm.

Maybe that was a cue she should take from her.

Glad they had managed to dance around the issue of her outburst, Eve ate dinner and contemplated the look on Nolan's face when she told him her mother had seen his butt.

The thought was almost as pleasing as the butter on her bread.

CHAPTER
EIGHT

"SO," Nolan said to Eve on the phone, "what are you doing tomorrow night?"

"Tomorrow night is Tuesday."

He was fairly aware of the days of the week. He rooted around in his refrigerator, trying to find something that was edible. So far he wasn't having much luck. "Yep. It's the day that follows Monday, which is today."

"I'm not doing anything after work, just getting my run in like usual."

Nolan got the impression she ran almost every day. He couldn't wait to run his hand along her slim muscular legs. Tomorrow night. Tuesday. "Well, what time should I come over then?"

There was a pause. "What are you coming over for?" she asked suspiciously.

"For sex. Guaranteed."

She snorted. "I've heard that before. And you should ask me, not tell me."

Eyeballing some cheddar cheese that looked a little like snow had been dusted on it, Nolan propped his phone on his shoulder. "Eve, can I come over and have sex with you tomorrow night? Tuesday night."

"You're an ass."

"So you've said." But he felt confident she would say yes. His gut told him she regretted not going to Dover with him. Plus she liked to plan things. So they would plan sex. It would appeal to her need to be in control. "So, what time? Allotting for time for a shower since you're so worried about washing your hair and all your girl bits."

"Did you really just say that to me?" She sounded indignant. "I mean seriously, Nolan, girl bits? Yuck."

"They're not yuck to me." At all. "And I'm only mentioning it because you mentioned that you didn't want to have sex without a shower. I'm trying to be accommodating." He pitched the cheddar cheese and eyed the clock. There was still time to go out for a steak.

"You're just weird. I don't know what to do with you, if you want to know the truth."

"Have sex with me." It wasn't that complicated. He washed his hands. Something slimy had touched him in the fridge. Or technically he had touched it.

She sighed. "Okay. Eight o'clock works."

That sigh was adorable. He loved the sound. It meant she was out of excuses to get out of doing what she really wanted to do but was fighting. "Prepare to be amazed."

"Uh-huh."

He'd make her eat those words of skepticism. "See you tomorrow, cupcake."

"Bye."

Nolan hung up his phone, feeling much better despite

his lack of food. He was finally going to get Eve in bed. It had only been a week, but it felt like years.

There was a knock on his door. Relieved to close the refrigerator door, he went to answer it. His brother was standing in the hallway.

"Hey, what's up?"

Rhett bounced on the balls of his feet. "Hey, uh, can I hang out for a while?"

Nolan wasn't sure what exactly that meant or why Rhett was asking it, but he nodded. "Sure. I'm about to go get something to eat. You hungry?"

"Yeah. You buying?"

"Just because I'm older doesn't mean I have any more money than you do." He wasn't broke, but he wasn't rolling in it either. Which niggled at him when it came to Eve. Was she the type of woman to care that he couldn't buy her jewelry?

Not that he wanted to buy her jewelry. But what if he did? At some point. He probably couldn't.

Then he thought about Eve's casual wear of sweatshirts and gym shoes and figured she probably didn't care. About jewelry. Maybe she did about the money.

"What?" he asked Rhett because he'd been too busy being neurotic to hear what his brother had said.

God, he was never neurotic. It was seriously annoying.

"I said are you charging admission to your apartment? Move out of the way, douche bag. I'm standing in the hallway."

"Oh." Right. Move out of the way. Nolan did that, following Rhett into his small living room. "Let me get my shoes then we can go. I want a steak."

His brother didn't respond, just moved a framed picture of the family at Christmas that their mother had given Nolan. There was obviously some brooding going on, but he figured Rhett would tell him when he was ready.

He was crossing the threshold into his bedroom when Rhett blurted out, "You know, I've never been in love."

O-kay. "You're what, twenty-five? You have plenty of time to fall in love." He kept walking, hoping that was the end of that.

"Have you been in love? Like, for real? Not in lust. Love."

Glad his brother was still in the other room and couldn't see his expression, which he was sure was horrified, Nolan bent into his closet for his shoes. This was not a conversation he wanted to have. But he figured the best way to end it was to just be honest and let Rhett at whatever it was he was digging for.

"I've been in love a time or two, yes." He had loved Lauren even if it had been an immature love. "But I was a kid and that kind of young love doesn't weather a storm, you know? For-keeps love, I haven't experienced that yet." But he was hoping he would sooner than later. It felt different this time with Eve.

"How did you know it wasn't the real thing?"

"Because it goes away as fast as it arrived." He emerged from his room with his shoes in his hand. "Is there someone you're involved with?"

"No." Rhett brushed that off. "So what's the deal with you and Eve Monroe? Are you in love with her?"

Nolan almost choked on his own spit. "Rhett, I've been out with her once. Plus two days we spent some time together for the derby and at the derby. I'm not in love with her."

His brother bit his fingernail and spit it out onto the floor.

"Rhett, that's disgusting. God, how does Mom put up with you?"

"What? What did I do?"

"You seriously don't know that you just spit your chewed-off fingernail onto my carpet?"

To his credit, Rhett actually looked bewildered. "I did?"

"Yes."

"Sorry. But mark my words, bro, you and Eve . . . it's going to get serious. And I don't know if that's such a good idea."

"How do you know it's going to get serious?"

"I'm psychic."

What the hell was the matter with his brother all of a sudden? Saying he should be a stripper, that he'd never been in love . . . it was all totally random and totally unlike Rhett. "Have you developed a drug habit? Because you sound like you've been smoking something."

Normally his brother would take a crack back at him, but Rhett just stared at him, studying him. It was fucking unnerving. "What?"

"Nothing. I'm just trying to remember what you look like as a single man. Because that's about to change."

That sounded more Rhett-like. Nolan shoved his shoes on his feet. "Let's go get you some steak, man, you sound anemic. And weird. Chicks don't dig weird."

"You would know."

"Eve doesn't seem to have a problem with me." Nolan clapped his hand on Rhett's shoulder. "Watch and learn, little brother."

"I'll watch how *not* to do it."

Nolan shot his hand out and punched Rhett in the arm. "Do you see that coming? Since you're psychic?"

Nolan felt better with them back on more familiar territory as brothers. He wasn't used to Rhett being anything but happy-go-lucky. Anything else worried him and he didn't want to worry. He wanted to enjoy the fact that he was getting to know Eve.

They were going to have a whole night to explore each other. In clothes and out.

WHEN the doorbell rang at quarter to eight, Eve jumped, almost blinding herself with the mascara wand. Really? Nolan was fifteen minutes early. What about that made sense?

But she should have known he would be early. It was just like him to give every appearance of being eager to see her. Which pissed her off. Didn't he understand she had no idea how to deal with a man who didn't get mad at her? Or more accurately, didn't rise to the bait when she pushed his buttons?

Yet Nolan didn't. At all. For that, and other reasons, she had found herself actually looking forward to tonight. Cutting short her run, she'd had plenty of time to take a leisurely shower, shaving every inch of her body that harbored unwanted hair. She had used a moisturizer that promised to make her silky and smooth and had blown out her hair with extra care, forcing the baby-fine hairs to have at least a little volume.

All that had been good. She had to admit, she liked knowing where she stood and where the night was going. She'd had time to prepare. Her place was clean, her bathroom toiletries hidden away, her garbage taken out.

Best of all, she was wearing skimpy underwear under her dark jeans and tight white shirt. They had been buried in her dresser with the tags still on them, a hot little lacy bright blue thong and bra, purchased with the idea of seducing her ex-boyfriend when their relationship had started to migrate south for the winter. Only she'd never had the chance, given that he'd canceled their plans over the phone and told her he was moving to Texas. Since she'd seen him in the grocery store two months later, she knew that had been a bunch of bullshit, but she hadn't cared so much about his lies or losing him as she did the fact that she'd spent a hundred bucks on lingerie that was never going to see the light of day.

Until tonight.

But Nolan was still early and she had mascara on only one eye. There was no way in hell she was answering the door with one eye looking open and alert with lustrous lashes, the other squinty with pale barely there lashes. She started to coat the naked side.

Her cell phone chimed on the bathroom counter. God, he was texting her. Cell phones were both liberating and annoying as hell. Torn between gratitude that he clearly wanted to see her and irritation that he couldn't just give her two seconds to get to the door, she answered him that she'd be there in a minute.

Finishing her eye at warp speed, Eve studied herself in the mirror. She was no supermodel, but she figured most women weren't. She was passably cute, especially with the mascara. Lip gloss would have helped as well, but she hated the stuff. It was like walking around with jelly on your lips. Not happening.

A spray of perfume and she was out of the bathroom and hightailing it to the door before he changed his mind and went for a burger.

Throwing open the door, Eve drank him in. Damn, he was a sexy guy.

He wasn't tremendously tall, but he was taller than her, and he had a chiseled jaw. Friendly eyes. Muscles. Lots of muscles. Had she mentioned the muscles?

"Hey," he said, his eyes running over her from head to foot, making her a little warm in her blue thong.

"Hi. Come on in."

She let Nolan into her condo, trying to ignore the fact that her heart was racing and her hand was shaking slightly. She was excited. Generally speaking, she didn't have a lot of men over to her place, and when she did, it wasn't like this. This was she and Nolan saying straight out they were going to have sex. Tonight. In her bed. Maybe even other places if things went according to plan.

Nolan was wearing his usual uniform of jeans and a T-shirt. It was the only way she could picture him. Well, that and in his track uniform. With his ass hanging out. Which reminded her . . .

"So," she told him, hiding her grin as he followed her into her living room. "My mother thinks you have a nice butt. In case you were wondering."

He winced. "Oh, Lord, are you kidding me? Okay, maybe now I see the problem with not wearing under-wear. I do not even want to think about you and your mother discussing my backside."

"She's the one who brought it up." Eve had to admit the look on his face was quite enjoyable. He managed to look both pained and pleased at the compliment all at once. "Apparently it made quite an impact on her."

"This is a nice place." He looked around her house, eyes drinking in her midcentury modern décor.

"Changing the subject?" she asked.

"Oh, hell, yeah, I am." Nolan held up a six-pack of beer he'd been holding. "Can I put this in your fridge?"

"Sure, if you let me drink one."

"Of course. And that wasn't just a diversionary tactic. I do think your place is great. It's huge."

"Is it?" Eve looked around her condo with an out-sider's eye. Her parents had a good-sized house. Not as grand as the drivers of today bought, but a large house designed for family gatherings and large-scale entertain-ing. To her, this condo seemed average-sized in compari-son, even small. But she realized that to someone who had grown up in twelve hundred square feet with eight siblings, it was downright enormous. "Yeah, I like it. I got a good deal on it before the housing market in Charlotte exploded. But that still doesn't change the fact that you have a cute butt and my mother knows it."

"Oh, God, stop saying that." He deposited his beer in her fridge, but not before he took two out of the six-pack. "Bottle opener?"

"Use your teeth."

"And ruin my Crest smile?" He gave her a model display of his teeth. "I don't think so."

She had to admit, he did have perfect teeth. "You are a poster child for dental hygiene. I would definitely feel guilty if you chipped a tooth." Rummaging in a drawer, she found a bottle opener. Taking a bottle from him, she set it on the granite island and popped the top off. But when she reached for the other bottle, he held on to it.

"I can do it," he told her.

"It's no big deal. I can open a bottle."

"I got it. Just give me the opener."

Frowning, she tried to read his intention. "What, you think I can't open a stupid bottle of beer?"

His eyebrows rose. "Uh, no. Of course you can open it. I just don't want you to have to wait on me. I was trying to be nice."

Oh. Well, how was she supposed to know that? "And I was trying to be freakin' nice, too, and open the bottle for you."

"I guess we're just a couple of considerate as hell people."

"Guess so."

He took a swig of his now opened beer.

She did the same.

Now what?

"Come here and give me a kiss," he said softly.

It was, she imagined, a very normal thing to say. But to

her, it sounded like a request for submission. Something she definitely wasn't good at. Her feet stayed rooted to her hardwood floors. What the hell was the matter with her? He didn't mean anything by it other than he wanted a kiss. Why couldn't she just do it?

Control, that's why. She had to be in control of everything she possibly could, since so many things were out of her control. It was insane, she knew that, frustrated with herself even as she willed her feet to just close the narrow gap between them.

Nolan didn't wait for her mental boxing match to conclude. He didn't even comment on why she was just standing there like she'd been hit by a stupid stick. Nolan just set his beer down on the island with a thunk and ate up the space between them in two purposeful steps.

When he kissed her, she recovered her sanity and kissed him back. It would have been a crime to blow this moment further than she already had, so she turned off her internal thoughts and just felt. She was really starting to fall for his mouth and the way he kissed her. It was always soft yet demanding, skilled but never too suave. It just . . . worked.

As his lips moved over hers, Eve leaned closer to him, wanting to feel his hard chest. Yanking up his T-shirt, she slid greedy fingers over that rock-hard hot surface. His skin was warm, such a contrast after holding her chilled beer that she wanted to taste him. Biting his bottom lip a little to get him to release her, Eve bent over and pressed her mouth against his abs, her tongue flicking out to swipe along his skin.

He gave a low groan. "What are you doing?"

She shrugged, not really sure. It wasn't normally like her to make a move like that. "I wanted a taste."

"Why don't you show me your bedroom then you can taste all you want. And just in case you were wondering, you're not restricted to the abs. Taste anything you want, I don't mind, really."

She gave him a wry smile. "I bet you don't. Bedroom is this way." But she wasn't about to let him dominate this seduction. As she strolled down the hall, she peeled off her shirt and tossed it on the floor behind her. She was wearing low-slung heels and she figured it gave him a good view of her butt in her jeans to dispense with her shirt. As well as catch him off guard.

It seemed to be working, given the strangled gasp he gave. "Damn, honey, you don't play around. I haven't even finished my beer yet and your shirt's off."

Was there an insult in there? For some stupid reason she'd thought he wanted her naked as quickly as possible. But hell, what did she know about seduction? She'd only gotten half a girlie gene and it wasn't the one that knew how to flirt.

"Did you bring your beer with you?" She'd abandoned hers on the island.

Pausing in the doorway, she shot him what she hoped was a seductive look. More likely she just looked insane.

"Yes." He raised his bottle. "Not sure why I did, but I did."

"Chug it and take your shirt off." Eve immediately regretted the words. God, she was trying to be sexy and she just sounded like a bitch.

But he didn't look off-put. "I can do that."

Somehow he drained the whole bottle in about four seconds. She was impressed. Then he turned around and went back down the hallway.

"Where the hell are you going?" She stood there, hands on her hips. This wasn't how she'd planned this night. She had planned on them tearing each other's clothes off in the foyer and doing it on the floor, to be honest. Scratching an itch. But only at the right moment, after they had relaxed and talked and sat on the couch. Suddenly it all seemed more complicated. Especially since ripping each other's clothes off wasn't really something you could plan.

He had disappeared into the kitchen but he called back to her, "I'm putting the empty bottle in the recycling bin. I wasn't going to just throw it on the floor."

That made sense. But it didn't make her feel any less ridiculous standing in her bedroom doorway with no shirt on. At least she had the blue lace bra on still. Being bra-less would have been truly awkward.

Nolan seemed to appreciate the bra. As he came back, he was staring at her chest, his eyes dark. "I like this," he told her, running his finger along the edge of the cup, his warm touch spilling over onto her breast.

So maybe the sexy bra and panties hadn't been a lost cause after all.

"It's like two blueberries I want to bite."

Blueberries? Really? There was nothing sexy about being compared to food. But she wasn't going to complain. That might distract him from his current task, which was stroking across her nipple, back and forth, slowly driving her wild. "So bite it."

Anticipation had been building in her all day. She wanted to have sex now. She wanted to skip all the preliminaries and get straight to the main event. It was a little embarrassing, but a couple of kisses and some nipple pulls and she was wet. Ready.

His eyebrows rose. "Well, well . . . sassy. I like that about you."

Then he yanked down the front of her bra with enough force that her breast burst free with comedic velocity. Only she wasn't laughing. She was gasping and aching. When his teeth grazed over her nipple, she dug her fingertips into his back. It had been way too long since a man had touched her. Just the view of him bending over her turned her on. Or maybe it was just that it was Nolan. From the first minute she'd seen his bare butt ten days earlier, she had been intrigued by him. Aroused, if you will. Which she was.

He bit. She moaned.

"Mmm. Juicy."

That distracted her again. Damn it, she was not a piece of fruit. Closing her eyes, she prayed he would keep his mouth shut. Then forgot to care when he started lapping across her breast, catching her nipple with each pass. It was slow, leisurely, maddening.

He raised his head, breaking contact. Eve sighed at the loss, but assumed he was going to switch to the other breast. He had a funny look on his face, though, one that didn't scream that he couldn't wait to slide his penis inside her.

"What?" she asked, her own ardor cooling a bit.

"Nothing."

"It's obviously something." Was there lint on her boob? Or something even more mortifying?

"I just don't like the taste of body lotion, that's all. I prefer the taste of your skin."

So the fifteen minutes she'd spent slathering slime all over her body had not served to make him in awe of her silky skin but actually turned him off? Yep, it was official. She sucked at seduction.

"I shouldn't have made you chug your beer. At least a swig now would wash the taste out of your mouth."

"It's not that bad. It's just very . . . floral."

Hot. Not. Between the blueberry bra and the floral lotion, she basically had garden tits.

The only thing she could think to do was to distract him so she undid the button on her jeans and pulled down the zipper. Bending over, she shoved the denim down to her ankles. Only she'd forgotten about the shoes. So the

jeans got stuck. And she was fighting with the heels, trying to wrest them off without falling over. Her hair fell in
her eyes. Sweat broke out between her floral boobs.

It was all very clumsy and bad and stupid.

"Can you go in the other room and come back when I
have a grip on this situation?" she asked, breathless, as she
tugged harder. One shoe off.

He grinned. "No."

Really? He couldn't spare her dignity just a little?
"You're an ass."

"And you need a new insult."

Eve managed to free the other shoe and ran through all
the various names she could call him, from the childish to
the gross to the downright rude. She settled on the one that
she knew would get him the most riled up, and land her
flat on her back with him buried deep inside her. "Wimp."

Kicking the damn jeans off with more violence than
finesse, she stood back up, trailing her hand across the
front of his jeans as she went. "You know a real man
would swallow a whole bottle of floral lotion and still
have an erection." Which Nolan did. But she did enjoy
teasing him. "He could eat dirt and still be turned on."

Nolan took her hand and pulled it back. He pressed it
hard, against his erection. "Feel that, cupcake? That is my
dick, rock solid for you."

Oh, my. Eve felt the heat of those forceful words deep
in her womb. She liked his bold reaction. She really liked
the feel of him thick and long beneath her hand. She
stroked, enjoying the way his body tensed at her touch.
"And while there's no way in hell I'm going to eat dirt to
prove any point, you can be damn sure I could and would
still have a massive hard-on around you. You make me
crazy."

Eve barely had a chance to say, "Good," before she
found herself swept off her feet. Nolan picked her up,

wrapping her legs around his waist and carrying her into her bedroom, all while kissing the curve of her breast. Yeah, he was definitely no wimp, and she was grateful for all the hours he'd logged at the gym.

Being carried like she weighed about as much as a Chihuahua was very sexy. She was wearing only the thong and her bra, dragged down so that half of her chest was exposed. He was still totally dressed. It should have been weird to be so exposed but it wasn't. It was just hot.

"I've had a hard-on since your button popped on your shirt."

As was that. "You have?"

"Yes."

They were in front of her bed, but he just stood there, holding her, nibbling at her neck. "I've had to take care of it a time or two."

"Really?" Eve felt breathless and her eyes were threatening to drift closed. She dug her fingers into his shoulders when he lowered his head to flick his tongue across her nipple. To think that she hadn't been the only one touching herself . . . it made her damp with desire.

"Really. All I could think about was you naked, you kissing me, you with your beautiful hair spread out around you while I use my tongue to make you come . . ."

Yes, please. Eve tugged at the bottom of his shirt. "Take your clothes off," she urged. She had gone from flustered to aroused to desperate. The sound of his voice was like an aphrodisiac. She wondered if they had been both in bed, thinking about each other at the same time.

Dropping her lightly onto the bed now, Nolan stripped off his shirt.

It was everything she had imagined and then some. Saliva pooled in her mouth, her inner thighs aching with want. God, he was nothing but muscles and masculinity, not an ounce of fat on him anywhere. Her legs drifted apart automatically. Nolan was unbuttoning his jeans when he paused, making her groan. She wanted to see what was under that denim. She wanted to feel it. With her hand, with her mouth, with her sex.

"Why are you stopping?"

Nolan let out a crack of laughter. "Nice tattoo."

Oh, damn. He'd spotted the visual display of her stubbornness. "Yeah, well, I have a hard time turning down a double dog dare."

"Who on earth dared you to have OPEN 24 HOURS tattooed on your inner thigh?"

Eve cursed her best friend in college all over again. "Don't worry about it right now. I'll tell you later."

"Was it a boyfriend?" he asked, still staring at her leg, his knuckles white on his zipper.

That made all of her annoyance disappear. She grinned. "Are you jealous?"

Most men would deny it and she was expecting that. But Nolan surprised her.

"Yes. I'm actually so jealous right now that I could chew nails. At first glance, the tat is funny, but to think that some guy wanted to stamp his claim on you like that . . ." Nolan seemed to check himself. His shoulders forcibly relaxed. "It's none of my business, though. Sorry."

If anyone else had said any of that, she probably would have tossed them out on their ass, no matter how fine. She normally hated jealousy. But Nolan had control over it and himself, and it was actually pretty damn satisfying to know that the idea of another man between her thighs bothered him. Which was why she was going to put him out of his misery and get back to the matter at hand— having an orgasm.

"It was actually a sorority sister thing. Picture intoxicated twenty-two-year-olds egging each other on about

their love lives. This is the ridiculous outcome. I don't
think I would tattoo myself for any man."

"Not even if I double dog dared ya?" Nolan grinned at
her and tugged his jeans down.

"You would never do that." He wouldn't. She was sure
of it. He would never force her to do something she might
regret, preying on her stubbornness. She didn't know how
she knew that, but she did.

The grin dissipated. "You're right. I wouldn't."
He looked down at her with such sincerity, such . . .
admiration. "You're beautiful."

Eve had never felt ugly, but she had never felt beautiful. The way he looked at her, the way he said it, she believed she was to him. To her, he was gorgeous, and it felt
good to be experiencing such mutual appreciation.

He stepped out of his jeans and stood in front of her in
his tight black jockeys. She wasn't normally a big fan of
anything but boxers, but when you filled the cotton like he
did, it would be a crying shame to wear droopy drawers.
He looked delicious. She wanted to touch every inch of
him, squeezing as she went.

She sat up on her elbows, determined to get her hands
on him.

But he pressed her back, moving in between her legs.
"I need to kiss you."

The difference between want and need was vast, and
she knew she was in the same camp as him. This wasn't
something that would be nice if it happened. It was something that had to happen or she was going to die.

When he took her mouth with his, she arched up to
meet him, wanting more, all of him. She wanted to touch
that chest and dig her nails into his back. But he pulled
back to strip off his briefs. Eve waited with bated breath,
knowing she'd felt something impressive. His erection

sprang up, as long as she'd suspected. Her vagina did a happy dance. Him inside her was all that mattered, and she reached out to stroke him.

He had stark white skin where shorts would normally be, his chest a deep rich tan. How he was still so tan in October amazed her, but she figured he probably worked on cars in the sun.

Whatever it was, the contrast amused her and only served to showcase his muscles all that much more. Her fingers rose up and down on his velvet skin and she couldn't prevent a smirk from squeaking out.

"What are you smiling about?" he asked her.

"You have quite the tan lines. Your thighs look electric white next to that bronzed chest. I'm surprised I didn't notice how lily white your ass was on YouTube." Talking helped her regain control over her body. She had been almost uncomfortably turned on by him. Aroused to the point that she might have been willing to do just about anything, and she wasn't sure how she felt about that.

This felt better. This was shoving back the veil of lust yet still enjoying touching him. She cupped his balls, aware of the irony of the position.

"Real men don't spray tan," he told her. Then he leaned over, forcing her hand to fall off his cock.

Eve's laughter died and she was about to ask what he was doing when his tongue landed on her clitoris. "Ooohh," she moaned, shocked at her instant reaction. He slid up and down her folds, lapping at her swollen button, and she marveled that something so simple could feel so damn good.

It was him, she realized. Him with her that felt so good.

Instead of freaking her out completely, the thought flipped a switch. She stopped trying to keep the lid on her control with both hands. She stopped worrying. She stopped trying to figure him out.

She just dug her fingers in his hair and came with the power of an eight-cylinder engine.

"Oh, God," she moaned.

"Oh, yes," he said as his tongue continued to do amazing and mystical things to her, his hands on her thighs holding her down when she would have jerked off the bed.

Her mind went blank, her only awareness the hot throbbing pulse of her body as she shuddered through the longest, hardest orgasm she'd had in a good long while. Maybe ever.

Okay, she'd give it to him. Longest orgasm ever.

As the shudders quieted to shivers, she thought she could get used to this.

Especially when suddenly his tongue was replaced by the thick probing head of his fully erect cock.

CHAPTER
NINE

NOLAN swallowed hard, the taste of Eve still on his tongue, ready to enter her. She was amazing. She looked, felt, tasted, even smelled amazing. It was tempting to just sink into her bareback, to have nothing between them but her slick moisture, but he couldn't do that obviously. So forcing himself away from temptation, he replayed her orgasm in his head while he bent over for his jeans.

She made a sound of frustration but he squeezed her foot, hoping that would reassure her he was coming back soon. Finding the trio of condoms he'd shoved in his pocket, he tore one off, the sound of her groans echoing in his head. That had been a hell of an orgasm. He could honestly say it was the hottest thing ever to know that he'd made her come undone like that.

Looking down at her, Nolan swallowed hard. She was beautiful and unexpected. Strong, yet vulnerable when he least suspected it. The tattoo, which he traced with his finger now, was ridiculous and hilarious. It actually suited her and her wonderful sense of sarcasm. She didn't back down from a challenge, even if it wasn't going to end well, and he admired that about her.

He hovered, poised right at her entrance, knowing there would never be this moment of anticipation again, this moment where he could only be amazed that she was opening herself to him, and only imagine how amazing she felt. He didn't know yet, and in a second he would, but he wanted to savor the tension, appreciate what was happening. It seemed unreal that she was as aroused by him as he was by her. It had just been a wish and an improbability until he'd taken a risk and asked her out. Now he was in her bed.

The first time, but hopefully not the last. Eve was different and he'd known that since he'd seen her take out the bull's-eye at the festival time after time, then donate the prizes to kids. Tough but soft, it was a combination he found irresistible.

"Are you having a stroke or a heart attack?" she asked him.

"What? No, of course not." Nolan slid a half inch inside her, then retreated. It was such a painfully perfect tease for himself and her.

"Those are the only legitimate reasons you should not already be inside me. Either call 911 for immediate medical assistance or thrust now."

Yeah, she was different. Nolan grinned. "So you want me, huh?"

She rolled her eyes, but she admitted it easily enough. "Yes. Though I'm starting to doubt you want me."

That couldn't possibly be in question. "Oh, I want you, trust me. All I've been thinking about all day is—"

Then hoping to catch her off guard, Nolan pushed inside her. His eyes closed shut on a groan as he sank into her moist heat. God, better than he could have ever imagined.

The sound she made was almost as satisfying as the way she felt. It was a sharp inhalation of her breath, followed by a hiss. On the heels of that was a rough curse under her breath. She liked it. No doubt about it.

So did he. "This . . . that's all I've been thinking about. Me, inside you."

"I think it's a good thought," she said, her voice breathy.

"It is." Nolan then gave up on talking and stroked inside her, feeling her tight body wrapping around him like a moist glove. Her passage was tight, clinging to him, drawing him in thrust after thrust.

He wasn't prepared for how good it felt. He wasn't prepared to see her shatter beneath him after a half-dozen pushes inside her welcoming body. But she did. He was barely there and she was arching her back, fingers clawing at his skin. He felt and saw her orgasm pull up, like a speeding semi, her eyes going wide in surprise.

"Oh, Nolan," she said.

She'd never said his name like that. It did strange things to him, making him thrust harder, his balls drawing up as his arousal wound tight inside him, building toward his own explosion.

"I'm going to . . ."

The sentence tapered off, like she forgot what she'd been about to say.

"I know, baby, come for me."

Without a sound, she did, a wordless eye-rolling orgasm that had her angling up toward him, her chin lifting like she was asking for a kiss to complete her ecstasy. Nolan bent his head and put his mouth on hers in a bruising kiss, his tongue plundering her mouth. As her body clenched on to his in orgasm, he pounded hard, once, twice, until his own release overtook him.

He felt feral, possessive, completely out of control as he poured into her, his moans loud and guttural through his clenched teeth. Freakin' amazing. He felt like he was drowning inside her sweetness, and when he finally came up for air, he was panting and sweating.

Eve finally came back down with a gasp, sucking in air, her body going limp on her bed. "OMG," she said.

That she would use that expression made him laugh. She always managed to surprise him. Nolan collapsed on top of her, wanting to feel her warm skin below his. Her arms came around his back and lazily stroked across his skin. He liked the way it felt, her nails triggering a shiver from him. It had been a while since he'd felt a woman's touch. This wasn't just any touch, though—it was Eve's.

Kissing the side of her jaw, Nolan snuggled as close as he could, expecting her to protest, but going for it anyway. She didn't complain, so he just lay on her and enjoyed feeling every inch of her body next to his. Her hand started to drift lower and she squeezed his backside.

"Excuse me," he said, pretending to be offended. "You can't just grab anything you want."

"If your penis has been inside me, and I want to point out it still is, I most certainly can grab anything I want."

"I'll give you that." Besides, he liked having her grope him. It made him feel virile. Manly. Wanted.

"It's too bad I didn't really get to see it . . . oh, wait. I actually have. On TV."

He bit her earlobe lightly. "Smart-ass."

"Jackass."

Nolan grinned as he pulled out of her, holding on to the end of the condom so he didn't leave it behind. "Apparently there's a lot of ass in this room."

She rolled onto her stomach with a sigh as he stood up, giving him an amazing view of *her* ass. Nolan paused, his hand on his cock as he removed the condom. He was getting hard again just looking at her. Those sweet curves were beckoning him.

"I'm going to sleep," she told him.

That gave him pause. "Are you serious?" They'd barely gotten started on all the ways they could lick each other and make each other come.

"Yes. I need my beauty sleep and I have an eight A.M. meeting tomorrow."

"It's like nine o'clock, Eve." Nolan stood there, disbelieving that she could actually be suggesting she was going to go to sleep now. He'd just walked in the door. Well, and had fucked them both senseless, but just once. He planned to do just that about three more times.

"Hmm," was her muffled response. Her face was in a pillow.

Was he supposed to stay? Did she expect him to leave? Awkward.

Heading into the bathroom that was connected to her bedroom, he tossed the condom in the toilet and flushed. Washing his hands, he frowned. Screw leaving. He wasn't going to nail her then slink out. One, because he wasn't the kind of guy who got his rocks off then ran. Two, because he wasn't going to be her itch-scratcher. They were dating, damn it, and he was going to get in her bed and spoon the hell out of her while she slept. If she didn't like it, she could wake up and tell him so. In the meantime, he was going to cuddle.

EVE couldn't sleep.

That wasn't part of the plan.

Her carefully orchestrated schedule of the evening's events had actually been to share a glass of wine, watch a movie, talk, have hot, efficient sex, then send him on his way home with her story about a morning meeting so she could avoid the whole awkward morning scene.

Instead they'd barely taken two swallows of their beers

before stripping naked to have mind-blowing sex. Which, while satisfying, left her wanting more, and it was only nine o'clock. Unsure what to do from there, and completely freaked by the intensity of her orgasms, she had tried to sleep. Sleep after sex made sense. Given that it was a boring thing to do, she had assumed he would leave. Any man in his right mind would have.

But Nolan was insane.

He was in bed again with her, all snuggled up against her like a muscular blanket.

How in the hell was she supposed to sleep? It was way too early and his semierection was nestled right between her butt cheeks. It seemed awfully intimate to have a man so casually insinuating himself into her ass crack. Her vagina was one thing, he was welcome there, but cuddling was unnerving.

Holding herself perfectly still, she curled her arms into her chest and stared at the wall. Having her eyes open was a risk—he might figure out she wasn't asleep—but she couldn't keep them closed without going insane. Though she was on the verge anyway. It was hard to breathe in an even pattern, and it reverberated in her ears as loud as when she had been scuba diving. In. Out. This was so boring. She wondered if her e-mails were racking up. Maybe once he fell asleep, she could slip out of bed and grab her phone. Why hadn't she left it on the nightstand? She should have been thinking ahead.

But then again, this hadn't gone according to plan, as she had already noted. They should just now be cozying up to each other on her couch for a few passionate kisses, not spooning naked.

"Can you quiet your thoughts? They're so loud, I can't sleep," Nolan told her, his breath tickling her ear.

He startled her and she jerked forward a little, then forced herself to be still again.

"Hmm?" she asked, feigning sleepiness, which was harder than she would have thought. She felt like a complete moron.

"You're thinking about getting out of bed and working, aren't you?"

Busted. "Of course not." She shifted a little.

"You're a terrible liar. You're reaching for your phone right now."

"I am not!" She wasn't. Only because it was in the other room. Unfortunately.

"You have two options here—sleep or have sex with me. Work is not happening."

Giving up on pretending, she complained, "I can't fall asleep."

"That's because it's nine fucking thirty! Of course you can't sleep. Only the senior crowd and toddlers go to bed this early, and I'm damn certain you're neither."

Eve sighed. "This isn't going at all how I planned."

"How did you plan this going?"

"I didn't think we'd have sex three minutes after you walked in the door."

He snorted. "Then I guess you haven't noticed how much I've been wanting you."

"I noticed." She had. Now she wasn't even sure why she'd thought the night would go one way or the other. She just felt like she wasn't controlling it, and that was hard for her. "You barely even saw that I put on sexy underwear." It hadn't been easy prepping for this date. Maybe she just wanted a little appreciation.

As if stripping her naked and taking her two minutes after walking in the door wasn't appreciation.

God, she needed therapy. Or a pill. Or more sex.

"Maybe you need to just do something on the fly now and again. Not plan it. Just have fun." He was suddenly stroking her nipple, and she had to admit, it felt good. It forced her to relax. "See, like I wasn't *planning* on touching you right now, but I just did it."

She did like that. She could admit it. "Nolan."

"Yes?"

"I'm a disaster. You do know that, don't you? I'm a neurotic control freak bitch."

It was sad, but true. She felt deflated, even as he aroused her by lightly pinching her nipple. Why couldn't she just enjoy herself? Why did she always have to borrow trouble? It really sucked that her brother Elec had gotten all the calm in the family.

"You just don't always remember to relax, that's all." His hand moved from her nipple down between her legs.

Eve sucked in a breath as his finger slipped inside her and hooked at her G spot. "You think it's really that simple?"

"Yep. Now just release all that tension on my finger. Work will still be there tomorrow. Take five minutes for yourself and let me get you off."

Could she do that? Eve felt his hard chest against her back, his growing erection no longer invasive, but arousing between her cheeks, his finger stroking her to increased pleasure, so steady, so sure, so determined. What did it matter if they watched a movie or not? The end result was the same. She was getting to feel him naked alongside her. She was having her first orgasms with a partner in a good long while. There was nothing to complain about here. Nothing.

Who gave a shit about the hundred-dollar underwear? Lingerie's sole purpose was to inspire a man to rip it off anyway. Nolan didn't need to remark on the effort she'd put into wearing it. Lame. She was lame and stupid and, oh crap, on the verge of another orgasm if Nolan kept doing what he was doing. She allowed herself a soft moan.

"Feel good?" Nolan murmured.

"Yes. Oh, don't stop." Eve started to move her hips so that she met his touch with each stroke, his finger moving slickly through her increasing moisture. She gripped the edge of the mattress, needing something to hold on to while she thrust against him.

"No worries, cupcake, I've got you."

He did. It was a weird realization that no matter how many ways she managed to be annoying, Nolan seemed unperturbed. He just rolled with it. For whatever reason, he seemed to like to be with her, so maybe she just needed to accept that and do a little of that rolling with it herself.

But first she needed to come. "Oh, damn," she said as her muscles started to tighten around his finger.

"That's it. Work it." He bit the soft flesh on her shoulder.

That sharp sting, coupled with his continued stroking inside her, sent her over the edge. She came, with great loud groans that filled the room, her hair flopping in her eye and her body dissolving into a wet pool of ecstasy.

Yeah, she could relax. Holy crap, that felt good. She rode the waves of her orgasm and his finger with abandonment, grabbing every ounce of pleasure it afforded her.

The inner spasms had barely stilled when his finger was replaced with his cock, nudging into her from behind. Oh, hell yeah. That's what she was talking about. He went deep inside, the angle hitting all the right spots. His strokes were leisurely, his grip on her waist light, his breath hot on her cheek.

"You feel so good," he told her, his voice holding a tone she couldn't quite decipher.

It was almost . . . awe.

She could say the same to him. He felt so full, so real, so attuned to her own body that she couldn't speak. It was then she realized he couldn't possibly be wearing a condom. Which was why he felt so amazing. There was nothing between them, just Nolan as close to her as he could possibly get.

Unless she'd been taking birth control pills without her knowledge, this was a dangerous situation that she needed to remedy immediately. In a minute. After she had an orgasm.

Eve came with a soft cry, arching her hips back toward him. Even as she was telling herself she shouldn't have allowed that to happen since it wasn't really fair to him, who wasn't going to be able to do the same, she was shuddering in ecstasy at the feel of him deep inside her body as she came. This was much better than any plans she'd had, she had to admit.

"Do I need to pull out?" he asked, his voice gravelly and intense. "I'm going to come."

"Probably a good idea," she told him, even though the timing was off. She was the kind of woman who charted her periods with a phone app because she didn't want any surprises and she knew she wasn't ovulating. But better to be safe than knocked up, she always said. Actually, she'd never said that. This was the first time in her entire sexual history she'd allowed a man to forgo a condom.

With a groan he was gone, and in her position she couldn't offer him a hand. By the time she rolled over to face him, he was flat on his back looking spent. But he did pry his eyes open and give her a grin. "I'm glad you couldn't sleep, cupcake."

"Well how could I with a penis in me?" she said, going for the smart-ass response. Climbing out of bed, she padded across the carpet to her bathroom to get a towel for Nolan. She should be freaking out about what they had just done, but for some reason she wasn't.

The worry would arrive later, when he was gone and she was alone with her thoughts. She was sure of it. She was capable of worrying about anything, from global warming

to what was floating in her soup. She most certainly was
going to worry about whether or not a stray sperm might
have rappelled his way up into her fallopian tube.

Balling it up, she tossed a hand towel at him as she
admired his naked body stretched out on her bed. Only
her aim was bad and it landed on his face.

"You trying to cover my ugly mug?" he said, voice
muffled behind the blue towel. He peeled it off his face.

Eve laughed. "Sorry."

He made no move to use the towel. He just lay there,
all muscular and sexy, his expression lazy and content.
She felt a pang for her phone, like she needed to check her
e-mail just in case, so she hovered for a second, admiring
the picture he made and trying to gauge how many e-mails
might have piled up in the last hour.

"Do not get your phone," he told her, snapping at her
thigh with the towel. "Lie down with me."

It was annoying the way he knew what she was about
to do all the time.

"I don't know what you're talking about." She slid into
bed next to him, wondering if she could grab her shirt off
the floor or at the very least her panties. Lifting her head,
she peered over the side to scan the carpet for blue lace.

"What are you doing?"

"Nothing."

"Then get over here and snuggle."

"I am here." She could feel his thigh touching hers.
That was a quality snuggle in her book. But in the spirit
of giving, she rolled onto her side and put her hand on his
chest. That was no hardship. It was a tactile orgasm feeling all that hot and hard muscle beneath her hand.

Nolan had tossed the towel down south so it looked
like he was wearing a blue loincloth. She loved that it
never occurred to him that he looked stupid. He didn't
care. She needed to borrow some of that attitude.

"I should probably jump in the shower."

"Probably." And take that towel with him.

He didn't take offense. She knew he wouldn't. He just laughed. Then startled her when he grabbed her waist and pulled her up on top of him. She landed on his chest, her breasts colliding with him, legs falling between his. "Ack! What are you doing?"

"Getting a kiss." He did just that, pressing his lips to hers in a nice smack.

Eve felt a little ridiculous, but at the same time, she liked it. Nolan didn't fight with her, he didn't get angry, he didn't try to cow her, and he seemed to think that she had a soft side under her prickly exterior.

It would seem he was right.

She kissed him back, a warm fuzzy feeling growing in her chest. Maybe cuddling didn't suck after all.

"You gonna party with me in Vegas?" he asked, nibbling on her shoulder.

"I think we'll both be working." She stared down at his face, amazed at how comfortable she felt. How easy it was to be with him like this. "But it is my birthday."

"It's your birthday? Well, hell, yeah, we have to party." He smacked her backside. "How old are you going to be?"

"You're not supposed to ask a woman that."

"Which is stupid. I know you're not eighteen or forty. So what difference does it make if you're twenty-eight or twenty-nine?"

It must have been so easy to be a man. They lived in a much simpler world than women. "Then why did you ask?"

He made a face. "Okay, you got me there. I was just curious." Then he gave her a grin. "Maybe I wanted to know how many spanks to give you."

"I'll break your hand if you try." She meant that most sincerely.

"But no, it really doesn't matter."

"And of course it matters. We live in a society where age is the enemy. So if you want to run for the hills, I'm going to be thirty-two." Eve paused. Wait. Was that right? It couldn't be, because Evan had just turned thirty and he was three years younger than her. "Oh, my God, no, I'm actually going to be thirty-three." She fell against Nolan's chest, horrified. How could she be thirty-three? She hadn't *done* anything yet in her life.

Maybe they should just forget her birthday was even happening. She could revisit turning thirty-three next year. Because right now she was feeling like she had a career she didn't enjoy, a ticking biological clock, and probably a rapidly developing ulcer.

Plus it was just lame that she had reached her current age and still didn't know how to date.

"Will you relax? Age is just a number. A birthday is a reason to celebrate with friends and family, nothing more. And you're lucky enough to be in Vegas for your birthday, so I say live it up."

Pfft. That's what she thought of that. "Yeah, well, we'll see. I have to be there earlier than usual because Elec has a morning show interview on Thursday. So maybe I can squeeze in time to hit the buffet."

"That is not a birthday celebration. You need to go out dancing."

He couldn't possibly be serious. "You saw me dancing at the Oktoberfest. No one wants me to go out dancing."

"Then see a show or something."

"Hmm." Eve laid her head down on his chest. She was starting to feel sleepy, and she'd much rather be unconscious when they discussed her birthday.

"I don't get in until Saturday but maybe we can grab a drink together."

"Sure." Chances were they'd both be too busy and he

knew it. But it was nice of Nolan to offer. Nice that he wanted to help her celebrate her birthday.

She'd just as soon celebrate a trip to the dentist but it was sweet.

He pinched her side.

Eve was yanked out of the dreamy almost asleep state she'd been in. "What the hell was that for?"

"A pinch to grow an inch."

The man was cute. She had to admit. Amused, Eve trailed her fingers down his chest until she found his penis. She cupped him in her hand. "I have all the inches I need right here."

His breath drew in sharply. "Damn, Eve."

"That's my name, don't wear it out." Since he was going with childhood phrases.

Suddenly she found herself on her back. The shock of the quick position change and how easily he could move her had her inner thighs humming to life.

"I'm going to wear *you* out," he told her, eyes dark with desire, arms enclosing her in a muscular cocoon.

He most definitely was not going to get an argument from her.

Eve wrapped her legs around his waist. "Is that how you treat an old lady?"

He plunged inside her without hesitation or preamble. "My old lady."

The possessiveness should have horrified her. Dried up her desire. Made her run from her own house.

Instead, she came almost immediately at the intensity of him taking her hard, his words reverberating around her. His. She wanted to be his.

CHAPTER
TEN

NOLAN cleared his throat and tried not to sound as awkward as he felt. "So," he said to Evan, "I'm guessing you might have heard that I'm seeing your sister."

He really wanted to just stare at the grease spot on his hands, but he forced himself to look Evan in the eye. He had no reason to be worried about anything. It was just everyone making him nervous about dating his bosses' sister. Or maybe he was nervous because after the night before, casually dating Eve was no longer an option. He wanted to date her for real. He wanted to kiss her senseless on a regular basis, massage away her worries, laugh with her.

It was safe to say he was falling hard for her, and that made him just a little nervous. It had been a while since he'd felt this way about a woman. If he needed to remember exactly how long, he could certainly ask his mother.

She seemed to have his dating history worked out on a spreadsheet.

Evan met his gaze straight on. He had stopped into the garage to check on his car for the Phoenix race. "Yeah, I might have heard about that."

"Did Eve tell you?"

"No. Elec did." Evan put his hands in the front pockets of his jeans.

He didn't look annoyed, which Nolan took as a good sign. "So you don't have a problem with that? From a work point of view, I mean."

"It's not really any of my business what you do in your free time. But Eve is my sister, and I'm going to be honest with you, she's not easy to get along with."

Why did everyone feel like they needed to warn him Eve was a pain in the butt? No one ever seemed to notice her good qualities. He did. "Eve and I get along just fine. We're having fun together." If he sounded a little defensive, well, he had a right to.

Evan's hand came up out of his pocket. "Whoa, alright, I'm not criticizing your relationship. I'm just saying dealing with her takes finessing, something I personally suck at. She and I fight all the time, but I love her. And I don't want her hurt. Nor do I want the two of you going at it at work."

Nolan wanted to argue. He wanted to say that they hadn't fought yet and he didn't plan on it. But he knew Evan had a legitimate concern and being defensive wasn't really Nolan's style.

"I think you can trust both of us to be professional. But you know what it's like—you can't help who you're attracted to." There really wasn't any explanation for why he and Eve hit it off, but they did.

Evan laughed. "Well, you've got that right. Some people were telling me that dating Kendall was a bad move for my career. I didn't listen. So I guess you shouldn't listen either."

"I plan on keeping my relationship with Eve separate from work. For the most part. That doesn't mean I'm not going to take advantage of the traveling." If he and Eve were both going to a race, he was sharing her hotel room, plain and simple. They had crazy schedules and he wanted to ensure they got to spend time together.

Evan made a face. "I really don't need to think about you and my sister sheet diving, okay?"

Yeah, he could see that. "I meant spending time together. I wasn't necessarily talking about sex." He had been talking about sex. Spending time together with Eve meant a lot of things, one of which should always include sex. Now that he'd dipped his toe in that water, he wanted to go swimming on a regular basis. But he didn't need to be discussing that with Eve's brother. He wouldn't want to hear that about his own sisters, so he needed to respect the boundaries before he ended up with Evan's fist in his jaw.

"Let's just not ever say the word 'sex' in relation to my sister and we'll be fine."

"No problem." This conversation wasn't going horribly, yet it was still making Nolan uncomfortable. "So let's talk about Eve's birthday instead. It's next weekend."

"Huh. I guess it is. I imagine we'll do a family dinner or something during the week. You angling for an invite?"

"No, no." Nolan had no idea how Eve would feel about him meeting her parents. That was for her to initiate, not him. But he had a few other tricks up his sleeve. "She's feeling bad about turning thirty-three, which is stupid, because she looks amazing. She is amazing. Anyway, I was thinking of throwing a surprise party for her in Vegas." Otherwise, knowing Eve, she'd sit in her hotel room and do push-ups.

"Oh, damn, Nolan, I don't know if that's a good idea." Evan was shaking his head. "Eve doesn't really like surprises. She's not a surprise kind of girl. She likes to know the ending of every movie and book in advance and she's a master at handling details. She could probably tell you every single article of clothing in her closet, categorized by color and type. No. No surprises."

"I get what you're saying." He did. "But that's the point. Eve has fun when she gets out of her comfort zone. Why let her stay home and dismiss her birthday when we can throw a party and she'll have a great time?"

He knew she liked to plan things herself. Hell, she'd planned their having sex. But that was also why she'd gotten upset when it hadn't gone according to plan. If there was no plan, then there was no way an event could disappoint. Not that he thought she'd been disappointed with their night together, but she hadn't completely let go either. He wanted her so relaxed that she forgot to worry. That she forgot her phone even existed, let alone where it was.

"I think you're insane," Evan told him. "This has the potential to completely backfire on you. And when Eve backfires, everything around her feels the sting."

Nolan was disappointed. "So are you saying you won't be there?"

Evan sighed. "Of course I'll be there. Kendall, too. She is my sister. But seriously, Ford, are you absolutely sure you want to do this?"

"Absolutely." It was brilliant, he was sure of it. "I'm telling her I won't be there until Saturday, but I'll come in on Thursday and we'll surprise her that night."

"Okay. Count us in. Who am I to interfere with your nut racking?"

Nolan laughed. "She'll be pleased. Trust me."

Tilting his head slightly, Evan studied him. "You really dig her, don't you?"

"Hell yeah, I do. She's a rare one and I aim to stick around as long as she'll let me." Nut racking or not. No pain, no gain.

"Good. I'm glad to hear that. Eve deserves someone who thinks she's the shit." Evan grinned. "And who can put up with her. So you need a list of people to invite?"

"That would be really helpful, man, thanks."

"I'll get it to you later today." Evan clapped him on the back. "I hope it works out for you. Now I'm taking off. I'll talk to you later."

"Thanks, I appreciate it." Nolan waved as Evan left.

Nolan had no clue how to go about planning a party in Vegas, but he had a feeling Suzanne Jefferson might be willing to help him. He seemed to recall she had done some wedding planning, and she and Eve were friends. Hopefully she'd be willing to give him some ideas on how to throw a party on a Big Mac budget. A room and a cake, that's all they really needed.

Rhett strolled over to him. "He didn't fire your dumb ass?"

"No, he didn't fire me. He's cool with me dating Eve, because he's an adult." It was starting to get really old that everyone seemed determined that he'd (1) lose his job, and (2) lose his sanity dating Eve. He didn't remember everyone ever having this much of an opinion regarding women he'd dated before.

"Doesn't it worry you that the Monroes are rich?"

Yes. "No. Eve doesn't seem materialistic. If that mattered to her, she wouldn't be seeing me." But he had to say, his brother had hit on a fear of his.

All of this was making him cranky. He just wanted to spend time with the woman and throw her a damn party. Why was everyone making it so difficult?

"I'm going back to work."

So there.

* * *

KENDALL looked at her husband skeptically. "A surprise party? For Eve? Does Nolan understand she's not really the type to get into surprises?"

"I tried to warn him."

Evan flopped on the couch of their motor coach next to her. They had arrived in Phoenix earlier, and with the time change, they were both tired and ready for bed. Or at least she was. But it was only seven o'clock, local time.

"He's kind of a stubborn guy. In a good way. Most men run away after one date with Eve."

"Oh, come on, be nice."

Evan put his hand up. "I'm not being a prick, I'm merely stating facts, babe. Eve is the kind of girl who makes men's testicles shrivel up. They hit on her and she hands them their asshole back."

"Why do you think she does that? I have my own theories, but as her brother, I'm sure you know her better."

"I don't know. She was born bitchy."

That was not the answer Kendall was looking for. "That's not a theory, that's laziness. Maybe you and Elec should have spent more time getting to know Eve, trying to understand her feelings."

Now he scoffed. "Yeah, sure, we'll just get right on that. You don't ask Eve about her feelings. Actually, I don't ask anyone about their feelings, and I'm not going to ask the one person who feels perfectly justified in giving me a right hook." Evan put his feet on the coffee table. "She has a mean right hook, by the way. Don't let her get the jump on you."

Kendall had knowledge of Evan being considerate enough to ask her about her feelings on multiple occasions, so she knew he was capable of it. "I think that Eve internalizes her stress. She needs an outlet and she's relied on arguing for that."

"Why would that be a stress reliever? It just makes my blood pressure go up."

Wishing she'd brought socks since it was cold in the AC, Kendall tucked her feet under her legs. "Everyone is different. I think for her that keeps her from bottling it all up."

"If Nolan is willing to argue back, then I guess I'm happy for them. I still think a party is a bad idea."

"Agreed." Kendall could visualize her sister-in-law's face turning eight shades of angry. "But then again, you should have seen her when we were out for girls' night and Nolan called her. She was so nervous. I think she really likes him." Which would be a first as far as Kendall knew. Back when she and Evan had dated right out of high school, she hadn't noticed Eve involved with anyone. Nor had she in the six months that Kendall and Evan had been back together. "How many boyfriends has Eve had?"

"I don't know." Evan's hand had landed on her upper thigh and was moving north. It was obvious he was losing interest in the conversation.

Tempted to throw a sofa pillow at him, Kendall put her hand over his to stop it. "I'm serious. I think it would be great if this worked out."

"I think that would be a good thing, too," he protested. "Seriously, I want Eve to be happy. It seems like the last few years she's been pretty damn miserable. If she can find a guy who can loosen her up and get her to have fun, I'll buy him a car."

Kendall laughed. "You'll buy him a car?" And the thing was, her husband might be flippant but she knew he meant it. He was at heart a very good guy.

"Yep."

"You'd better not mention that in front of Eve. She might tell you she's happy just to stick it to you."

He drained his drink and moved his hand farther up her thigh. "Good point. Now can we get to the real subject at hand?"

"What subject would that be?" Kendall felt the heat of his touch immediately. It always amazed her how just a stroke across her leg could have her glancing around for the nearest mattress.

"My horniness."

Kendall laughed. She loved her husband, that was for sure. "Well, let's get to work on that subject right now."

He leaned over and kissed her. "Did you buy condoms? We're out, remember."

She ran her fingers through his hair and kissed him back. "No. Let's just skip the condom this time." They'd been talking about starting a family for months. It felt like time to pull the trigger.

Evan pulled back and stared at her. "Are you serious?"

She nodded. "Yeah, what do you think?" The urge to be a mother had been growing steadily, and she loved her husband so much. She wanted to start a family with him.

He hugged her so tightly her ribs hurt. "I think we should do it."

The way her heart swelled amazed her. She wasn't sure she could love him any more than she did right then. "I love you."

"I love you, too."

Then hopefully what they did in the next hour would result in baby makes three.

Or at the very least an orgasm.

NOLAN glanced around the hotel suite in amazement. Suzanne was barking out orders, her infant son in her arms. The room was a whirlwind of activity with at least half a dozen women running around transforming the space into an explosion of pink and purple and yellow.

Suzanne came over to him. "So what do you think? How does it look so far?"

"It looks . . . amazing." It looked like a whole lot of a whole lot. Nolan couldn't believe what Suzanne had pulled off in such a short time. "I really appreciate you doing this."

"It's a fun challenge for me. You know you can't rent a bathroom stall in Vegas on your budget, so using our suite for the night allows us to use all your cash for the décor and food."

The budget that Suzanne had thought was so insanely small was going to give him a heart attack if he thought about it too long. Never in his life had he spent so much money on a party and certainly not on a woman he'd been dating for two weeks. But once the ball had started rolling, he hadn't been able to catch it.

So now he was giving Eve a surprise birthday party in Ryder and Suzanne's Vegas suite, and there was no turning back. It looked like a bakery had exploded in the room. When Suzanne had asked him if he had a theme in mind, he had told her no. But then she had tricked him by asking him if he had a nickname for Eve. He had answered "cupcake" without thinking why she might be asking that.

Now he knew. She had made the entire room look like an actual cupcake, with fluffy fabrics hanging from the ceiling and a giant towering display of individual cupcakes made to look like an enormous cupcake. There were dozens of colorful balloons and a table full of paper favors, including stick-on tattoos of baked goods. Plus hanging over all of it, like a giant sugary declaration of his feelings, was a sign that said HAPPY BIRTHDAY, CUPCAKE in sprinkles.

No backing out now.

He liked her and now everyone and his brother was going to figure that out.

While he was a little nervous as to Eve's reaction, he couldn't help feeling a little pleased. This was a surprise party. This was a whole table of food and desserts and ten bottles of champagne. If he had done this himself, it would have been a few cases of beer, some chips, and a cake.

"Thanks, Suzanne. I have a mother and seven sisters, so they always muscle me out of anything like this. I had no idea what I was doing."

"You have seven sisters?" Suzanne looked down at her baby, who was sleeping, his tiny hand clenched into a fist. "Lord, I can't imagine squeezing out eight of him."

"Actually nine. Rhett is also my brother." Who was supposed to be showing up for the party, but had been oddly silent all day. Then he forgot all about his brother entirely as a terrible thought hit him. "Shit. I didn't actually get a gift for Eve. What the hell is wrong with me?"

What guy doesn't get his girl a gift for her birthday?

Of course, she wasn't even his girl. Which made him wonder what the hell he was even doing. But you know what? Screw it. He was in it to win it.

"You'd better hit the pavement," Suzanne told him. "You have forty minutes before Eve gets here."

What the hell could he buy in forty minutes? It would be a nightmare if he wasn't actually in the room when Eve got there, and God knew she would be on time. She thought she was arriving at the Jeffersons' suite for a photo shoot of the Hinder Motors drivers, and he knew full well she took her job seriously.

But he didn't really know Eve's tastes that well. He'd only been to her condo once, and he'd spent most of his time in the bedroom. Added to that was the fact that he was only going to be able to shop in the hotel retail spots. So he ran and discovered as he slid into the lobby that his options were Vegas shot glasses or beaded bags that brought to mind older ladies on tour buses.

"Can I help you?" A blue-haired woman who was wearing a beaded top that matched half the bags on the wall next to her approached him with a beaming smile.

"I'm just looking, thanks." He scanned the shelves, hoping something would miraculously pop out at him and guarantee that Eve would fall in love with him.

He almost knocked a Vegas Strip ashtray onto the floor. Did he want Eve to fall in love with him?

Duh. The answer was pretty fricking obvious. He had allowed himself to stroke inside her condom free, something he hadn't ever done. Not once. Plus he was throwing her a surprise birthday party in Vegas with all of his last paycheck. There was no way he'd do that for a roll in the hay. Sex just wasn't that hard to come by. No, he wanted her to want him. He wanted her to love him.

It should have been a terrifying realization, but instead he just felt exhilarated as he stared at T-shirts with tigers on them.

"I'm buying a birthday gift for my girlfriend," he blurted out to the clerk. "I'm throwing her a party but I forgot to get an actual gift."

Maybe if he called her his girlfriend, he could make it so. Or maybe that was a psychotic junior high thing to do. Either way, it felt pretty damn good to speak the words out loud.

"Oh, dear." The clerk gave him an admonishing look. "What does she like? Jewelry?"

"No." Eve wore very basic jewelry and makeup. "She likes cars. Being on time. Salads." His tongue between her thighs.

"Oh, dear," she repeated. "That's not a lot to go on.

How about a scented candle? Does she like poker? We have a bedazzled set of poker chips."

Maybe he shouldn't buy her a gift after all. Looking around, the pickings did seem to be on the wrong side of tacky. Though there were worse gifts than an Elvis poster. Nolan distinctly recalled the Christmas his father had bought his mother a Shop-Vac. That had not been a pleasant dinner. Or the time his brother-in-law had gotten his sister a rifle for her birthday when she'd never been hunting a day in her life. Those were fuck-up gifts. He didn't want to give Eve a fuck-up gift.

Then he turned and he was fairly certain applause sounded as he spotted a leopard print bra and panties. It was the kind of bra that pushed everything up and out. What woman didn't want that? Plus it was an inside joke between them that she'd popped her button and this thing would cause her whole blouse to burst. The panties said PUSSYCAT across the front of them, which was perfect. It was like the whole set was designed for Eve. She would appreciate the humor in it.

Plus if she was a good sport and actually put them on, he was going to have a very happy ending to this shopping excursion.

"I'll take this," he told the clerk, lifting the bra off the rack. "With the panties."

She looked dubious. "Are you sure? Most women want something more personal for their birthday."

What was more personal than underwear? Besides, it was essentially a joke. Eve would get that. "No, this is good."

"What size?"

"Um." Like he knew. "Small panties. Big bra."

"Like a D cup big?"

Nolan put his hands in front of him. Eve had a nice rack. "Like this big." He was going to have to make sure he looked at the tags on her clothes next time they were all lying on the floor. He'd put them in his phone for future gift giving, of which he planned to do plenty.

"I'd say that's a large C."

Noted. Though he might need a second job. The register read $97.23 when the clerk was done ringing the bra and panties. Seriously? For two inches of leopard print material? Nolan swallowed his doubts and tried not to think about how much money he had spent today alone. More than he normally spent in a month.

Nope. He wasn't going to think about it.

"I hope she enjoys it."

"Thanks, I'm sure she will." He may not have a lot of money, but he'd always had a fair amount of confidence, and Nolan took the package and strolled out of the store.

He had a feeling this was going to be a night to remember.

CHAPTER
ELEVEN

EVE sat in the car with Evan and Kendall, feeling cranky as hell. She didn't want to be going to this photo shoot. She wanted to eat dinner, go for a run, then lie in her hotel room feeling sorry for herself.

She'd barely heard from Nolan in the last three days. There had been a couple of text messages every day, but he hadn't called her and she hadn't seen him. He kept saying they would see each other on Saturday, but she didn't believe it. What she believed was that men sucked.

This was just so typical. He had pursued her, gotten her into bed, and now he was retreating. Asshole.

Not to mention that even right now at this moment cells could be dividing into a fetus in her uterus since he'd been inside her without a condom. Oh, so it hadn't been the right time, but that wasn't foolproof. Nor was pulling out. He should have talked it over with her before sticking it in. Asshole.

What was she going to do with a baby? Nolan was on the road all the time. Asshole.

She noticed Evan was looking at her. "What?" she snapped at him.

He put his hands up. "Nothing. Jesus Christ, you're in a mood."

"I am not." Okay, she totally was, but fuck him. Why did Evan have to always point out her crankiness? Like he was never cranky? "Tell me this—why do men have sex with women then disappear?"

"They don't always do that."

"No, but they do a lot of times." They were in a limo coming directly from the airport so Eve was across from both her brother and sister-in-law. "Don't they, Kendall?"

"It seems like a stereotype, the commitment-phobe guy, but stereotypes are usually based on something."

"I don't think it's a commitment issue. I think most men are just seeing an opportunity and taking it."

"But why can't they at least hang around long enough to see if they like the woman or not? Why is it like, 'Well, I've touched her vagina, now she can't possibly be interesting.'"

"Where is this coming from? Are you worried that Nolan is blowing you off?" Kendall asked.

Yes. Eve just made a sound with her lips. "I'm not worried about it. I know he is."

They exchanged looks. Great, they felt sorry for her.

"Eve, that is most definitely not the case." Evan nudged her foot with his boot. "Trust me."

"He mentioned you all are going out for your birthday on Saturday," Kendall said.

She appreciated the pep talks, but really, she was just determined to be miserable. It was all for the best really.

The sooner he shit on her, the sooner she could stop seeing him, and the less she would get hurt.

God, that was seriously the most pathetic thought she'd ever had.

Maybe she should just assume they were going out on Saturday and stop worrying about it. That couldn't honestly be that hard.

Though she wouldn't mind a drink. It had been a long flight to Vegas the day before and an early morning press event today. She was tired. Crossing her leg, she flicked lint off her pencil skirt. She wanted to ditch the heels, too. Work clothes after 5 p.m. were just rude.

"You're right. He did say that. Though I'd rather forget about my birthday."

They exchanged another look as the limo pulled up in front of the hotel. "What?" she asked again.

"Nothing." Evan opened the door and put his foot out onto the pavement. "But if there winds up being something of a celebration for your birthday at any point this weekend, don't be pissed."

That gave her pause. "Are Mom and Dad here?"

He didn't answer, just hopped out of the limo.

She looked at Kendall, who shook her head. "I'm not saying a word."

"My parents planned a party for me?" That was sweet, she had to say, but at the same time, she didn't want any attention paid to her impending old age. "Wait, is it tonight?"

Kendall exited the limo right behind Evan without saying a word, which to Eve was confirmation.

Great, she was tired from traveling and dressed like the wait staff. But it was nice to know she was loved, that was for sure. Sometimes she questioned why her family didn't just wash their hands of her.

Climbing out of the car, she felt a wave of nostalgia

wash over her. She had no right to bitch. She had a good life, a family that loved her, financial security, and a career a lot of women would love to have.

Plus she was getting jackman action.

Maybe thirty-three wasn't so bad after all.

As they went up in the elevator together, Eve brushed her hair and put on a neutral lipstick. "Thanks for giving me the heads-up. I'm not big on surprises, you know."

"I know. I told No—"

Evan stopped talking when Kendall elbowed him in the gut.

Suddenly suspicious, Eve followed them down the hallway. "What are you two not telling me? Is there a male stripper here or something? I don't do male strippers, you know that."

Evan snorted. "No, there isn't a male stripper. Why would any of us order that? I don't want to be anywhere near male strippers. And by the way, how would I know you don't do male strippers?"

He knocked on the suite door then opened it.

Eve muscled past him, ready to get this over with. "Because you should know if I have a dollar, I'm not sticking it in a G-string."

She entered the room, pasting a smile on her face. And was met with neither a male stripper nor her parents.

It was Nolan, surrounded by a lot of pink and yellow tulle, and a giant sign behind him proclaiming, HAPPY BIRTHDAY, CUPCAKE.

Oh. My. God.

Stunned speechless, she stared blankly at him beaming at her, then looked left and right. There were balloons and a giant towering cupcake display. Elec was there, as well as the Jeffersons, Tuesday and Diesel, Ty and Imogen. Behind an explosion of flowers were her parents, the table next to them lined with a shit-ton of champagne bottles. The owner of Hinder Motors, Carl, was there with his wife, Trudy, and both of her brothers' secretaries. Even Nolan's brother, Rhett, was there, already popping cheese cubes in his mouth.

"What the hell . . ." was all she managed before they all launched into a rousing, but off-key version of "Happy Birthday."

Nolan came toward her as they sang, and she found herself both hard-core blushing and fighting the urge to turn and run back to the elevator. Everyone was staring at her. No one ever stared at her. Certainly fifteen people didn't ever at the same time. She was the background fader, the woman with the clipboard and the phone, in the most nondescript outfits possible.

So while part of her wanted to crawl into a hole in the carpet and die, the other part was squealing in girlish delight.

Nolan wasn't a commitment phobe. He hadn't blown her off.

He was so into her that he was wearing a cupcake button on his shirt and had pulled off a surprise party on just a few days' notice.

It was equal parts mortification and magic.

Everyone was smiling and singing, and she was blushing. No one had ever thrown her a surprise party before. They knew her better. But Nolan didn't walk on eggshells with her. He just dove in, forcing her to enjoy herself.

It was both messed up and touching.

"Wow," she said, while everyone was still singing, because it seemed like she should say something.

Nolan was almost to her, and to give herself credit, she didn't run away. She met his smile with a smile of her own. Truthfully, it was easy to smile at him. He was so damn cute. You'd have to have no soul not to respond to his sheer adorableness. He was like a kitten you had to touch and pet and soothe. Only he was a lot hotter than a kitten and mostly she wanted to kiss him, not soothe him. So maybe he wasn't like a kitten at all. He was like a hot jackman who was adorable and he had thrown her a surprise birthday party. There were no words for that.

"Happy Birthday, baby," he told her, leaning in and kissing her cheek as the singing petered off.

"Holy shit, Nolan," she told him, because that was how she was feeling.

He laughed.

"Thank you. This is . . . unexpected."

He took her hand and turned so he wasn't blocking the room from her view.

"Thank you," she repeated to everyone. "Wow, this is awesome." The weird thing was, she actually meant it. It was very cool to know that everyone had managed to fit her birthday into their busy schedules. She hadn't had a thirtieth birthday party because she hadn't wanted one, and to see everyone here, beaming at her, for such an uneventful birthday as thirty-three really touched her. "I really appreciate you all coming, this is amazing."

What was equally amazing was that she was holding hands with Nolan and didn't want to throw up in her mouth. Everyone could see they were holding hands, too. That was a first.

They were all still sort of staring at her expectantly, so Eve realized she needed to make a bigger statement. "So let's party! Have some of this delicious-looking food and a glass of bubbly. It will keep you all from noticing my growing crow's-feet."

They all laughed and Eve squeezed Nolan's hand. "You're a nut," she told him. "You didn't have to do this."

"I wanted to. I just happen to like you a whole lot, you know."

He did. And it was making her feel a bit giddy. "I like you, too. As much as I like champagne."

Nolan leaned closer to her, his eyes dropping to her mouth. "Lucky you, you get to have both on your birthday."

Her heart rate was increasing and she felt warm in her pencil skirt. Her nipples pushed against her blouse. "You weren't supposed to be here until Saturday."

"I know. But my boss happens to be your brother." He winked. "I pulled the family card with him, and he was more than willing to let me come early. I just have to promise never to talk about our sex life."

Eve laughed. "That sounds like Evan. Now I'm going to get a glass of champagne and mingle with my guests."

If she expected him to just wander off, she was dead wrong. Nolan stayed with her like he was, well, her boyfriend. It should have been unnerving but instead it felt good. Like finally she wasn't the odd one out, the cranky single girl. Like she was capable of having fun with someone.

Admittedly she could have done without the hand-holding at a certain point—was she fifteen?—but overall she was feeling pretty damn happy with the whole situation. She approached Suzanne, who was jiggling her baby. "I know you had something to do with this. Nolan did not put tulle on the ceiling by himself."

Suzanne laughed. "No, he did not."

"I don't even know what tulle is, so I can't argue with either of you." He let go of her hand and asked Suzanne, "Can I hold the baby?"

"Hell, yes, you can hold the baby. My arm is about to fall off." Suzanne passed baby Track over to Nolan and rolled her shoulders. "Lord, Eve, you need to hold on to this man. He plans surprise parties and holds babies."

"He is something." Eve wasn't sure what he was exactly

but she was starting to really like the idea that he was hers. At the moment he was holding the baby and cooing down into his face, making goofy expressions, which pleased her more than she liked to consider.

"Yes, you're a handsome little dude, aren't you? Don't look a thing like your daddy. You're all your mommy." Nolan leaned forward and put his ear toward Track's mouth, like the baby was actually talking to him. "What's that? Yeah? Eve is beautiful? Yeah, I think so, too."

Eve rolled her eyes, blushing again. She blushed more around Nolan than she had in her entire puberty.

Suzanne laughed. "If my son was going to say anything about Eve, it would probably be to express regret that she's not the one breast-feeding him."

"Suzanne!" Now Eve was totally horrified.

"What? You have what women pay big bucks for. You should display them more prominently. I'm envious myself."

"I wholeheartedly agree with Suzanne," Nolan said, nodding seriously. "You should display them more."

Awkward. "Can we stop talking about my breasts in front of an infant?"

Ryder strolled up. "Do you want me to take Track so you can talk about your breasts?" He held his hands out to Nolan for the baby.

"No. I want no one talking about my breasts." In fact, Eve crossed her arms across her chest to emphasize her point.

"The baby's asleep. I don't think we've scarred him." Nolan leaned down and kissed his petite nose. "You're a cute little man."

"You're good with babies," Ryder said.

"Seriously." Suzanne looked awed. "I've been trying to get him to sleep for the last hour."

"I have fourteen nieces and nephews."

Suzanne gave Eve a searching look that made her uncomfortable. "I see," Suzanne said.

Eve didn't want to see anything. How had this turned from her birthday party to Nolan's potential as a father?

"I'm getting a glass of champagne." She beat a path across the carpet for the makeshift bar that had been set up. Nolan was good with babies. He looked very natural and very, well, sexy holding baby Track so easily in his arms. It was scary as hell.

Especially considering that their condom-free incident meant she could be pregnant right now. Of course, she wasn't. She knew it wasn't possible, given her ovulation app on her smartphone. So she wasn't going to worry about the fact that for a split second she had liked the idea. Nor was she going to stop herself from indulging in a glass of champagne. They said you should drink wine if you were trying to get pregnant so surely if wouldn't be harmful if she was.

There wasn't an open bottle yet, but she unwrapped the foil and untwisted it until the cork was accessible. Then grabbing a hotel napkin off the sideboard, she covered the cork and yanked and pulled until it popped. Unceremonious, but that suited her style better. She was pouring herself a glass when her mother appeared at her side.

"Hi, Mom."

Her mom bussed her cheek. "Happy Birthday."

"Thanks. Thanks for coming." She took a big sip, a gulp really, of her bubbly. "Were you planning to be here this weekend?" She honestly couldn't remember. She'd been too preoccupied with a certain jackman to make note of her parents' schedule. They usually attended half a dozen races or more a year, especially the big ones like Daytona. Vegas offered more than just racing, too, so it wasn't out of the question they'd already been planning to attend this race.

"We were on the fence, but once we heard about the party, we decided to come. Tamara was sorry she couldn't make it, but she has the kids and work."

"I understand." Elec's wife was a college professor and her schedule wasn't flexible. "I didn't expect any of this. This was really sweet of everybody."

"Well, that man of yours was so determined to do this, how could we say no?" Her mother leaned closer and murmured in her ear. "He's even cuter in person than he is on TV."

Amused, Eve laughed. "Back off, Cindy," she told her mother. "He's mine."

"Fine," her mother grumbled. "But in all seriousness, you might want to hang on to him. Someone will snap him up if you don't."

Her father came up behind her mother. "Well, I guess Nolan's alright. I still don't think you should date him, but I see the attraction."

"He's pretty cute, isn't he?" Eve said, nudging her dad in the chest.

"That's not what I meant. I meant he seems like a good guy. I mean, he's wearing a pin with a cupcake on it. That either means he's a nice guy or a total pansy. Now that I think about it, I'm leaning towards pansy."

"Be nice."

"Nice is overrated." With that, her dad grabbed a beer and strolled off.

It occurred to Eve that she was more like her father than she cared to admit. He could be a real grump. She didn't want to be that person. But she already was that person. She took another sip of her drink.

Fabulous.

"Don't listen to your father. He's just never going to think anyone is good enough for you."

It was more like she wasn't good enough for anyone.

Eve drained her glass and refilled it. She wasn't going to do this. She wasn't going to feel bad on her birthday when all these people had taken the time to wish her well.

She wasn't going to do this to Nolan, who was the nicest man she'd ever dated. She'd been fine until two seconds earlier when her dad had served as a mirror to her own flaws.

Tonight wasn't about flaws. Tonight was about celebrating. About being with the people she cared the most about.

About being free . . . free to enjoy herself, free of worry.

"Nolan's more than good enough for me," she told her mother sincerely. "I can't believe he did this for me."

"My pleasure."

Eve jumped when she heard Nolan's voice right behind her. God, had she said anything embarrassing? But a quick glance showed he was the same as always—smiling and calm. How did he achieve that sense of easiness? She'd give her condo and everything in her bank account if she could figure out how not to stress.

"It's nice to meet you, Mrs. Monroe." Nolan stuck his hand out to her mother, still comfortably holding the sleeping baby in the crook of his left arm.

"Call me Cindy, please." Her mother shook his hand and smiled.

Oh, Lord, her mother was thinking about Nolan's ass. It was as clear as the nose on her face.

He seemed to realize it, too, because he looked a little flustered and cut the handshake short. It was amusing enough to dash off the remains of her bad feelings.

"I'll leave you two kids alone," her mom said with a wink. "Let me take that baby from you."

She didn't wait for an answer, just took the baby from Nolan and left with a "Don't do anything I wouldn't do."

"Your mom is a firecracker," Nolan told her.

"You seem to bring out the flirt in her. It's your sexy factor." She raised her glass to him. "Want a drink?"

"I want a kiss."

"I'm not kissing you in front of a roomful of people." Displays of affection were reserved for private. Holding hands had been enough for her, thank you very much.

"Even after I threw this party for you?"

Eve rolled her eyes. "Please, like I'm falling for that emotional blackmail. You should know me better."

"I know you well enough to know that you want to kiss me, you're just being uptight about it."

Shit. He also knew her well enough to know that she was bound to react to that precisely the way he wanted her to. "I'm not uptight." Might as well play out their roles.

"So kiss me and prove it."

The worm smiled because he knew he had her. He knew he was going to win this round.

Eve gave him a kiss, nice and long and juicy, even biting his bottom lip as she retreated. It was a calculated move to make him horny, but unfortunately it made her horny as well. But she could ignore that for the moment.

"Hey, save that for later," Elec said, coming up next to her.

She refused to blush. She was older than Elec. "It's my party, I can kiss if I want to."

"You always do whatever you want. Happy Birthday." Elec kissed her cheek.

"Thanks, Eyeball." She used his stupid childhood nickname just to keep their relationship on its natural trajectory. But his words gave her pause. Did her family really think that she got everything she wanted? Because in all truth, she hadn't gotten anything she wanted.

What she had wanted was to drive a stock car in the Cup series. Hell, not even on that level. Just to drive for enough money to pay the rent. Just feel that adrenaline, the freedom, the beautiful solitude of her and a powerful machine.

Nor did she have a family. A husband, children of her own.

But whose fault was that? She couldn't blame her father or men in the business for shaking their heads at her driving ambitions. If she had wanted it badly enough, she could have gone for it. She hadn't even tried because she hadn't wanted to fail. She'd known she would be good at managing her brother's careers, and she was, but it had been a cop-out. She hadn't tried to find a quality relationship either. She had bullied her way into a few unsuccessful attempts with men she thought she could control. That wasn't trying either.

That was setting herself up to fail. Intentionally. Because maybe she was afraid to succeed. It was easier to stomp around and say she'd been given a raw deal. Easier, yes. Happier? Hell no.

Elec was telling Nolan he'd done a great job with the party and Nolan was shaking his head. "It was just my idea. Suzanne did all the hard work."

"Is your nickname for my sister really cupcake? Because that's nauseating."

"Mind your own business," Eve told him. Cupcake was starting to grow on her mainly because it was so nauseating. There was a certain sincerity to any nickname that was so saccharine Nolan was setting himself up for ridicule.

"It's because she's so damn sweet." Nolan gave her a loud smacking kiss right in front of her brother.

She could admit it. She was pleased. Giddy. Pink in the cheeks. Feeling as sugary sweet as he was proclaiming her to be.

"Oh, Lord," was Elec's opinion. "I'm going to eat, though I'm not sure I can stomach anything after that."

Eve watched him walk away, then looked at Nolan. "I guess I should stop calling you jackass. This was a really sweet thing for you to do."

"If you stop calling me jackass, I'll start to think you're mad at me. Jackass works." He smiled at her. "And you're welcome. It was my pleasure." He gestured for her to come closer. "I have a secret to tell you."

"Yeah?" she asked suspiciously. Was he going to tell her he wanted to have a threesome for her birthday or something that would equally piss her off? Or was he going to give her a wet willy by sticking his tongue in her ear?

"I really like you."

Oh. Right. He was showing no signs of being an ass-hole yet. Maybe she needed to trust that. The champagne and the party were warming her from the inside out. Instead of a smart-ass response, she told the truth. "I really like you, too."

"Good. Now do you want a cupcake, Cupcake?"

She did. And she wanted him.

NOLAN watched Eve waving good-bye to the last few party guests, feeling pretty damn pleased. He had been right. Despite Evan's declarations otherwise, Eve had enjoyed the surprise and the party. She had been shocked and maybe a little embarrassed, but she had been sincerely touched that all these people had showed up for her birthday celebration.

He was starting to think that her family took her for granted. They just assumed she would always be there, cheering them on, yet no one cheered her on. It wasn't always easy to understand how to do that with someone who didn't have a career that had an applauding audience, but Nolan got the impression they didn't show Eve a whole lot of appreciation.

It was easy not to give praise and thanks when someone was prickly. But was Eve prickly because she was taken for granted?

Nolan didn't know what the truth of her family dynamics was. He just knew that Eve had somehow gotten herself wound up tight, and he was taking great pleasure in watching her unwind slowly and surely. He felt privileged to see her in raw, unguarded moments.

Looking around at the remnants of food and empty bottles of champagne, the balloons floating silently in the mostly empty suite, Nolan was satisfied. He no longer gave a shit how much the party had cost. It had been worth it.

"Thanks again for everything," he told Suzanne. She had put Track to sleep in the portable crib and was sharing a glass of wine with Ryder. "We'll get out of your hair so you two can enjoy some alone time."

"You're welcome. I had fun. I felt like an adult tonight instead of a milk spigot."

Ryder laughed. "You make motherhood sound so glamorous, babe."

"That it's not. It's wonderful. I wouldn't trade it for anything. But I miss conversation that doesn't revolve around burps and bowel movements."

"So motherhood is like the boys' locker room in seventh grade?" Nolan asked.

"I wouldn't know since I've never been in the boys' locker room, but I'm going to say yes."

"Lucky you." The comparison amused Nolan. Suzanne was always entertaining. "I'll come by tomorrow and clean all this mess up. Unless you want me to take care of it now."

"Oh, no, who cares? It will still be there tomorrow. Go have fun."

"Thanks, both of you, seriously. This was amazing."

Suzanne waved her hand, her feet on the coffee table. "Go on now."

He could do that. Eve turned back from the front door as he approached her. She looked flushed, happy. Maybe slightly drunk.

"I think that was everybody," she said. "Let me clean up this food, then we can go."

"Leave the food. I'll take care of it later. Suzanne and Ryder want to be alone, I think." Nolan wanted to be alone with Eve, too, but he figured this was a better card to play.

She looked past him to the couch, where the couple was getting cozy, heads bent close to each other. "Oh, right. Let me just get my purse. I left it somewhere." She went over and said good-bye, found her purse, then they were standing in the hushed hallway together.

"Thank you," she said again, smiling up at him in a way that made his heart and other parts swell.

"This was a great night, Nolan."

So naïve if she thought this was the end of the night. "It's not over yet."

"No?" She cocked her head. "Are you going to give me a birthday treat?"

"Oh, yeah. But first, let's go out. Let's hit the Strip, go dancing, do some gambling." He just didn't want this night to end. He was enjoying her so much he wanted it to last as long as possible.

"What? Are you nuts? I have to work tomorrow."

"Come on. It will be fun. How many times do you turn thirty-three?"

She rolled her eyes. "You turn every age only once."

"Which is why each one should be celebrated."

"That's insane logic."

"No, it's not." Nolan pulled her close, enjoying the feel of her breasts pushing against his chest. She was warm, her eyes dancing as she tried to protest.

"You can sleep when you're dead," he told her. "You have a good buzz and we should go out."

She laughed, a sound that was so free and goofy Nolan couldn't help laughing himself. "Okay," she said. "Fine. I'll hate you tomorrow, but fine."

"No, you won't." There was no hate involved between the two of them. There was something growing that he thought was more like the opposite of hate.

"No," she admitted, her fingers stroking across the front of his shirt. "I probably won't."

Nolan was holding the gift bag the clerk had put the bra and panties set in, and he held it up for her. "A little something for you for later. After the dancing and the gambling and a few more drinks."

"You got me a gift, too? Nolan . . . seriously, that's too much." She looked touched.

And she was touching him. Her hand was sliding across his ass. Hello. He liked that. "It's just a little something I thought you would find entertaining." Or at least he would find entertaining.

"Give it to me." She backed up and held her hand out.

He laughed. That was Eve. "I love your patience."

"You offered it to me." She tore the tissue off the top and threw it down on the floor. A second later she had the bra in her hands. Her jaw dropped. "What the hell is this?"

"It's a bra. With a jungle theme. It's hot. Or should I say, you'll be hot in it." His mouth was starting to water just thinking about her breasts pushed up in leopard print.

"I should be offended. I think I am. But at the same time, I have a hard time resisting you when I know it was well meaning."

"You're offended?" He supposed he wasn't really

shocked by that. It had been a gamble. "It was meant to be fun. To compliment you on your assets. The panties say PUSSYCAT on them. I mean, come on, that's funny."

She laughed, holding the bra up to her chest. His mouth watered a bit.

"You bought this last minute, didn't you?"

"Yes."

Eve leaned forward and kissed him softly. "Well, that was very sweet. Unnecessary, but sweet."

"You're going to wear them, right?" He'd return the set if she was just going to throw them in a drawer. This wasn't a gag gift, he actually wanted to see her fine behind in those panties.

"Because you were well intentioned and because I'm drunk, yes, I'll wear them."

Fair enough. "Hey, that's all any man can ever hope for. To get his girl drunk enough that she'll wear tacky underwear for him."

Her finger came up and she grinned. "So you admit they're tacky?"

"I never said they weren't. That's kind of the point. Now come on, put those back in the bag and let's hit the Strip."

"I'm not carrying around a gift bag all night." Eve ripped the tags off with her teeth and spit them into the bag. She then stuffed the bra and panties in her purse and put the gift bag outside Suzanne and Ryder's door. "All set."

Oh, man, she made him laugh. He appreciated that she saw a problem and just solved it, without drama. "Perfect."

"Though I wish I wasn't wearing this outfit. It's boring."

"So take your panties off," he told her as they moved toward the elevator.

The look on her face was hilarious. "How the hell would that make my outfit more exciting?"

"It wouldn't, but you'd feel dirty. Sexy. Which would

automatically give you more swagger. On second thought, don't do that. I don't want to get into a fight tonight with some punk hitting on you."

She snorted. "Yeah, right. Though I don't understand how women go without panties. I mean, don't they . . ."

"Don't they what?" He pushed the down button. This could go in interesting directions.

"Don't they ever get *wet*?"

Holy crap. Nolan had an insta-erection. "Do you?"

"Well, yeah. I mean, we're going out together, and if I'm not wearing panties and you're giving me that look like the one you're giving me right now, I'm going to get wet. It just happens. That's awkward when you're not wearing panties."

She was killing him. "What's awkward is now for the rest of the night I'm going to be wanting to slip my finger inside you to see if you're wet."

Her eyes went wide. "I might be already."

The elevator doors slid open. Damn. Nolan nudged her inside then spun her around.

"What are you doing?" she asked, clutching her purse, her tongue dragging across her bottom lip.

"Doing a spot check." Blocking her with his body in case the doors opened unexpectedly, Nolan slid his hand up her knee, under the fabric of her narrow skirt. Her breath hitched.

"You can't be serious."

"Very." Kissing her jaw, he stroked higher under he found the apex of her thighs. A quick shift of her panties and his thumb was inside her. She gave a sharp inhale. Nolan fought the urge to close his eyes. She felt so good, so open to him, her nipples beading in her blouse, her sex in reality very, very wet.

"Am I wet?" she asked, rocking her hips forward onto him.

"Soaking wet." He wanted to pursue the point, but they were rapidly approaching the first floor. Nolan pulled away and adjusted her skirt right as the doors open.

Eve stood there for a second, blinking, then she moved off the elevator, shaking her head. "I can't believe I wasn't even worried about getting caught."

"That's because you've been drinking."

"No." She turned and looked at him, her expression serious. "That's not it. It's you. You and me. For some reason."

He knew what she meant. "It's like we bring out the best in each other, isn't it?"

"Is letting you feel me up on the elevator the best in me?"

He laughed. "It means you're not worrying. So yes, that is what's best for you. I would never suggest you blow off responsibilities. But hell, Eve, you deserve to have some fun."

She nodded. "Yeah, I do. So where are we going, Mr. Happy?"

"We're hitting the clubs, girl." Nolan gave a mock strut. "Checking out the scene."

"If you keep walking like that, you'll be going alone."

"Come on, you know you think I'm sexy."

"I think you're insane. But yeah, you're sexy."

He put his hands up like a touchdown, walking backward so he could see her. "Score."

"You're about to walk into the door."

He smacked right into the curve of the revolving door and stumbled forward. "Whoa, hey, now watch it there, buddy."

Eve laughed.

"You could have warned me sooner," he grumbled. But he didn't really mean it. He was enjoying himself too much to care if he fell flat on his face. Eve had enjoyed his efforts to give her a fun party, and now they were going for more fun. "I need a beer." He wasn't much of a wine or champagne drinker so he'd only had one glass. Now he wanted a nice cold one.

"So where are we going? Since you seem to think you know the scene?"

"I don't know anything about the scene, but hell, it's Vegas. If we walk a few feet, we should hit a nightclub, right?" He was just going to head right, a gorgeous woman on his arm, and figure it out from there.

The first place they walked into was a sports bar. "Not what I had in mind," he told Eve as his shoe stuck to the floor by the hostess station and three guys burst into cheers at the bar, a baseball game on the big screen.

"But you can definitely order a beer here. If we end up in a nightclub, you'll only be able to get Christal, Petron, or a mixed drink with a name like the Tantini."

"Good point." He wasn't ever going to drink anything with "ini" on the end of it. They took a seat at the bar and she ordered vodka, him his longneck. "So, excluding this birthday, which is clearly awesome, what is your best birthday memory?"

She swung her legs and fingered her purse resting on the bar. He was impressed that she hadn't pulled her phone out of it.

"Hmm. Best memory. I would say sixteen. My dad gave me a vintage Ferrari. I loved that car. I drove it into a ditch going a hundred and ten at seventeen. My dad was pissed. I cried. But for twelve months I drove that car hard."

"Are you kidding me?" Nolan took his beer from the bartender and shook his head. "You suck. You got a Ferrari and you wrecked it?" He was pretty sure he'd gotten a pair of Levi's and a twenty for his sixteenth birthday and had been damn happy with that. Not that he begrudged

Eve her family's money, but he'd have given his left nut to get a Ferrari as a teenager. He'd give both nuts to have Eve and a Ferrari right now.

"I was a little more of a risk taker in those days. But I did pay my dad back when I was twenty-five. I always felt bad that the insurance never covered the full cost of the car."

He couldn't fault her for that. "That's cool."

"What was your favorite birthday?"

That he could answer without hesitation. "My eighth birthday. For some reason my mom gave in to my pleas for a birthday party. I didn't usually have a kids' party, just family, but that year she let me have my guy friends over. The girls were banned and we had a camouflage theme. My friends and I just ran around the yard with guns and screamed at the top of our lungs. It was great."

"Then this cupcake party must have been your worst nightmare. Very girly."

Nolan nudged her leg with his knee. "Nah. I can hang with some pink for you. And the cupcakes were freaking awesome. It was like an orgasm in my mouth."

"I'll give you an orgasm in your mouth."

He didn't know what that meant exactly, but he liked the sound of it. "Oh, yeah? Right now?"

"We should probably wait until later. Are we going back to my place or your place?"

It didn't matter to him. "Whatever you prefer."

"Are you ready?" Eve drained her drink.

Nolan looked at his half-full beer and raised an eyebrow. He wanted to be flattered by her clear desire to get into the sack with him, but he suspected she had other motivations. "Are you trying to get out of dancing?"

Guilt made her cheeks flush pink. "No. I was just trying to establish what we're doing for the rest of the night."

"There's no planning on your birthday. We're just rolling with it, remember? We stay here until we're done with this place, and we move on to the next."

"What time are we going back?"

She wasn't getting the principle of go with the flow at all. "Why does it matter?"

Eve gave a soft laugh. "I don't know. It seems like it should."

Nolan finished his beer and threw down a twenty on the bar. It was time for them to move before Eve had too much time to think. "Don't worry, cupcake, there will be plenty of time for me to worship your body in leopard underwear."

"Don't get corny."

He snorted as he stood up. "How is that corny?"

"People don't worship each other. It's an overblown term."

That was where he was going to prove her wrong. "Hold on to your socks then, because I'm going to worship up one side of you and down the other. I'm going to teach you the meaning of the word 'worship.'"

Just the thought was actually getting him a little hot under the collar. He must have made it clear to Eve that he wasn't playing around, because she sucked in her breath.

"So why aren't we going back now?" she asked again.

Nolan laughed. "Because we're having fun getting to know each other better."

"You're just trying to get me drunk enough that I'll wear the leopard underwear."

"Honey, I really don't care what you wear as long as it's off you for ninety-nine percent of the night."

Eve acted like she wasn't a seductress, but the truth was she was a natural at it. Her desire lit her eyes, and while she may not have the hair toss moves of some women, it was way sexier to him because it was just raw sexuality.

"We seem to have the same goal," she said, her voice

husky. "So explain to me again why we're not in your hotel room right now."

Frankly, he was starting to wonder the same thing himself. But he still said, "Patience isn't your strong suit, is it?"

Then Eve shocked the hell out of him as usual with her boldness.

"Blow jobs are my strong suit."

Damn. Double damn.

Eve was going to kill him.

But he'd be smiling up from his coffin.

CHAPTER
TWELVE

EVE couldn't really blame the liquor for her words. It was safe to say she very well might have said them stone cold sober. She didn't believe in not saying what you were thinking.

And what she was thinking was that she wanted to suck his cock.

"Oh, yeah? Those are big words. Let's see if you can live up to them."

Nolan certainly knew how to play the game with her. Eve would never even have thought she was playing games, but there was a truth that she wanted a certain response from a man. Everyone wanted a particular reaction from their partner when they were dating—it was natural. But no one ever seemed to be able to produce what Eve was seeking. Maybe because she'd never even really known what it was she wanted.

Now she knew.

She wanted Nolan.

"I don't think you'll be disappointed." She moved her leg in between his and bit the straw in her drink. The sports bar hadn't had champagne, so she had switched to vodka. Now she used the straw to demonstrate her point, drawing it up into her mouth, the tip of her tongue trailing alongside it.

"Finish your drink," he told her, obviously well aware of what she was doing.

"Are we going back?" she asked hopefully. She had a slight buzz going on, and she was seriously horny. She wanted to show Nolan how much she appreciated his birthday efforts.

"No, we're going to the next bar. It's called drawing out the anticipation."

In her mind, it was called stupid, but she wasn't going to argue. He'd done a lot of work and spent a lot of money to pull off that party. If he wanted to hoof it all over the Strip, she was going to let him.

Finishing her vodka, she paused, awed at her own thoughts. Holy shit, she was being considerate. She was compromising. Sharing. Having fun.

It was absolutely amazing.

What was equally amazing was that when he dragged her onto the dance floor at the club next door, she let him. Even in her black skirt and plain white blouse, she managed to ignore the fact that people might be judging her and just went with it. They gyrated together to a slower song and Nolan spun her in insane circles to a faster song that had her laughing and breathless.

"Fun, huh?" he yelled in her ear.

She nodded. It was fun. It was even fun when he started doing the lawn mower. "You're a dork!" she shouted over the music, her sides aching from laughing. He was a dork. A completely wonderful, endearing, sexy, sincere dork.

Eve wanted him. In bed. Out of bed. Dancing next to her like this for spontaneous nights out. She wanted to glance across a room and lock eyes with him and know that he would wink at her because she was his.

Together. A couple.

The strobe lights of the dance floor flashed and the bass beat pumped hard. The music was loud, the room hot, her hair damp across her forehead, her feet pinched in her work pumps. She clutched her purse awkwardly on her shoulder and her throat was dry, her drink long gone.

But none of that mattered. She was having the time of her life.

"Call me Dr. Dork," he told her, mugging like a rap artist.

Oh, God, that was even funnier. Eve laughed and jumped up and down in her heels. "I'm thirty-fucking-three! Can you believe it?" She was having a hard time accepting that three years had passed since her thirtieth birthday. What the hell had she done in those three years? A whole lot of nothing. The same old, same old. Day in, day out.

Not anymore.

Never again.

"I know. You're the hottest piece of thirty-three-year-old ass I've ever seen!" Nolan pulled her tight up against him, moving his hips with hers.

She grabbed his ass. "Speaking of ass, have I told you that yours is awesome? It's like the ass of all ages."

"You have the best breasts I've ever had the pleasure to touch. I would take a bullet for your breasts."

Eve snorted. God, he was fucking funny. "That's the sweetest thing you've ever said to me."

He dipped her low to the ground. Eve shrieked, afraid

he would drop her. It was a vulnerable position and she didn't like it.

"Relax," he told her. "I have your back, I promise."

Eve looked up at him from her awkward position of resistance, half up, half down. His eyes flashed in the blue strobe lights with an emotion she was sure she wasn't imagining.

He did have her back. More so than any man she'd ever met before. Eve swallowed and nodded her consent.

Closing her eyes tight, she let go of her muscles, letting her body and head drop, leg coming up.

Nolan didn't drop her.

His lips brushed over hers and he held her, solid and steady.

Her hair swept the floor and she opened her eyes, amazed at how intriguing it felt to be upside down, to let go of all her inhibitions and just enjoy the music. He spun her around and it felt like a merry-go-round, a natural high from the freedom of her body rushing through air, her view of the room upside down.

When he lifted her back up, she took a second to focus, her heart racing. Nolan kissed her and Eve felt like her body was still spinning. She was dizzy and not just from the dancing.

"Would it be crazy if I told you that I'm falling in love with you?" Nolan murmured in her ear.

She shivered. She wanted to scoff. She should push him away and tell him it absolutely was crazy. Insane. Certifiable. Stupid.

But she didn't.

She couldn't.

Because she felt the same way. "I would tell you you're nuts except for the fact that I think I might actually be falling in love with you, too."

God, she couldn't believe she had said that. It made her feel light, breathless. Blissful.

"Are you serious?" He looked awed by the fact and he kissed her hard. "You're amazing. You're the most amazing woman I've ever met."

Eve kissed him back, slipping her tongue into his mouth, her hands still on his backside. It took her a solid thirty seconds to remember that they were still on the dance floor in a very public place and that making out at a club was for teenagers. Gesturing to Nolan that she needed a drink, she managed to pull away and stumble off in the direction of the bar, unsteady on her feet not from alcohol but from the enormity of her feelings. She had never felt this way about a man ever. She'd never had this much fun. Ever.

"Let's do a shot together," he said.

For some mysterious reason she said yes. Nolan ordered them vodka. Eve took a shot glass from the bartender and lifted it to Nolan. "To the best birthday I've ever had."

Nolan lifted his glass up next to hers. "To us."

If she hadn't already thought she was falling in love with him, that would have done it. He was so damn sweet, he was the one who should have the nickname "cupcake." Or "fudge ripple." Between the two of them, they were a goddamn bakery and she was as happy as she had ever been.

"To us." Eve tossed back her shot and let the fire of the vodka burn down her throat.

"Woo. Good stuff. I'll be right back, gorgeous." Nolan kissed the top of her head before heading to the restroom.

A woman standing next to her at the bar smiled when Eve glanced her way.

"You're so lucky," she said, her cherry red lips glowing

in the artificial light. "My boyfriend would never dance with me." She gestured to a thin guy behind her dressed in black who looked bored and pretentious.

"I'm not sure we can really call that dancing. It was more like flinging our bodies around."

"Yeah, but you're having fun. Some people don't know how to let go." She shrugged. "Have a good night, I'm heading out for a cigarette."

"Thanks, you, too."

The woman, who was pretty in a forties pinup dress, said something to her boyfriend. He made a face and stayed put, surveying the room. She continued on to the front door by herself.

Eve knew without a doubt that if she was going to stand outside a club in Vegas at midnight, Nolan would go stand with her. It was the gentlemanly thing to do. Hell, the human thing to do. If one of her girlfriends went outside, she would go with them just out of courtesy.

She was lucky. She was super astonishingly lucky.

Nolan was walking back toward her, smiling.

She was lucky to have this man, this night, this birthday.

NOLAN was feeling like the luckiest guy on the planet as he walked across the bar to Eve, who was standing there looking like a stone cold freaking fox. He wanted to fist pump. Break dance. Drop to the ground and do twenty.

She—that amazingly hot and super cool chick—was falling in love with him.

It was unbelievable.

Awesome. On the scale of great nights, this one was off the charts, and she hadn't even put the leopard underwear on yet. He was so pumped up with energy and emotion he was sure he could dance for another six hours or so. But first he wanted to buy his lady another drink.

"Want a drink?" he asked her, leaning in for a kiss before she could possibly answer. He couldn't help himself. Her lips were just there asking for it.

"Actually, let's step outside for a second. It's hot in here and I want to check on this woman I was talking to. She went outside by herself and that doesn't seem like a good idea to me."

"Sure, of course." He followed her lead and they headed to the door. It was cooler outside and he took a deep breath of the crisp night air as Eve greeted a cute girl with a black and red patterned dress.

It wasn't a good idea for her to be out there alone. Nolan could see the street was still busy, but to the right of the club was an area that during the day served as al fresco dining for a restaurant. Now it was full of shadows and potential dangers for a woman by herself. He was glad Eve had thought to come out and check on her. But that was the side of Eve he saw and understood more so than a lot of people, it seemed. She was a worrier because she cared. If she didn't give a shit, she'd be a whole lot less stressed. But she cared about people, about her family, her brothers' careers.

The woman dropped her cigarette to the ground, said good-bye to Eve, then went back into the club.

"Everything okay?" he asked Eve.

"Yeah. It's just her boyfriend seems like a bit of a jerk."

"That happens. I'm glad she was okay, though."

Me, too."

"Want that drink now?"

"Let's go somewhere else where it's a little quieter. I think I'm done dancing for the night." She smiled at him.

The look on her face squeezed Nolan's heart. God, she was beautiful and she didn't even understand how much. "Sure. We can go wherever you want, birthday girl."

Eve took his hand. All on her own. Without his suggesting it. "Thanks for making this such a great birthday. I really appreciate it."

"I told you, it's my pleasure. And we can do whatever you want." They were passing a classic Vegas wedding chapel. "Hell, we can get married even if you want."

He meant it as flippant, since they were passing the place, two gigantic hearts bursting out of the building in neon red lighting. But the minute the words came out of his mouth, he meant them. He would marry Eve. He would marry her in a heartbeat.

"What?" She stopped walking and stared up at him, her expression more amazed than horrified. "Are you serious?"

Was he serious? Nolan looked at Eve, her chestnut hair blowing across her face in the night air, her cheeks flushed from the dancing and from, he'd like to think, being around him. Oh, hell yeah, he was serious.

"Yes. I know it doesn't make any sense and it's insane, but cupcake, if you want to walk into that chapel with me right now, I'd be honored to marry you." It was possible the liquor might be influencing him a little, but he didn't really think that was it. He didn't see any point in beating around the bush. If you wanted something, you should go for it. Grab it, enjoy it, hold it as long as you could.

There was a reason he'd fallen in love with Eve so easily. That didn't just happen overnight all the time. It was special. She was meant to be the woman he had as his wife, and whether that was a year from then or right in the next thirty minutes, it was a definite. There was no doubt in his mind. He wasn't twenty-two anymore, going gaga for the first girl in a skirt who giggled at him. He'd watched Eve for years. He'd worked for this. It was real, and it was going to stick.

Eve would say no, he was fairly certain. She didn't do

impulsive. She needed to think and process and plan. Which was okay. But a small part of him wanted her to say yes.

"That is insane." Eve glanced back at the chapel, clutching her purse tightly against her chest. "How can you be sure you want to marry me?"

He was sure. Nolan took her hand. "It's called trusting my gut. It's never once let me down. When I stop thinking and just hear what my gut is telling me, it says that I love you and that at some point you're going to be my wife."

Never would he have thought he'd go down onto the sidewalk on the Strip but he found himself doing just that. "Eve, will you marry me?"

If she said no, they'd have another drink and still have some smoking hot sex.

But what she said was simply, "Yes."

Nolan was so stunned he just stayed on the sidewalk, staring up at her in shock. Yes. Her answer was yes. An emotion he could only describe as exhilaration bloomed in his chest. Holy crap. She'd said yes. Now it was his turn to ask, "Are you serious?"

She nodded rapidly. "Yes. Let's do it. Now. Now get off the sidewalk, God only knows what is getting on your pants."

That was his Eve. Nolan jumped up and pulled her into his arms. "Woot! That's fantastic, cupcake. Let's go get married."

Eve let Nolan scoop her into a bone-crushing hug. Frackity-frickin-frack. She'd said yes. And she wasn't even having a panic attack. She was . . . happy. Excited. How the hell had that happened? Why wasn't her mind racing to negatives and positives and roadblocks and stumbling blocks and mental blocks?

Because she was in love with Nolan. It was as simple

as the nose on her face. She was in love with him, and therefore, it made perfect sense to accept his marriage proposal.

"Look, they're open twenty-four hours. Just like your thighs, babe." He gave her a grin.

If any other man had said that to her, she would have ripped off his junk and stuffed it into his nostrils. But the fact that she just thought Nolan was funny showed her that she was in love with him. There was no other explanation for it. "Ha ha. You're just amazing, aren't you? Jackman, party planner, comedian . . . what's next, dolphin trainer?"

"Sex machine."

Oh, Lord. She would not laugh. She would not . . . she laughed. "You're an—"

He cut her off. "Ass. I know. But I'm you're ass. Want a piece of this?" He lifted the bottom of his shirt up and turned around so she could see the seat of his jeans.

Drool formed in her mouth. Yes, she wanted some of that. Immediately, if not sooner. "I wouldn't mind having some of that."

"Then get on in that chapel and let's do this thing."

Somehow that was not how Eve had envisioned her wedding. Getting on in and doing it. But it was right. Listen to her gut—that was what Nolan had told her. When she quieted the jet engine buzz of worries assaulting her brain, when she stopped thinking altogether and just felt, she knew this was right. Feeling the silence of peace and conviction was so foreign to her she wasn't even sure what to do with it. It was akin to an out-of-body experience, and she really wanted to be fully in her body for the rest of the night, so she actually pinched her left wrist. Yep, that hurt.

"Did you just pinch yourself?"

"Yes, and if you make any comment about it, I will cut you."

"God, I love you." Nolan took her hand and kissed it hard.

Seriously. She had to marry him. What other man on the planet would be a better fit for her?

They entered the chapel, both grinning and holding hands. The chapel wasn't hopping, given that it was a Thursday night, so the woman behind the desk greeted them, looking relieved to have something to do.

"Welcome, welcome! Are you interested in purchasing a wedding package for the future or as a walk-in right now?"

"Right now," Nolan told her.

Eve fought the urge to giggle. She didn't even get her hair cut on a walk-in basis. But now she was getting married. Without an appointment. She sort of expected her calendar app on her phone to open and swallow her whole in protest.

"I take it it's just the two of you?" The woman was in her fifties and she was old school Vegas showgirl. Big hair. Long acrylic nails. Chandelier earrings. Bright lipstick. And lots and lots of cleavage. It was a slightly outrageous effect, but her smile was warm and her eyes were genuine.

"Yes, it's just us. This wasn't planned. It's my birthday," Eve told her. Which technically it was the next day, but that was beside the point. It seemed like some kind of explanation was required. Though now that she thought about it, it was after midnight so it was her birthday.

"Well, Happy Birthday!" She beamed at her. "That's a nice way to celebrate, for sure. I'm Kat, by the way."

"Eve. This is Nolan."

"Nice to meet both of you. What type of ceremony are you looking for? Would you like a theme?"

Eve glanced over at Nolan. If he said he wanted a theme wedding, she might have to rethink the whole thing.

But he just shook his head. "I think we just wanted something simple. Eve and I, some flowers, a kiss. We already had cupcakes earlier, so we don't need cake or anything. What do you think, babe?"

Could it really be that easy? It seemed it was. "I totally agree." She figured everyone had the right to get married however they wanted, but she would find an Elvis impersonator irritating. She'd never dreamed of a big wedding either, come to think of it. Being a bridesmaid in Elec's wedding had been stressful enough. She'd probably implode if she spent a year planning a wedding for four hundred guests. "And some champagne." If she could make her tongue unstick from the roof of her mouth, this whole thing would work better.

"Sounds perfect. Has either of you been married before?"

"No," Nolan said. "First and last time."

There was suddenly a massive lump in Eve's throat. She wasn't sure where it came from or what point it was trying to make but she couldn't speak. So she just shook her head desperately at Kat.

Nolan squeezed her hand. She didn't respond in any way, focusing on the book Kat had set in front of them, outlining the packages available to them. The Traditional Package swam in front of her eyes. Fresh floral bouquet, disc of photos, framed marriage certificate . . . she didn't care about any of it. She just wanted to be Nolan's wife. That was what her gut and her throat lump and her heart were telling her.

"Hey, are you okay?" Nolan pulled her slightly away from Kat. "Excuse us a second." He studied her face. "Are you sure about this? We can leave if you want."

There were tears in her eyes and she never cried. Impatient with their presence, she brushed at them. "If you think you can get out of this that easily, forget it. You can't propose then take it back."

He grinned. "I wasn't taking it back. I was offering you an out."

"I don't want an out." She didn't. "And if you try to walk out that door, I'll haul your sorry ass back in here."

"I love it when you make false threats."

Eve softened her voice. "Do you love me? You're sure?" She found it so hard to believe. It was like the ultimate birthday gift, this amazing guy who had dropped into her lap out of nowhere.

"Oh, babe, yes, I'm sure. I love you. I wouldn't be standing here if I didn't."

He kissed her, and she felt the tenderness of his lips on hers. Yeah, he loved her. She could taste it.

"I love you, too." It wasn't even that hard to say it. The words just sailed out of her mouth without any hesitation whatsoever.

She turned back to Kat. "What do we need to fill out?"

After five minutes and a minor tussle with Nolan when she tried to pay the fees and he told her that her money was no good there and threw her purse under a chair, they were standing in front of a woman named Susan something-or-other who had appeared from the back. Another five minutes and a couple of "I do's" and that was it. They were married. It took longer to buy car insurance than it did to get married.

She looked at him. He looked at her. They were both grinning.

"You can kiss the bride, you know," Susan told Nolan.

"Can I kiss you?" Nolan asked her.

It was perfect, the way he asked her.

"Hell, yeah," she told him.

When their lips touched, all Eve could think was that

she wanted to freeze this moment and hold on to it forever. She wanted to breathe in the perfection, the love, the
certainty, the giddiness, the desire to be as close to Nolan
as physically and emotionally possible.

Nolan broke away and looked down at her, his eyes
dark with desire. "That was our first married kiss."

Married. She grinned at him. "Did it seem any different to you?"

"It was like just as amazing, but with a dash of Tabasco
on top."

"For me, it was like peanut butter fudge ripple."

He laughed. "That's a fine compliment."

Eve looked over at Susan, who was looking bored.
Kat was back at the front desk doing something on her
computer.

"So now what?" she asked him.

"We get out of here and have married sex."

Her nipples instantly went hard and her inner thighs
warmed. "I'm cool with that." Or hot with that, more accurately.

He grabbed her hand and dragged her toward the door.
Eve jogged to keep up with him, laughing. "Slow down!"

"No." Nolan was carrying the bottle of complimentary
champagne Kat had given them. Then suddenly he was
carrying her.

Eve shrieked, her ass suddenly in the air as he scooped
her up with one of those impressive arms. "Oh, my God!
Put me down." She was a good three feet off the ground
and she squeezed his shoulders to keep her balance, her
purse strap tumbling off her shoulder. "You're going to
drop me."

"Don't insult me. This is like bench pressing a cotton
ball to me."

She realized that she probably wasn't all that heavy to

him compared to jacking up a stock car. Now that was hot. Her man could *carry* her. Take that, bitches. Wait. Not just her man. Her husband.

A shiver stole up her spine and a serious jolt of heat kicked her down south. Her clit was pressed against his chest. There might be several layers of fabric between it and him but now she very aware of it. Of his hand on the underside of her ass. He was strong, no question about it. Muscular. She felt her inner thighs growing damp as he juggled the bottle of booze and her and yet still managed to open the front door of the chapel and take her onto the Strip.

She almost lost her balance completely, though, when he let out a loud yell and bounced her up and down in his grip.

"Whew!" he repeated.

"What the hell are you yelling for?" she asked, laughing, though it was obvious it was something of a victory yell.

"Because I love you and you're hot and we're married!"

Really, was there anything else that mattered? She didn't think so.

She gave a whoop of her own, regardless of the curious stares they were getting from people on the street. "Your place or mine?"

"Where are you staying? I'm out by the track in a Holiday Inn."

"I'm in the same hotel we just had the party at."

"Your place then. It's closer." Nolan set her down on the sidewalk.

Eve took stock to make sure she had everything— purse, shoes still on her feet despite being dangled in the air, marriage certificate. Her husband holding her hand. Yep. That was everything.

There was nothing else she needed.
Except for an orgasm. Or two.
Which, given the look on his face, was within her grasp.
Eve smiled as Nolan hailed a taxi.
Best. Birthday. Ever.

CHAPTER
THIRTEEN

NOLAN wasn't sure how he had started off the day throwing a surprise party for a woman he wasn't sure he was allowed to call his girlfriend, and ending it with her as his wife, but he wasn't going to argue. He'd gotten everything he had wanted and then some.

He knew that other people would say they were insane, but he didn't believe it. Insane was letting an opportunity pass you by. Insane was debating so long over what you wanted that it disappeared.

Eve was his wife and he couldn't think of a better end to the day.

Well, except for the upcoming leopard underwear show.

"I'll get you a ring tomorrow," he told her between kisses in the backseat of the cab.

"Whatever," she said, her hands gripping the front of his shirt. "There's no hurry."

But a wife needed a wedding ring. Nolan had a split second of panic when he thought about the cost, but he figured he just wouldn't think about the cost. Problem solved.

"Why did we get a cab?" she asked. "We're only like two blocks from the hotel."

Nolan processed that. God, she was right. He shrugged. "Hell if I know. I guess I was thinking we're in a hurry. Or maybe I just wasn't thinking. You have a way of making me forget to think."

She laughed. "I'm not sure if that's a compliment or not."

"It is." Nolan slid his hand up her skirt, flicking his thumb across the front of her panties.

She sucked in her breath.

"See? If I was thinking, I wouldn't have just done that."

The corner of her mouth tilted up. "Oh, I think you knew exactly what you were doing."

"Maybe." He started to peel back the side of her panties, need suddenly gripping him. He wanted her now. Not in five minutes. Now.

"You're here. Ten bucks," the driver said.

Really? Nolan pulled his hand out from under Eve's skirt, sorely disappointed.

"Two blocks," Eve said with a significant amount of regret. "Told you."

Ten bucks was a lot of money for that short of a distance, but Nolan wasn't going to waste time arguing. Not when he felt like if he didn't get Eve upstairs and naked, his dick was going to snap off and hit the ground.

They made out on the sidewalk. They made out in the elevator. They made out in the hallway while Eve fumbled for her key.

Then they were in.

So they made out.

Nolan hadn't spent this much time in a frantic lip-lock with a girl since high school. He'd forgotten how exciting it was to just kiss and not skip straight to the good stuff. Kissing his wife had that same feeling as kissing his girl-friend back in the day had. It was worshipful, awed, desperate, wanting more, yet at the same time, wanting the moment to never end. It was kissing with the intensity of knowing that this was really happening, everything you had wanted and desired.

When he was sixteen, he hadn't been able to grasp that Carrie had been willing to let him stick his tongue in her mouth. Now he couldn't quite wrap his head around the fact that Eve Monroe had said "I do" to him.

So he kissed her over and over.

Eventually her hands started to wander across his chest and down around his ass. When she squeezed, he felt a serious kick of desire. Then he couldn't control his own hands anymore. Fortunately, her shirt had buttons, so he undid them as quickly as his somewhat drunk fingers would allow. When they were all free, he yanked her blouse apart and just took a minute to stare at her breasts. Eve produced effortless cleavage. It wasn't polished and packaged and put on display. It was just *au naturel*, baby, some seriously nice tits in a basic bra. He leaned forward and sucked the side of one. Her response was to cup his ass tighter.

"Wait!"

Nolan froze. That better mean pause for fifteen seconds or less. Not stop. Because he would die. "What's wrong?"

"I believe I have some new underwear I'd like to try on."

Hot damn. Nolan pulled back. He gestured to the bathroom. "By all means. As long as you model them for me."

Eve threw her purse back onto her shoulder and kicked her shoes off. "Of course." Then she bent back over and grabbed. "Shit. I need these."

"For what?" Though he knew what she meant.

"For height. So my legs look sexier." She laughed. "Not that I'm any expert on seduction. Did I ever tell you my first kiss was when I was twelve after I bullied my crush into doing it?"

Nolan couldn't help it—he laughed. That was so Eve. And so Eve to tell him. "I bet he liked it in the end, didn't he?"

"I'm not really sure."

"I can assure you I'm going to enjoy this." He was practically drooling in anticipation of the show.

"Why are you so different?" she asked, her voice dropping almost to a whisper, her eyes wide and curious. "No man could ever handle me."

His heart melted all over again. God, he thought she was so beautiful. "Because maybe I'm the first man to realize that you don't need to be 'handled.' You just need to be loved. And that's all I need, too—I just want to be loved."

"I do love you, strongman."

"And I love you." He started toward her, wanting to hold her. Now. Forever.

But Eve squawked and ran away. "No! I have to change now or it will never happen. And my slutty birthday underwear will be irrelevant."

"Irrelevant?" Nolan sat down on the bed and took his shoes off. "Honey, sometimes I don't know what the hell you're talking about."

"I can't hear you."

Why she needed to close the bathroom door was beyond him. It wasn't like he hadn't already seen her naked, but he had learned in life that women liked to do certain things in private. They also liked the presentation, to have a big moment of arrival. The man's role was to appreciate the effort that had gone into it. He could do that.

Naked. Nolan stripped off his shirt and socks. He tossed his jeans in the direction of the desk chair and debated taking his boxers off. He went commando fairly frequently, but he'd worn underwear today and now he was regretting it. If he hadn't been wearing them, he wouldn't have to debate anything. Which made his decision for him. Screw it. The underwear was gone.

When Eve stepped into the doorway, every ounce of blood in Nolan's body rushed south. Holy hottie. She looked amazing. Like a Vegas showgirl, only with less makeup. Her hair was flowing over her shoulders and her eyes were bright. The leopard set had been worth every single penny. The panties barely covered her sex and showed off her long, lean legs and flat stomach. Then there was the bra. There were no words to describe how glorious her chest looked. The word "bombshell" came to mind when he stared at all that astonishing cleavage. She looked so juicy and ripe and ready for the taking. He wanted to lick and bite every inch of her.

He was grateful for her putting the shoes back on. It gave a definite sex kitten air about her. His sex kitten.

"Meow," he told her. "You are one sexy honey."

She posed in the doorway. "Thanks. And that is one fine erection you're sporting."

Nolan glanced down. Yep. Steel post reaching for the sky. "I could say something really corny right now but I don't want to ruin the mood."

"Oh, come on, let's hear it." Eve had her arms up on the door frame and she dropped them slightly. "I don't know how women hold these poses, it's exhausting." Suddenly she was doing an Egyptian walk with her hands. "This is more me. I'm not the best at seduction."

He wasn't necessarily into the whole setup either. His fantasy was get naked as fast as possible. "It's working for me."

"I feel like a stripper."

"Then come on over here and dance on my pole, girl." Nolan gave her an exaggerated lecherous nod. "I'll make it worth your while."

He patted his thighs.

They both laughed. Eve kicked off her shoes. "Okay, I don't think this is us. I'm just going to jump your bones."

"Sounds good to me. Or I could meet you halfway."

"Nope. Bone jumping. That's what I'm doing."

He loved her go-get-'em attitude. Or go get him, technically. "Alright, you won't catch any interference from me."

When Eve sidled up to him, her breasts were almost level with his mouth. He would have liked to bury his lips in that cleavage, but she tilted his head up to her and kissed him on the mouth. Then she dropped down and kissed the tip of his penis. His leg twitched involuntarily.

This was a pleasant turn of events. He suspected he knew where she was going with this. Eve shot him a wicked look over the head of his cock. Oh, yeah, she definitely had plans for him. Nolan leaned back, palms down on the bed to let her do her thing. It was going to be hard not to grab on to her and just fling her on the bed, but if she wanted to bone jump, he was going to let her.

Only when she slid her mouth down over him and took him deep, Nolan couldn't prevent a groan. "Oh, yeah, baby, that's perfect."

Her response was to cup his balls in her hand lightly, her fingers brushing across his thighs, then the end of his shaft all while her mouth moved up and down on him. The stimulation, the tease, had him gripping the bedspread and fighting to keep his eyes open. But he wanted to watch her. He wanted to see those pink lips sliding up and down on his hardness, her hair falling across her face. She hadn't gone on her knees, she was bent over the bed and him, and it made her ass rise behind her head in a perfect leopard print exclamation point to the picture she presented.

"You are so hot," he told her.

All that hotness and intelligence and she had chosen him.

Seemed like it was her birthday, but his lucky day.

CHAPTER
FOURTEEN

THE persistent sound of "Dude Looks Like a Lady" blasting out from her phone forced Eve to pry her eyes open and feel around on the nightstand for her cell. That was Evan's ringtone. Why the hell was he calling her so early?

Or not so early. As the call disconnected, a one-eyed squint at her screen showed it was almost noon.

Noon?

Eve sat straight up in bed, her breathing kicking into high gear like she'd run a marathon, her heart stuttering a beat before ramping up into overdrive.

Oh, my God.

She was married.

Glancing over at Nolan, who was snoring lightly, the sheet barely covering his nakedness, she tried to remember how to breathe. Her head was pounding and her sinuses felt clogged. Her mouth was dry. It would seem maybe she had been slightly more tipsy the night before than she had realized. Because she was married.

She had married a man she'd been dating for two weeks at midnight in a Vegas chapel.

Who did that? People did that. Impulsive people. Not her people. She didn't do spontaneous.

But she clearly had last night.

For thirty-three years she'd gone without behaving impulsively and she picked marriage as the thing to break her pattern? The last thing in the world you should do without planning, counseling, serious thought, and extensive time and research.

Oh, Lord.

The phone rang again, causing her to jump, the sheet clutched to her chest.

"You gonna answer that?" Nolan asked, his eyes still closed.

"Um, yeah." How had he known she was awake? His ability to read her was scary.

The last thing in the world she wanted to do was talk to her brother, but if he had called twice in a row, it must be important. Better to get it over with.

"Hello?"

"Where the hell are you?"

Eve swallowed. She would love to drink anything liquid that wasn't champagne. It felt like her tongue had been painted with sugar. "My room."

"Your room? It's noon. Are you sick or something?"

"No." She didn't think she was sick, even though she felt a little ill.

"Hungover? You did drink a lot last night."

She wasn't even sure she was hungover. More like in a state of shock. "I just overslept." Because she'd been up until four o'clock in the morning having sex with her *husband*.

Her husband, whose hand was on her thigh now under the sheet, rubbing, rubbing. Even as her brain panicked, her body purred like a kitten. She could feel arousal spiraling up and out from her inner thighs just from a few simple strokes.

"You overslept?" He snorted. "You mean you were knocking boots with my jackman all night and ignored your alarm this morning. Get your ass down here."

"I'll be there in a half an hour."

Nolan's finger slid inside her warm core. She tried desperately not to moan.

"Or more like an hour. I have to shower." Naked. With her husband.

"God knows we don't want you to skip a shower. Tell Ford just because he wasn't supposed to be here until tomorrow doesn't mean I can't find something for him to do at the test run today."

Normally she would have put up a fight that Nolan wasn't with her, but she wasn't that good of a liar. Not when he was lazily petting her to an orgasm. Not when he was her husband.

And had she mentioned he was her husband?

When she hung up, Nolan kissed her, his skin warm, chin stubbly. "You didn't tell him we got married."

"I need coffee first. A shower. Some clothes on. Your finger not inside of me." And a vatful of courage to tell her brother that she of all people had gotten hitched in Vegas.

Plus an orgasm. She could use one of those.

Nolan bent over her chest and flicked his tongue across her nipple. Eve had a nice, slow, delicious morning orgasm that had her eyes drifting shut.

"Good morning," he murmured in her ear.

Eve struggled to recover. What was she doing? Wondering why she was married? Well, there you had it. The man had the distinction of being the first in recorded history to get her off five minutes after she had woken up.

"Morning. How are you?" she asked inanely. What did you say to your shotgun groom? She had no idea, and for some reason she just felt embarrassed.

The truth was she had fallen in love with Nolan. Champagne or not, she never would have married him if she hadn't, and that was just embarrassing. She wasn't a flaky chick. She didn't fall in love in less than nine months. That's how long it took to cook a baby start to finish. That's at least how long it should take to fall in love.

"You're thinking, aren't you?" Nolan asked. He touched the spot between her eyebrows. "This trench is so deep we could bury a gas line in it."

"Thanks." She rolled her eyes. "I'm just thinking that I can't believe we got married last night. What were we thinking?"

"We weren't thinking, we were feeling. Are you having buyer's remorse?"

One of his big, warm hands was on her tummy, the other on her shoulder. His rich brown eyes were right in front of her, so close she could see the tiny gold flecks in them. See the love he had for her. His contentment. It was amazing. Beautiful.

Bizarre.

"No," she answered truthfully. "Not exactly. But I'm not sure it was a wise thing to do."

"Fuck wise. We can be wise when we're ninety. Let's just be happy."

Which was why he was so good for her. She needed that reminder. She needed to live a different way than she had been.

Could she do this?

She wanted to. But she wasn't sure.

Her heart was still beating double time. Maybe she'd just have a heart attack and she wouldn't have to worry about telling anyone. There was a plan.

"Aren't you worried about telling your family?"

She had expected him to say no with enough vehemence and confidence to make her feel better.

But he shrugged. "Maybe a little. My mom might express some concern."

"My dad's going to burst a blood vessel." Eve glanced at her phone. It was twelve eleven. "We have to go. Evan wants you at the track."

Nolan gave a lazy yawn, pulling her hand over to his erection.

Eve automatically stroked it. Maybe there was time . . .

She yanked her hand away, determined to get out of bed. It was preventing her from rational thought. Sitting up too fast, she paused when dizziness overtook her. "We have to go," she told him.

"So that's how it is now that we're married?" he teased. "I get you off then none for me?"

Bristling, because there was some truth to it, given her orgasm, she told him, "I didn't ask for you to get me off. You just did it."

"I was kidding."

She knew that, but she didn't care. She wasn't feeling particularly rational and now her stomach was twisted up in knots. Her mouth felt hot and she swallowed hard. "Besides, I'm easy to get off. That took like a minute and a half. It will take twenty minutes for you and then we'll really be late."

Nolan burst out laughing. "Cupcake, you are not like most women, that's for sure. It's why I love you."

Not sure if that was as much of a compliment as he was trying to make it sound, Eve bent over, groping around on the floor for some clothes to wear to the bathroom. She felt vulnerable and incapable of walking across the room naked. Her hands were shaking as she plucked her shirt off the carpet.

"I'll make some coffee while you're in the shower." Nolan gave another yawn and stretched his arms over his head.

Eve stole a look at his chest. The man had the most amazing arms and chest she'd ever touched. Her husband had a body to die for. Husband. She made an involuntary sound and rushed to the bathroom regardless of her nudity. She needed a second before she had a full-fledged panic attack.

He followed her. Eve was turning on the shower when he strolled in and shook the dew off the lily. Really? Adjusting the temperature of the water, she tried not to watch, but there was a giant mirror in front of him causing the reflection to bounce around the room. Everywhere she tried to look she caught a flash of his stream of urine.

Ick. She wasn't ready for that. At all. A little too much reality for her first thing in the morning.

"So that's how it is now that we're married?" she parroted back to him, stepping into the shower. "You pee in front of me?"

"There's only one bathroom," he said. "And I had to go. Sorry. At least your place has two bathrooms, so if it bugs you, I can make sure I use the other one."

"Thanks," she managed as hot water hit her face. A thought had occurred to her as he was speaking and she suddenly felt like she was going to faint.

They were married. He would assume that they were going to live together. That's what married people did.

He was going to move into her condo. With his stuff. His shoes. His underwear. His deodorant. His shaving stubble in her sink.

Eve clung to the shower wall, the cool tiles welcome against her hot body. The soap tray was the only thing holding her up, and she held on to it for dear life.

"Eve?"

She didn't really think she could speak without vomiting so she didn't even try. The shower curtain was yanked back.

"Holy shit, what's wrong?"

"I'm going to puke," she told him, hoping he would go away. She didn't want him to see her hurl. "Close the curtain."

"I don't think so." Nolan put one foot into the tub and suddenly she was in his arms.

The motion was jarring and her stomach rebelled, but she kept the nausea down as he carried her out of the tub. She had to admit it was nice not to be standing on her gelatinous legs anymore.

"Just relax. Close your eyes," he murmured.

She did exactly that and she felt better without the hot water pelting her.

"You drank a wee bit too much and then didn't get enough sleep. Plus you haven't eaten. Once you've had breakfast you'll feel better. I'm going to order room service."

It probably was all of those things. But it was also the reality of being married that had nearly dropped her to her knees. And the realization that she couldn't do it.

"Should I call Evan and tell him you can't make it today?"

"No. I'll be fine." She sighed as Nolan deposited her on the bed. "I just need a minute." Her wet hair stuck to her cheek and she peeled it off.

Nolan had disappeared and she opened her eyes to see what he was doing. He emerged from the bathroom with a towel and proceeded to dry her off like a little kid. Eve was slightly embarrassed, mostly touched. God, he was a good guy, even if the vigorous rubbing he was giving her arms was bringing her nausea back full force.

How could she tell him she couldn't be married to him?

Or could she?

Nolan tenderly pulled a hank of her hair off her chest so she wouldn't get cold. "Damn. I was hoping to go ring shopping today."

The rubbing and his words accomplished what she'd been staving off for half an hour. Eve leaned over and threw up on the bed, a nice dry heave that sounded like an adult male lion burping to impress his peers.

She was officially the least sexy newlywed on the planet.

Oh, and today was actually her birthday.

Thirty-three. And not so fabulous.

Eve closed her eyes and wished she had fainted in the shower. At least she wouldn't be conscious for any of this.

"Wow," Nolan told Eve, fairly amazed that she had managed to create that kind of sound with her vomiting. If she didn't look so miserable, he would have laughed.

But he noted for future reference that she didn't seem to be able to hold her liquor. Nor was she happy about it. When he tried to adjust her towel, she smacked at his hand.

Now what? If he tried to call Evan, she would snarl at him. But she didn't look like she was moving anytime soon. He decided to jump in the shower himself. Her breathing had slowed, like she was falling asleep.

As he shampooed his hair, Nolan whistled. This wasn't at all how he had envisioned their first day married, but he wasn't going to let it destroy his good mood. Eve would sleep it off, then they would go out for a nice dinner, tell all their friends and family, and have another night of smoking hot sex.

As a married couple.

He was still having a hard time wrapping his head around the fact that they were actually married. It was mind-boggling but in a good way.

His mother was not going to be happy. He was going to get an earful from her. At least half of his sisters would follow suit. But that would just be a speed bump. They would get to know Eve and love her like he did. Hopefully Evan wouldn't have an issue with it. Nolan did not want to lose his job. He loved it. Plus the thought of his bank account, which was sporting a balance of about twenty bucks until payday, was enough to give him a pang or two. He hadn't thought about the possibility of being fired when he'd gone down on one knee in front of Eve.

Hell, he hadn't thought about anything.

He certainly hadn't thought about the logistics of living together or working in the same business. Having kids together.

But it would work out.

He was almost sure of it.

EVE got out of the taxi, squinting against the bright sunlight, pulling her cardigan tighter around her. She was cold. Tired. Hungover.

Nolan had left her to sleep for a couple of hours in the hotel room, heading over to the track. He'd left her a note explaining, along with a room service tray, two aspirin, and a hand-drawn heart with her name in it. It was so freaking considerate it was disgusting. For at least the tenth time she asked herself why he couldn't just be a total jerk like every other man she'd dated. It was going to make it really difficult to explain to him that getting married had been a serious mistake. That they couldn't live together. That normal intelligent people knew you couldn't make a marriage work on two weeks of infatuation.

She knew that. Accepted. Hated it. A tiny part of her that she was choosing to ignore doubted that logic. That part of her wanted to believe that you could fall in love that quickly, that you could sustain the sense of fun and passion into a long-term deal. She wanted to buy into the romance of it all.

But that was stupid. Romance didn't exist outside of books and movies.

Then again . . . Nolan's note had been pretty damn romantic.

She sighed as she flashed her credentials to the security guard and headed into the garage behind pit road. Never in her whole life had she been so confused. It was like she was turning into Sybil, the chick with multiple personalities. The Eve she knew wanted to just retreat from all of this, slamming the door on her emotions and telling Nolan it wasn't going to work. Cupcake, on the other hand, wanted to plan a honeymoon with him and find him room in her closet.

Which officially made her insane. Aging had caused her to crack. First the demolition derby, now a marriage in Vegas. What was next? A drive-thru nose job? A shanty in the Australian outback where she raised alpaca?

Even through her sunglasses she could see her brother was walking toward her. Damn. She'd been hoping he was on the track. He was suited up but he didn't have his helmet.

"Hey, you feeling better?" he asked her.

"No," she told him accurately.

"I didn't think so. You look like shit. And you're dressed like Grandma Monroe."

Eve was wearing a turtleneck with a cardigan. Not

something she would usually layer together but she was cold, the aftereffects of the alcohol. "I skipped the brooch and the white Keds, so I don't think this qualifies me for granny status."

"I have to say Nolan looks a hell of a lot better than you do today. He's been whistling and bouncing around happy as a clam. A well-fucked clam." Evan clapped her on the arm, almost knocking her over. "I'm impressed, big sis. I guess you don't suck in bed."

She could not handle his teasing. Normally she would give it right back, but she wasn't capable of doing anything other than standing upright and breathing. "Can you please stop talking? Permanently?"

"Oh, come on, it's your birthday. Perk up. You just need a little hair of the dog, that's all. Though maybe stop at one drink instead of eight."

"I didn't really drink that much. I'm not sure why I'm so hungover."

"Did you and Nolan go out after the party?"

Eve felt her cheeks start to burn. "Yes."

"Did you drink?"

"Yes."

"Then you drank enough to be hungover. Where did you guys go?"

"A bar. A nightclub." Then because she was going to have to admit it sooner or later, she murmured, "A wedding chapel."

"Come again?"

Blushing furiously, she darted her gaze around to make sure no one was within hearing distance. "We might have gotten married last night."

Evan stared at her blankly for a second, then he burst out laughing. "Are you shitting me?"

"I wish I was."

His laughter revved up until he was snorting. "Oh my God, that's the best thing I've heard in a long time. You of all people . . . damn, that's funny."

She glared at her brother. "I'm glad you find it so amusing. But notice I'm not laughing?"

It obviously took some effort, but Evan reined in his glee. "So, um, congratulations?" he said.

Eve took her sunglasses off and crammed them onto her head, tired of trying to see her brother through the dark lenses. "No. No congratulations. We obviously can't stay married."

"What? You're not even going to give it a shot?" Evan asked. "You might as well since you've already done the deed."

"Are you nuts? No. You know this won't work."

"I don't know anything about what would work for you and Nolan, and I don't think you do either. You rushed into it, why rush out? Kendall and I eloped and look how well that turned out. We're awesome."

Was her brother serious? He had always been just like her—cut and run when things got uncomfortable. Though it had always been different with Kendall. He had never doubted his feelings for Kendall, which was why her own situation wasn't comparable. She did doubt her feelings for Nolan.

Didn't she?

"You and Kendall knew each other."

He shrugged. "How well do you ever know anybody? I say go for it and enjoy the ride for as long as it lasts."

"We're getting this annulled as soon as possible. So don't tell anybody. We can't have anyone getting wind of this, or it will look bad for you and the team."

"How will your quickie wedding look bad for me?"

"It ruins the squeaky-clean image of the Monroe family and Hinder Motors if I get hitched with the naked jackman." The more she thought about it, the more that aspect of the situation freaked her out. That hadn't even crossed her mind the night before.

"We have a squeaky-clean image?" Evan asked dubiously.

"We should!" she snapped, her stomach starting to churn again. This had the potential to be a PR nightmare. "Just don't breathe a word of this. No one can know."

"Hey, Eve!"

Eve raised her head, hoping whoever was calling her would go away and die.

It was Jim, Evan's car chief, a good twenty feet away from her with a crowd of crew members. "Congratulations, girl! Heard you got hitched last night to my jackman! Always knew there was a spark between you two."

Oh, shit. Eve hunched deeper into her sweater. "Thanks," she called weakly because what the hell else was she supposed to say?

She was going to kill Nolan. He must have told. Without asking her if it was okay. Without her telling her family first. She was going to rip his nuts off and stuff them in his pocket.

"Well, I guess the cat is out of the bag," her brother said, stating the very obvious.

"Where's Nolan?" she asked Evan under her breath. "And Elec?"

"Elec's test lap was this morning. I imagine he's in his RV by now. You better send a fast text to Mom and Dad. You don't want them to hear this from someone else."

"I don't want them to hear it, period. I'll talk to you later." Striding over to the crew, she demanded, "Where's Nolan?"

A couple of them grinned at her. "Damn. Already territorial," Jim said.

She really wanted to tell him to go screw himself hard

and repeatedly, but she restrained herself. "How did you find out about our marriage?" she asked.

"My wife told me."

Jim's wife knew? What the hell?

"She gets that gossip blog about racing, and you know, Ford is kind of a hot ticket since his ass was on YouTube, and with you being a Monroe and all, it was the featured story this morning, right next to Junior's blowing an engine on his test lap."

They were blogworthy? That was seriously bizarre. But how had the blogger found out? And oh, my God, was that blogger Tuesday? Would her friend really do that to her?

Her phone was blowing up in her pocket. Eve was afraid to look at it.

"Oh," she said brilliantly to Jim. "I see."

They were looking at her expectantly.

"What?" she snapped.

"Whew." Jim made a big deal out of pretending to wipe his forehead. "For a second there I was afraid marriage had stripped you of your sass. Which would be a damn shame."

That astonished her. "You like me bitching all the time? I thought you said I was a battle-ax."

"That's just to rib you. Yeah, I like your mouthiness. It keeps it from getting boring around here."

All the guys were nodding. "My day just wouldn't be the same without you telling me to get the fucking lead out," Ace, the tire man, said.

She was almost touched. Not. "Today I'm just going to tell you that if you don't inform me where Nolan is in the next thirty seconds, I will prevent you from ever being a father."

Ace instinctively moved his hand over his man parts. "He's heading this way right now."

Eve turned. Nolan was striding toward them, with an awful lot of swagger in his step. He looked pleased as freaking punch with himself and his life. The guys around her broke out into whoops and catcalls. She winced. Both because of the sound coming at her still not quite recovered head hurt and from the fact that they were hooting because they knew she had married Nolan.

Braving a glance at her phone, she saw she had two missed calls from her mother and six texts, one of which was from Tuesday. She couldn't call her mother back right now, but she was curious to see what Tuesday had written.

Is it true? How does some upstart gossip blogger know and I don't?

So now she knew it wasn't Tuesday, which was a relief. She would have thought Tuesday would run something like that past her first for her permission, but it wasn't Tuesday. So who was it?

Nolan was grinning and shaking hands with everyone. Then in the midst of all the melee he leaned over and gave her a big wet kiss. "How are you feeling?" he asked.

The roar of approval around her was deafening. Really? If Nolan knew her at all—which he clearly didn't, making their marriage even more insane—he would know she did not like to be in the spotlight like that. Especially not involving physical contact.

But she managed to say, "I'm fine," which was a big fat lie.

"You look beautiful."

"You're still drunk," she told him.

He laughed. "Nope. Just happy." He turned to the other crew members. "You all need to buy me a drink when we get back home since we didn't have a wedding reception." He turned back to her. "Or should we have a wedding reception? That might be fun."

Having four hundred people staring at her all night

questioning what drugs she had slipped to Nolan to get him to marry her? No thanks. The very thought of a reception and what it represented made her want to have a heart attack. She pulled her sweater so tight it was practically a straitjacket. "We can talk about that later," she told him. Like never.

She looked at the other guys. They needed to go away. "Can you all go away? I want to talk to Nolan alone."

That was met with chortles and laughs. But hey, she wasn't going to waste time being polite. Today was not the day for polite. Today was the day for a two-by-four she could knock herself unconscious with.

The guys wandered off with a few last words of congratulations.

Once they were alone, Eve asked Nolan, "How did a blogger find out we got married?"

He looked bewildered. "A blogger knows?"

"Yeah, that's how the crew knows."

"Really? I have no idea. The only person I told was my brother."

"The only person I told was my brother and that was five minutes ago."

"Huh. I just told Rhett like an hour ago. Neither of our brothers would call the gossip rags anyway. Maybe someone saw us? But who would recognize us?"

"I don't know. It's weird."

But Nolan just shrugged. "I guess it doesn't matter, though I guess we both need to call our mothers before they are mortally wounded and even more pissed off than they would be anyway."

The thought made shivers of dread trounce up her spine. "Ugh." She needed more aspirin. "My mom already called me twice. I'm guessing she knows."

It was safe to say the low-key birthday Eve had envisioned wasn't going according to plan. Which was evidence that spontaneity wasn't wise. Now she couldn't even just get a quickie annulment with no one knowing. Everyone knew. She did not want to be the subject of even more gossip by turning around and filing to annul the marriage.

Though she wasn't even sure she wanted to annul the marriage. She did have very strong feelings for Nolan, which might be love if it wasn't completely nutty to be in love after two weeks.

She didn't know what she wanted other than about six more hours of sleep. In her granny clothes.

"I like this look, babe," Nolan said, pulling the edges of her sweater closed. "It makes me want to unwrap you."

"You're nuts. I look like hell."

"No, you don't. You look delicious." He nuzzled in her neck.

Eve didn't do nuzzling. Not in the garage. Hell, not anywhere. But she let him do it.

And she *liked* it.

God, she didn't even know herself anymore.

With more effort than should be necessary, Eve dragged herself away from him. "Call your mother. What time will you be done working?"

"Six or so. What are you going to do until then?"

"Sleep in an empty car." She was only half-kidding. "No, I have to call some people."

"Hey." Nolan took his thumbs and drew them along her eyebrows and down to her temples, where he massaged her gently. "Don't worry. Our families will be fine once they get over the shock."

Maybe. But the real question was would she be fine? And was she ever going to get over the shock?

She was married. Lord have mercy.

CHAPTER FIFTEEN

THE garage and pit road weren't exactly the quietest places to have a phone conversation, but Nolan knew he had to call his mother sooner than later. So he found the remotest corner and hit dial for his mother. She answered on the second ring.

"You didn't really get married in Vegas, did you?"

Apparently she knew.

The key to dealing with his mother was not to get riled up and not to buckle under her pressure. "As a matter of fact, I did. I'm very happy."

"Why would she do that? Why would that girl just up and marry you? Is she on drugs?"

"Gee, thanks, Mom." Nolan felt his bubble burst with a loud pop as his mother managed to hone in on his most elemental fears and doubts. Why had Eve married him? What did he have to offer?

"I didn't mean that the way it sounded."

There weren't a whole lot of ways that could be inter-preted. "So how did you mean it?"

"I just mean that she comes from a wealthy family and I'm sure she's been around drivers and team owners and corporate sponsors her whole life. It seems like she'd be more comfortable dating someone like that."

"Someone who isn't beneath her, you mean?" It was a deep worry that he had, and he didn't need to be reminded of it. Not eighteen hours after their wedding.

"Don't go getting all sensitive, Nolan Junior. You know exactly what I'm saying and you know it's true. I just think that a woman who can truly appreciate you is not going to be some rich career woman."

Nolan loved his mother. He had been taught from birth to respect her. Never even in his hormonal teen years had he yelled at her or said anything cruel. For the first time ever, he was sorely tempted to hang up the phone before he said something he would regret.

"Well, Eve certainly seemed to appreciate me last night." Let her think what she wanted of that one.

There was a shocked silence. "Junior, I'm going to trust you weren't referencing bedroom activities to your mother."

Part of him was feeling petulant enough that he wanted to say what of it? Most people had sex on their wedding night. But he stopped himself in the nick of time. He did not want to fight with his mother. He didn't want to fight with anyone. He wanted to just revel in his marriage, but it seemed all reveling was on hold. "Mom, I married Eve. I'm asking you to be happy for me. To accept her and be nice."

The pause was so long that he actually said, "Hello?"

"I'm here," she said begrudgingly. "I don't know what

to say. How can I be happy for you when I think you've made a huge mistake?"

"One, you can trust me. Two, you can shrug your shoulders and be happy I'm happy. If it doesn't work out, what is the big deal? Is it the end of the world?" He wanted it to work out, more than anything. But if it didn't, at least he would have had whatever time he did with Eve. "Better to have loved and lost and all that, right, Momma?"

His mother gave a massive sigh. "Just don't knock her up for a while, you hear me?"

Nolan almost laughed. Almost. "Trust me, that's the last thing on my mind. What did Dad say?"

"That you're a damn fool but she's a looker."

Figured. "Well at least I have his support."

"Your sister wants to talk to you."

"Which one?" Actually, he didn't want to talk to any of them at the moment. "I'm at work, I should go. I'll call her later. I'll call you on Monday when I'm back home. Love you. Bye."

Nolan bum-rushed his mother off the phone and frowned.

This was going to be harder than he thought.

He didn't really like things to be hard, unless it was his penis.

Suddenly he wanted his wife.

"*DAD,* calm down, you're going to have a heart attack." Eve was standing outside talking on the phone, sunglasses firmly back on her eyes to protect her from the fading, but still painful, Vegas sun. "It's not that big of a deal." Truthfully, it was, but she wasn't about to admit that to her father.

"We had this conversation about driving in the demolition derby. You told me that was no big deal, and in retro-spect it probably wasn't. This, Eve Alexandra, is a very big deal!"

She sighed, rubbing her temple. She needed Nolan to massage her again. "You had to assume that I was going to get married at some point in my life. I know I sort of scream old maid, but you can't have thought it was totally out of the realm of possibilities."

"Of course I figured you would get married, but I thought you would have the sense to do it the right way."

"What is the right way? In a church?"

"The right way is with someone you've been dating for at least a year, and you think about it and plan it. What do you really know about this guy?"

That her father thought there was a time minimum to knowing someone before you could marry him amused her because truthfully, a few weeks ago, she would have said the exact same thing. She definitely had quite a bit of her father in her. "Dad, he's a nice guy." What else could she really say? She wasn't going to stomp her feet and cry and declare herself wildly in love. She may have gotten a little more impulsive, but she hadn't regressed to a teen-age girl in a vampire film.

"Well, you're going to have to write up a postnup and have him sign it. I'll put a call into the lawyer."

"A postnup for what?" That had never even occurred to her.

"You have a lot more money than he does, and you're going to inherit half of my estate someday."

Her head really was pounding again. This sounded like way more than she wanted to deal with. Her father's even-tual death and Nolan trying to take her money. That was cheerful. "Half? Don't you mean a third?"

"No. I'm giving you half, and a quarter for each of the

boys. Their incomes are ten times higher than yours—they don't need it."

Eve was sincerely touched. "Thanks, Daddy."

Her father cleared his throat. "You would have been an excellent driver, you know. One of the best. You have the fire."

Tears suddenly were in her eyes. She didn't realize until that very second how much she had needed to hear that her father had believed in her. The truth was, maybe she hadn't believed in herself. Maybe it had been easier to blame the system than try and fail.

"Which is why you shouldn't settle, Eve. You're a wonderful woman capable of great things. You're the best PR rep for your brothers we could have ever hired, and I don't want to see you lose everything."

Somehow buried in the compliments and the concern was still the implication that she'd been dumb enough to fall for a gold digger. She had no doubt that Nolan was anything but. "Dad, I appreciate your concern, but Nolan is not after my money. Any in my bank account now or what I might have in the future."

"Maybe not now, but things get ugly when people get divorced."

So now he had them already getting divorced. Granted, Eve had been contemplating an annulment, but she still found it annoying. So no one thought she and Nolan were anything more than a Vegas flash in the pan.

"Dad, I will sign a postnup if it makes you feel better, and I'm sure Nolan will, too. Now I'm going to go and eat large amounts of chocolate."

It took a couple more minutes and guarantees from her father that the postnuptial agreement would be on her desk first thing Monday morning before she could get off the phone.

She wasn't kidding about the chocolate. If she didn't get some creamy goodness in her mouth in the next five minutes, she wasn't responsible for her actions. It had been a stressful head-pounding day and she hadn't even been awake for most of it.

Eve checked her e-mails and answered a bunch of stupid people asking stupid questions. Questions if they had just read her last e-mail with anything other than half a brain they wouldn't have needed to ask. She crammed her phone back in her pocket. She was not in the mood for work, obviously. In fact, she wanted to go home and back to bed. Only now, she had a husband and she had to wait for him. It was weird. Kind of annoying.

Flagging down Evan, she told him, "Nolan and I are leaving."

"I think he's in the middle of a run-through."

"Screw that. It's my birthday and I got married last night. He wasn't even supposed to be here today originally. He's leaving with me *now*." She didn't do waiting very well, especially not when she felt like ass.

Evan raised an eyebrow. "Somebody wants to get laid."

Horrifically, that wasn't even her motivation. Mostly she wanted chocolate and her fleece pajama pants. "Think of it as a birthday present for me," she told her brother.

"Fine. I'll go get him since apparently I'm your errand boy now." But Evan did lean over and ruffle her hair. "Congrats again. I hope you guys will be as happy as me and Kendall."

Hopefully he meant after he and his wife had reunited, not when she had been locking herself in the RV bedroom and telling him to F off through the door.

Speaking of his wife, Kendall came over, a grin on her face. "Eve, Eve, Eve . . . I didn't know you had it in you."

"What, stupidity?"

"No. Spontaneity. The ability to listen to your emotions."

At the time, that was what she thought she had been doing. Now she wasn't so sure what exactly had been going on in her head. "Well, thanks for not calling me an idiot like everyone else basically has. I just had to listen to my dad tell me that Nolan married me for my money."

Kendall paused in tightening the ponytail her auburn hair was in. She started laughing. "I'm sorry, I know I shouldn't laugh, but that's just ridiculous. Parents mean well, but where do they come up with this stuff? It's not like you're independently wealthy."

"I know. Hanging around for twenty years waiting for my dad to kick so he can get his hands on some of my inheritance seems like a lot of work."

"Well, just try to ignore everyone's opinions because you're going to get a lot of them. You should call Tuesday and have her blog with the details so it's accurate, unlike that other one that came out this morning that said after you spent the night at a strip club together you got married."

"What?" Charming. "That didn't happen! We were at a nightclub."

Kendall shrugged. "You know how that goes. Nightclub wasn't exciting enough. So it became a strip club. But seriously, it's all just white noise. Just enjoy your relationship with Nolan. Don't let gossip ruin your honeymoon phase. I speak from experience."

Was this the honeymoon phase? Holy crap, that wasn't promising.

Thank God Kendall wasn't a touchy-feely kind of chick, because Eve was fairly certain if she had tried to hug her, Eve would have burst into tears. Which would have pissed her off.

"See you later. Call me if you need to talk."

"Thanks."

Nolan came up behind her and hugged her. Hadn't she just thought she didn't want a hug? But his was more like a bear hug from behind, and while it was mildly embarrassing to be hugged in the garage in front of a half-dozen people, a small part of her kind of liked it, too.

"Evan says I'm sprung. You want to go to dinner?"

"What I really want is a giant chocolate bar, room service, and bed," she told him truthfully. "How did your call with your mom go?"

She could feel him shrug. Finding it weird to be talking to him when he was behind her, Eve pulled away and turned around. "My dad was pissed. My mom seems okay with it."

"Yeah, my mom was not thrilled either," he said. "But she'll come around."

His eyes were dark, and there was a reserve to him when he spoke that she wasn't used to. Obviously there was more to the conversation than he was willing to share. Fabulous. But she wasn't going to pry when she didn't really want to share the details either. *Hey, my dad thinks you're a gold digger.* What everyone wanted to hear.

"I wish we could teleport to the hotel."

He snapped his fingers. "Shit, it didn't work. I guess we have to take a cab."

But he had the taxi stop after a block at a convenience store. "I need a soda, I'll be two minutes."

Eve sat in the cab and used the time to call Tuesday. "I can't believe someone scooped you on this," she told her. "I didn't tell anyone. Hell, I wasn't planning to tell anyone ever."

"It's that little upstart, Mary Jane, Cooper Brickman's little sister. She's like twelve! This is infuriating. But she's in Vegas because her brother has custody of her and she travels the circuit with him. Apparently she and her so-called nanny were out hitting the clubs last night."

A driver's teenage sister was responsible for everyone

in the universe finding out about her midnight wedding? "That's weird and completely wrong. Someone should have a chat with Cooper. It's ridiculous that his sister is posting lies on the Internet. But whatever, what's done is done. Please correct the bullshit about the strip club. You can post that Nolan threw a surprise birthday party for me at the W Hotel and that we were married at a Vegas chapel afterwards."

"Will do. So, uh, are you happy?"

"I'm more freaked out than happy. I'm debating options." Actually, she was debating getting out of the cab and going into the store and screaming like a fish wife for Nolan to hurry up. But lucky for him, he emerged from the store, a giant brown bag in his hand. "Okay, here's Nolan, I'll talk to you later."

As he got in the car, she asked him, "What the hell did you buy? Is there a small child in that bag?"

He gestured for the driver to start moving again, then he opened the bag. "You said you wanted chocolate, so I grabbed a couple of different options for you. I don't know what kind you like so . . . hopefully one of these will work."

A half-dozen different candy bars spilled into her lap. Eve looked down at them, shocked. He had actually listened to what she had said. Not only had he listened, but he'd attempted to correct the situation. Her lip started to tremble and her eyes got moist. "Thanks."

"What's wrong?" he asked, alarmed, pausing in opening his bottle of Coke.

"Nothing." Then she did something so weird it almost beat marrying Nolan without warning. She clutched the candy to her chest and lay down on the seat so that her head was in his lap. Staring up at him, she fought tears.

What the frickin-frack was the matter with her?

"Hey." Nolan looked down at her, his hand stroking her hair off her forehead. "In case you didn't know, you're beautiful."

She really did start crying then. Maybe she was just tired. Maybe it was her hangover. Maybe it was the stress of dealing with everyone's reaction. Not only was there her family, but Nolan's mother apparently hated her guts.

Or maybe it was love. Was it love if a man could make you cry with his thoughtfulness?

Was it love if you could allow yourself to be vulnerable in front of him?

She didn't know.

But as he wiped the tears rolling down her cheeks with his callused thumb, Eve knew she wasn't ready to file any annulment papers just yet.

NOLAN knocked on the bathroom door and opened it a crack. Eve was still in the bathtub, bubbles up to her chin, several empty candy bar wrappers on the ledge next to her. "Do you need anything?"

"I wouldn't mind another candy bar," she said, hair piled high on her head with a rubber band. "Something with peanut butter in it."

"Sure." Nolan hid his grin. Eve wasn't much of a drinker, but it seemed she sure loved her chocolate. Especially when she had a hangover. "Can I get in the tub with you?"

There was a slight pause as she licked a flake on chocolate off her finger. "Are you going to try to have sex with me? Because I'm not really in the mood."

"Wow, we really are married," he teased her. "Twenty-four hours in and you already won't put out."

The look she cut him was so scathing he had to laugh. "If you want to have sex with a rag doll, go for it, jackass."

Tender Eve, who had made an appearance in the cab, was gone again. This Eve he knew and understood. A crying Eve had almost made him panic. He hadn't known what to do. But this sarcasm, this he could deal with. "Maybe I dig rag doll sex. And maybe you know that I was kidding."

She threw a balled-up wrapper at him. It missed by a mile. "You're a lousy shot. Now scoot your ass over. I'm coming in."

Nolan stripped his shirt off as he went back into the hotel room for the requested candy. He grabbed a jumbo peanut butter cup pack and two bottles of soda and headed back. Plunking the spoils down next to her right arm, he took off his jeans and stepped into the tub on the opposite end from Eve.

"You don't wear underwear very often, do you?" she asked.

He closed his eyes briefly as he sank into the hot water. Damn, that felt good. "Nope. It's overrated."

"Don't you risk injury?"

"Nope. I don't work out commando, it's just for my days off."

"And when you have a fire retardant suit on."

"Yep. Those things are snug. I'm in no danger of racking myself." He tickled her foot, which was next to his hip. "Why are we talking about my nuts? Don't turn me on if you're not going to follow through."

"Talking about your nuts turns you on?" She tore the candy wrapper open with her teeth.

"Everything about you turns me on. Like right now, using your teeth, turns me on." He wasn't lying. Just seeing the aggressive biting had him working on a boner.

She licked her lips.

"Even worse," he told her. "Look." His erection had broken free of the bubbles and was aiming for the sky.

"I have a way of making that go away. Hey, what happens when we get home on Monday?"

Trust Eve to cut to the chase. "What do you mean?" Even though he knew exactly what she meant.

"We're married. What do we do with that back in Charlotte?"

This was a trick question, and he suspected no matter what he said, it would be wrong. So he just shrugged. "We be married."

She flung a handful of bubbles at him.

"Quit throwing shit at me," he told her. "You're going to give me a complex."

Eve snorted. "Right. I mean, I don't even know where you live. We haven't planned anything."

"Planning is as overrated as underwear. My apartment is small and crappy and I can either break my lease or see if Rhett wants to take it over since you own your place. I can split your mortgage payment with you and the other bills."

"My mortgage is twenty-five hundred a month."

Nolan almost drowned in the tub water. Was she serious? "Um. Really? My rent's six hundred." He couldn't double that. He wouldn't be able to make his truck payments. Or buy food. But he didn't want to admit that.

She looked as uncomfortable with the conversation as he felt. "You could give me six hundred and I could use it for all the other bills and I could just keep the condo in my name only."

He hadn't even thought about adding his name to her condo. That didn't seem right, since it was her place, so he nodded. "Sure, sure, that would work. So what is your schedule like? When should I move in? If Rhett wants to sublet my apartment, I'll just leave all my furniture there. It's not exactly your style and your condo looks perfect the way it is." He wasn't going to mess up her space with his flea market finds and hand-me-down furniture.

"Oh, okay, sounds good." She looked super relieved. "If you're just bringing clothes and personal stuff, whenever you want. I have a full workload this week, but then I always do."

"Next weekend is the derby." Nolan was still a little stunned by the steep cost of her mortgage. She hadn't blinked when she'd said it, and maybe he was living out of touch with reality, but it just seemed to him like that was a hell of a lot of money for a single woman to be shelling out every month. "Think you can make it?"

"Sure." Though she looked less than thrilled with the prospect.

Nolan remembered her feelings on being a cheerleader. He almost told her she didn't have to come, but then he decided that he wanted her there, so why should he pretend he didn't? If they were going to be married, which they were, then they had to spend time together. Support each other. Live together.

His foot brushed between her thighs.

Have sex.

That's what married people did. Despite the jokes, studies showed married couples were getting it on more frequently than singles did. It made sense given the convenience factor. He wanted to conveniently have a lot of sex with Eve.

"Watch it, Ford," she told him.

"What? This tub isn't that big. I needed to stretch."

"You're a terrible liar."

He winked at her. "But a wonderful lover."

"Oh, Lord," was her thought on that.

But damned if her slippery little fingers didn't reach out and stroke his cock.

By the time she was done with him, they were both wrinkled like a couple of raisins and were as limp as the rag doll she had claimed to be.

So far, he had no complaints about marriage whatsoever.

CHAPTER
SIXTEEN

EVE glanced at her watch as they stood at the desk, waiting to check out. They were going to store their things in Elec's coach since they were both flying back to Charlotte that night. They'd grab their bags after the race and head to the airport. It was nine in the morning. They had plenty of time, but she was still impatient. Worried. She sincerely hoped there wouldn't be anyone in the media asking her any questions about her marriage. It probably wasn't newsworthy. Her coworkers would be ribbing her, she was sure. But at least the crew had said their piece the day before.

As they reached the counter and Eve gave her room number, the clerk asked if she wanted to use the card she had given at check-in.

"Sure, that's fine."

"Here, let me get it," Nolan said, pulling out his wallet.

Eve was startled. "No, the company is paying for it. This is a business expense."

"Our room service was a couple hundred bucks. At least let me pay that."

It seemed important to him for whatever testosterone-driven reason, so Eve agreed. "Okay, thanks."

She was back to fiddling with her phone, checking e-mail, when she realized there was a problem. "What's wrong?"

The clerk was punching numbers repeatedly. "His card has been declined, Ms. Monroe."

Oh, shit. Eve knew that it was possible it was a weird electronic glitch, but given the look on Nolan's face, that wasn't the case. She tried to brush it off. "Just put it all on my business card then." She turned to Nolan. "You should call your credit card company. Sometimes when you travel they put a freeze on it if it seems like an unusual charge."

She meant it to soothe his ego, because she suspected his card was maxed out. But somehow he managed to take her words as an insult as well.

"Yeah, I guess this isn't my usual scene. The Motel 6 is more my speed."

"That's not what I meant. I meant how often do you come to Vegas? Credit card companies watch your patterns, and if you're traveling and they don't know it, they'll put a freeze on your card."

"It doesn't matter." Nolan slung his duffel bag over his shoulder. "Thanks for buying our wedding dinner."

Oh, God, was she going to have to deal with this all the time? She was sympathetic to ego, but at the same time she wasn't going to feel bad because she could afford a dinner here and there. "Hey, guess what?" she told him as they'd left the desk, the clerk looking noticeably uncomfortable. "I'm successful in my career and I'm not going to apologize for it. You are too, I might add. Hundreds of guys would kill to be a pro jackman. I doubt I make that much more than you do at the end of the day. So drop the macho bullshit and get over it if I pay for my share."

"Remember that conversation we had way back when about telling people something honest but with a little sugar thrown on top?" He slapped the hotel door open, waving off the bellman. "That wasn't it."

"So sue me." She stomped out after him, wearing a stupid skirt with tights and booties to go to the track. Her feet hurt and she was exhausted from all the freaking congratulations she had heard the previous day. Did everyone and their mother have to seek her out to comment on her nuptials? Apparently yes, and she wasn't good at doing the pretty. Never had been. She was better at opening up an engine and taking a curve on two wheels. Not wearing stupid tights and smiling at people who thought she was stupid for marrying Nolan. "Or divorce me."

Okay, that was childish. She knew it. But it slid out before she could stop it.

He whirled around on her. "Oh, is that how it's going to be? Every time we disagree about something you're going to throw that in my face? Don't be passive-aggressive. It doesn't suit you."

"Why don't you sleep at your place tonight? Does that suit me?"

"Whatever."

"Don't whatever me." That was the one thing guaranteed to piss her off. Okay, a lot of things were guaranteed to piss her off. But that one always did it.

Nolan opened the door of a cab and gestured for her to get in.

She hesitated, well aware she was being irrational.

"Get your ass in the cab or I'll throw it in there."

"You wouldn't dare." The idea kind of stole some of her anger and turned her on a little. She had to admit, she liked that he didn't cower under her venom.

"Are you daring me?"

"Yes."

Nolan threw his bag in the backseat, then he picked her up by her upper thighs and flung her over his shoulder.

Holy crap. Eve grabbed on to his waist, terrified she was going to fall onto the concrete. But that was superseded by the sheer hotness factor of what he had just done. He'd picked her up like she weighed no more than a kitten. He wasn't stomping off washing his hands of her, nor was he tolerating what she knew was completely bitchy behavior.

Her husband was a hottie, no doubt about it. She was face-first into the ass of his jeans. She went with impulse and bit his butt cheek.

"Jesus!" He jerked forward a little. "Do you want me to drop you?"

"No," she murmured, squeezing the backs of his thighs a little. His muscular body was truly a work of art.

Her view changed as he lifted her into the cab. She landed on the seat on her back. "Mmm, strongman," she told him, licking her lips. Regardless of the driver in the front seat, she was seriously hoping he was going to cover her body with his and kiss her spitless.

He climbed in beside her and slammed the door shut. "I have to be to handle you."

Mood ruined. Eve sat up and crossed her arms over her chest. She could say what she wanted to, but that would just make her sound petty, so she kept very quiet and very still.

"Nothing to say?"

"Nope. Not a thing."

"There's a first."

Eve decided the problem was when you got married impulsively, you then treated every day as a possible breaking point for your relationship. It wasn't healthy.

Because in the last thirty-six hours she had decided to annul her marriage about six times then waffled and changed her mind.

She was back to wanting to make the whole thing go away.

NOLAN didn't go away. He moved into her condo with two duffel bags of clothes, mostly jeans and T-shirts since he didn't appear to own a whole lot of underwear. There were four pairs of sneakers suddenly in her closet, which was insane, because who needed four pairs of sneakers, but Eve was handling it. As long as they didn't talk about the future, she was okay with it all, for the most part.

The sex was great. Getting laid every night was working for her.

And a secret part of her couldn't help being pleased that he was still hanging in there, that he had married her and seemed to actually like her.

It was weird, but there it was.

Now they were on their way to her parents' house on Wednesday for a dinner with Nolan's family. Her mother had insisted on doing it, even though Eve had explained that Nolan's family wasn't exactly small. But her mother had thought it would be beyond rude not to know the parents of her son-in-law.

Eve didn't bother to point out that she didn't even know her son-in-law.

"I hope your mom is okay with this," Nolan said as he pulled his truck into her parents' driveway. "There's almost thirty of us showing up here tonight."

"There's only nine of us, so the Fords definitely outnumber the Monroes, but I warned my mom. She's all jazzed about it. After the initial shock, she's all on board with the fact that I won't be an old maid after all. I wouldn't be surprised if she starts hinting that we should have children."

He grinned at her. "My mother told me not to knock you up."

"Fabulous. Everyone is involved in our sex life."

"That's reproduction. Our sex life has nothing to do with that." His eyebrows went up and down. "Our smoking hot sex life."

"That it is." She couldn't deny that they were burning up her sheets every night.

"It's the best thing about living together." He immediately seemed to realize how that sounded. "I mean, after waking up next to you every morning."

"Epic fail," she told him. "You're lucky you're cute."

He leaned over and gave her a loud smacking kiss, nearly giving her whiplash. "I love you," he told her.

"I actually love you, too," she said, still marveling over that fact. But there was no other man she had ever met who she would let hug her the way Nolan did.

"Don't sound so surprised."

"I'm not." She was.

"I think we're late." The driveway looked like a used car lot. Nolan wasn't going to be nervous about seeing his in-laws again. He refused. They were either going to like him or not, and there wasn't a whole lot he could do about that. They had seemed friendly enough at Eve's birthday party, but that was before he'd up and married their daughter. So he wasn't really expecting them to be overjoyed, but obviously Mrs. Monroe wanted to make an effort, since this dinner party was her idea. Though she might already be regretting it, since his nieces and nephews were probably destroying the Monroes' house as they spoke.

"It's not my fault you wanted to have sex."

"Yeah, I can take the fall for that one." He'd managed to get Eve to put her ankles on his shoulders. That was worth being late for.

When he stepped into the house behind Eve, he was greeted by a fair amount of chaos and the smell of chili in the air.

His niece Asher raced up to him. "Hi!" She jumped into the arms he wasn't holding out yet. Good thing he had quick reflexes. As he held her squirming form, he marveled that kids were so trusting, so sure no harm would befall them.

Had Eve been like that as a girl? Somehow he thought she had been. So when had she become such a worrier? He saw it, how she internalized all of her stress, her fears, her concerns. They took up residence in her eyes and her forehead, and he wanted to just hold on to her shoulders and absorb some of that away from her. She was doing it now—worrying. Her hands were crammed in the pockets of her black dress pants as she scanned the room.

"Asher, this is Eve, my new wife. Eve, this is Asher, who's thirteen."

Asher giggled. "I am not. I'm seven, Uncle Nolan."

"Oh, that's right! It's Georgia who's thirteen."

"She's only three!" Asher punched him in the stomach.

"Geez, you're not Asher, you're Rocky." He swatted her on the butt and said, "Go play."

She ran off. "I hope your parents aren't fond of their carpet," he told Eve.

"They did raise two boys and me, who was half boy. I'm sure they're fine. And now we have Pete and Hunter here from time to time and my mom loves it. I'm sure she's thrilled."

Eve's mother did look like she was enjoying herself. She was on the couch talking to his mother, who seemed content if not exactly overjoyed. There were no men in the

room at all, just Nolan's sisters and Tamara. Children ran
all over the place, ranging from toddlers to tweens. His
nephew Owen was crying at the top of his lungs.

Eve greeted her mother with a wave. Nolan kissed his
mother on the cheek. Then because it seemed appropriate,
he did the same to Eve's mother. Mrs. Monroe looked up
at him in surprise. "Well, nice to see you again, Nolan.
You sure had us fooled the other night. We thought you
were just planning a birthday party for Eve, not a sketchy
Vegas wedding."

"Mom." Eve gave her mother a warning look before
turning to his mother. "Hi, Mrs. Ford, it's good to see you
again."

"Kind of unusual circumstances, isn't it?" his mother
said, and if Nolan wasn't mistaken, she was eyeing Eve's
middle like she could ascertain if there was a baby growing in there.

Yeah, this was going to be a fun night. Nolan said,
"Well, it looks like everyone made it. I really appreciate
them being here."

"It was short notice," his mother said. "But then the
marriage was short notice."

"Yep," he said cheerfully, determined to bluster his
way through this. "Thank you very much, Mrs. Monroe,
for hosting this."

"Remember, call me Cindy, especially now that you're
married to my daughter."

"Excellent, Cindy."

Eve looked distracted. She kept glancing over at Owen,
who was squalling so loud they all had to raise their
voices. Owen was on his mother's lap and she was jiggling
him and shushing him, but it wasn't having any effect.

"Can I hold him?" Eve asked.

"Absolutely," she said, holding her son out with relief.

"I'm Dawn, by the way. One of the middle sisters. And this is Owen, who is usually much cuter."

"How old is he?"

"Ten months."

"He's adorable." Eve took him and shushed him and swayed back and forth, making funny faces until Owen stopped crying and just stared at her, probably wondering who the hell was holding him.

It did something weird to his gut to see Eve looking maternal. He'd never seen this side of her, and it was eye-opening. She looked . . . peaceful.

He sank down onto the couch next to his mother, the rug metaphorically pulled out from under him. God, he really did love Eve. How was that possible? He kept knowing it was true, yet he kept questioning how he could feel this much after such a short period of time. But the more he learned about her, the more deeply he fell in love with her, even when she was trying to annoy him.

His face must have revealed something, because when Eve glanced over at him, she blushed. "I do like babies." She might as well have added, "What of it?" to the end of her sentence.

"You're good with him," Nolan murmured. "My ear-drums thank you."

"Don't get any ideas," his mother said. "Let us all re-cover from the shock of your elopement before you throw a baby into the mix."

Nice. "Mom, please."

Eve's mother laughed. "I don't think babies are the first thing on Eve's to-do list."

The words seemed to have the opposite effect her mother intended. Eve made a face and it made Nolan wonder how much her family knew about what made Eve happy. Hell, what did he know about it?

Unnerved by his thoughts in general, he asked his mother, "Where is Dad and Mr. Monroe? I want to say hi."

"They're in the backyard starting a bonfire for after dinner. We'll be eating in a few minutes," Cindy said. "Tell them to come back in, please."

"Okay, great, thanks."

"Go through the kitchen and out the French doors."

When he passed Eve, Nolan couldn't help leaning over and kissing her on the top of her head. She just looked so . . . beautiful. Man, he was whipped. Maybe if he went into the backyard with the other guys and threw wood on a fire he'd grow his balls back.

It took longer to get there than he'd anticipated. The Monroes' house was enormous, his boots squeaking on some elegant-looking tile that probably had a fancy name. The kitchen was the size of his own parents' whole house and probably cost about the same. But he did finally step out onto the patio and found all his sisters' husbands out there with both his and Eve's fathers and Evan and Elec. There seemed to be some debate waging over how to stack the wood properly.

"Hey, there he is, the lucky groom!" his sister Danny's husband, Jared, said. "Congrats, bro!"

"Thanks, man." At least someone was happy for him.

Jared and Danny's son, Simon, who was cruising toward double digits, was poking a log with a stick. "Mom said you've lost your ever-lovin' mind, Uncle Nolan."

"Simon!" his father chided.

"It's good to know my sister talks about me in front of her kids." Nolan just grinned and shook Mr. Monroe's hand. "It's a pleasure to see you again, sir. You have a wonderful daughter."

"You don't need to tell me that, son. Just make sure you treat her right."

"I plan to."

"Don't mind him," Elec said, coming over and clapping him on the back. "Dad is like an older male version of Eve herself. Just ignore his crankiness. Want a beer?"

"Sure." He wanted Eve's family to completely accept him, but he'd settle for a Heineken at the moment. "Hey, Jared, where's Rhett?"

"Your mom said he stayed home. Something about a headache."

"A headache? Are you kidding me?" He didn't understand what was going on with Rhett. He'd called him a half-dozen times since Monday trying to see if Rhett wanted his apartment or not, and his brother had yet to call him back. He was both concerned about his brother and worried about his personal finances. He couldn't afford to help Eve out with the mortgage and pay his rent until his lease was up.

Another of his brothers-in-law, Dave, hauled his son back from the woodpile, where he was in danger of having the whole thing collapse on him. "Maybe he's jealous that we're all married and settled down except for him."

Simon started yelling that he'd gotten a splinter.

"Yeah, because who wouldn't be envious of this?" Jared said with a grin. He studied Simon's hand. "Yep. It's a splinter."

"Do something!" Simon demanded.

"Go show your mother."

Simon ran off into the house. Jared shrugged. "Danny will punish me later for that one, but I don't want my beer going warm."

"Hunter Jean, get down out of that tree! It's dark out!" Elec moved out into the yard.

"How did he even see her there?" Nolan asked, squinting into the darkness. He briefly caught a glimpse of something white moving on a tree branch.

"Dad radar," his own father said. "I could pick you out

of a crowd of two hundred kids at a hundred feet. In the rain."

Maybe someday he would be able to do that himself. Maybe sooner than later. "Hey, the ladies said to tell you all that dinner is ready."

"Thank God," Evan said. "I'm about to eat my arm."

Nolan went into the house last, lingering on the dark patio for a second. He was happy. Genuinely, truly happy.

Despite his declined credit card and his empty bank account.

EVE chewed her Texas toast and tried not to frown. From somewhere her mother had managed to secure some folding tables and all forty of them were sitting in two long rows, banquet style, one for adults and one for the sixteen kids, minus Owen, who was still in Eve's arms. He'd seemed to have taken a shine to her, and she to him. There was plenty of conversation flowing all around them, but Eve still felt like she was in the hot seat, which was her least favorite chair.

"So are you guys going to have a reception or anything?" one of Nolan's sisters asked. Eve honestly couldn't keep them apart. There were six of them present, and they were all about the same height and weight, except for one who was noticeably shorter. One was blond, but the rest had the same caramel-colored hair as Nolan.

Whoever they were, they were all peppering her with questions that she didn't have any answers to. "Oh, we haven't really talked about that, but I'm thinking probably no. It seems an unnecessary expense."

"But it would be fun," Nolan said. "And most people have a wedding reception of some kind."

And maybe thirty grand would fall out of the sky onto her head and they could do that. Eve thought it was an enormous waste of money. "We're already married. It seems pointless to have like a retroactive wedding reception. And did I mention it's expensive?"

"Yeah, you're right, I suppose." He was seated across from her and he looked crestfallen that she'd put the kibosh on his party fun.

She found herself resenting that she had to be the practical one. Wasn't that what she had been her entire adult life?

"Are you taking a honeymoon?" another sister asked.

Eve needed freaking note cards to remember their names. "It's kind of impossible to take a honeymoon with our work schedule." They hadn't even talked about it. Another unnecessary expense, in her opinion.

"Maybe we can manage something in December after the season is over," Nolan said. "That's not too long to wait."

"Maybe." She bounced Owen on her knee and took another spoonful of her chili. Did anyone notice she did not want to be having this conversation?

"Do you have a ring yet?" her own mother asked.

Traitor. Couldn't her mother see she did not want to talk about any of this?

"Not yet."

"Probably next week," Nolan said.

"You don't look upset, Eve," the short sister said. Eve thought her name was Danny. "I would be harassing my husband for a ring like right now."

"I know you would," her husband said.

She made a face at him.

"We'll get to it when we get to it," Eve said, because that was really how she felt about it. They could ignore the fact that they were married indefinitely as far as she was concerned.

"Eve's not really a girly-girl. That stuff doesn't matter to her," her own husband said.

Really? Eve put her spoon down carefully in her bowl. Her irritation had been repressed all night. She couldn't contain it any longer. "So what, I'm like a man? You married a man?"

Evan coughed in his palm. "Here we go."

She really wanted to throw her bread at her brother, but she restrained herself because her mother would die of humiliation.

"Of course not," Nolan said. "But if you are trying to tell me that you'll squeal in delight over a new purse or shoes, or in this case, a ring, I'm not going to believe you."

He had her there. "You're right. I don't squeal. I can't argue with that."

Evan reached around Kendall and fist-bumped Nolan. "Dude, you're like an evil genius. I can't believe you defused her that easily."

Trust her brother to make her sound like a loose cannon.

"Are you changing your last name?" Mrs. Ford asked.

"Uh . . ." How the hell did she answer that one? Truthfully. "I don't know." The thought hadn't even crossed her mind. Did she want to be Eve Ford? Eve Monroe Ford? Her palms felt sweaty and she felt Owen slipping in her grasp. She forced herself to relax and put both her hands on his waist. He was warm and smelled like crackers.

"It seems to me," Nolan's father said, as cheerfully as Nolan himself usually sounded, "that the two of you have a lot to talk about."

That might be the understatement of the year.

But Eve couldn't help but feel that there was something really wonderful about being a part of the club finally. She was at the adult table, a baby in her lap, and a husband across the table from her. It felt . . . right. Like all the pesky details would fall into place if they just ignored them.

Nolan smiled at her. "We haven't really spent a lot of our time talking."

Whether or not he meant it to be sexual, everyone at the table seemed to perceive it that way. There were a few gasps and chuckles.

"I mean, we've just been having fun."

That wasn't any better.

"Getting to know each other." Nolan actually looked a little red in the cheeks.

Eve laughed. "You're making it worse, babe. Let's just change the subject."

"Good idea. How about those Panthers? Not looking too shabby."

"True, true," Tamara chimed in, and Eve made a note to thank her brother's wife later.

Elec raised an eyebrow, clearly wondering what in the Sam Hill his wife knew about football, which was probably nothing. "Tamara, what do you think of that quarterback?"

Nolan's foot lightly kicked Eve's under the table. When she looked at him, he was making a face that she easily read as relief that he was no longer under scrutiny. She knew that feeling. She kicked him back to let him know she sympathized.

She did love this man.

And when her father slipped her an envelope from the lawyer later, she just shoved it in her purse to deal with later. Tonight she didn't want to think about postnuptial legal documents.

Or wedding receptions. Or rings.

She just wanted to eat chili and bounce a baby on her lap while her husband looked at her like she was a supermodel.

Nothing wrong with that.

CHAPTER
SEVENTEEN

EVE had talked Tuesday into going to the demolition derby with her and they sat in the stands, freezing their butts off and eating a ridiculous amount of saltwater taffy. Eve's teeth were practically cemented together from the six pieces she'd eaten. Excess saliva pooled in the corner of her mouth and she stomped her feet, trying to get the blood flow going. "Is it supposed to be this cold?"

"It's almost November. I think it's allowed."

"I should have brought a blanket." She was wearing jeans and a sweatshirt, but it wasn't enough to combat the wind or the metal bleachers under her butt. Tuesday was better prepared with a trench coat on over a thick sweater, her hair tucked under a jaunty knit cap, matching gloves on her hands. "I'm going to steal your hat."

"Try it. I'm tougher than I look."

Eve didn't doubt it. Tuesday had gone through a rough

patch after she'd lost her father, but she was now staying totally away from alcohol, going to counseling, and planning her wedding to Diesel Lange. Eve was glad things had worked out so well for her.

"Shouldn't this have started by now?"

"How should I know?" Tuesday plucked another piece of taffy out of the bag Eve held. "You do realize we're two of the most impatient women on the planet, don't you?"

"I'm not impatient, I just appreciate efficiency. I mean if I were running this event, I would have an emcee explaining to the crowd what is going on. I would have the track better lit, too. How are we supposed to see the hits if it's half in shadow out there?" God, she wanted a coffee. With whiskey in it. But she wouldn't do that, not while sitting with Tuesday. She wouldn't really do it anyway. She mostly found she just liked to complain and then she felt better.

"Of course it would be running better if you and I were involved. That's a given. Oh, look, here comes Nolan. You said he's number 20, right?"

"Yep." A trio of girls in their early twenties turned around and glanced at her. Okay. Tuesday gave Eve a look, indicating she had noticed the girls' behavior, too.

"Nolan Ford is totally hot," one of them said, and it wasn't a whisper. "He has the best ass I've ever seen."

Hello. That twit was talking about her husband. Though she couldn't deny he had a fabulous ass, she wanted to know how this girl knew that.

"I've watched that video like seven thousand times."

Ah. The infamous video. She wondered if they could sue someone to get it taken off the Internet. These pit lizards didn't need to be seeing her husband's rear end. Eve made a mental note to check on that.

"I'm totally going home with him tonight."

Eve snorted. The one glanced back at her again. She

wasn't going to say anything. It wasn't important or necessary. They probably had no idea Nolan was married.

Tuesday, however, had no such problem saying something. "Excuse me," she said, tapping the girl on the shoulder. "I'm sorry, I couldn't help but overhearing your conversation and I'm sure Nolan would be totally flattered that you think he's hot, but he does happen to be married."

Eve was less inclined to hate the girl when her jaw dropped. "He's married? Oh, shit, that sucks."

"Yes, he's married." She shot her thumb in Eve's direction. "This is his wife."

Three sets of eyes swiveled onto her. Eve tried to give a smile, but there was still taffy on her teeth, so she just nodded and gave a close-mouthed smile.

"*You're* his wife?"

She didn't need to act so damn surprised. Why couldn't she be his wife?

Because she wasn't coiffed and tanned and tweezed to within an inch of her life like they were, their feet covered in fuzzy boots, cleavage still displayed in arctic hoodies.

"Where's your wedding ring?" one had the nerve to ask her.

It was on the tip of her tongue to say, "Up your ass," but she didn't. She was just going to let all of this slide right off her back. She wasn't going to feel inadequate in any way. "It's being sized." Which was a lie. But they didn't need to know that. "We just got married last Friday."

"Well. Congratulations."

If looks could kill, she'd be six feet under. Plus she suspected they didn't even believe her. Not that she could blame them. She probably wouldn't believe some random chick in the stands either. "Thanks."

When the derby started, Eve found herself chewing her taffy even faster, nearly pulling out a tooth a time or two. She was both nervous for Nolan, wanting him to win, and second-guessing his strategy. "Oh, my God, does he not see that yellow car? He needs to get a hit in on him. That's his strongest competition."

Tuesday seemed to find the whole event more entertaining than stressful. She cackled with glee whenever a collision was hard and loud. "This is so bizarre, I love it. Where else can you intentionally slam into another car? God, I haven't been to the derby since I was a kid."

"Oh, shit, he needs to watch 42. He's trouble. Did you see that? He just went out of bounds and no one noticed. Geez. Where were the officials on that one?"

By the time it was just Nolan and the yellow car, Eve had dislocated her jaw from violent chewing and her palms had ridges from where she had dug her nails into them.

"He's going to win," Tuesday said, looking calm and unconcerned. "He's cleared the field and the other dude still running has two flat tires and his bumper is dragging."

Her stomach hurt. Which was either stress or the eight pounds of taffy her body was trying to digest. She wasn't as confident as Tuesday.

But Nolan won, and when he climbed out of his car and bounced on the hood a few times, fist pumping, she was grinning like a fool. "He is so sexy. Isn't he sexy?" she asked Tuesday.

"Uh, sure, if you say so." Tuesday licked her mitten. "Shit, I got taffy on my glove. But he did drive well, I have to admit."

"He did." Though if she were honest with herself, Eve would have much preferred being down there behind the wheel herself than sitting in the stands. "I'm proud of him."

They started down the steps, heading toward where Nolan was getting his picture taken with his trophy.

The girls in front of them had beaten them to the ropes. One was leaning over, displaying her cleavage. "Hey,

Nolan, can I get an autograph? Right here?" She fondled the top of her breast.

Eve wanted to yank her back by her processed hair, but Tuesday put a hand on her arm. "Chill out. You know it happens all the time in racing, big or small track. Doesn't mean anything."

Except that Eve didn't know how to handle it. She'd never been the prettiest or the sexiest or friendliest. She was used to being passed over for women like the three in front of her, and she didn't understand why Nolan wouldn't have done the same thing. Maybe that's part of what had driven her in competition in her youth. She couldn't compete with the girls and win, but she could with the boys.

"So I'm supposed to just stand here and wait until he's done being fawned over by big-boobed women?"

"Yes."

"Well, that sucks." She felt ridiculous. Like a groupie.

Nolan didn't make it any easier by taking the girl's Sharpie and signing his name on her cleavage. Really? Was he a rock star?

He must have felt the penetrating spikes of her glare because he glanced over at her and smiled. "Hey, cupcake!"

She didn't feel like being cupcaked at the moment. "Congrats," she told him. "You did awesome."

"Thanks." Then his finger came up. "Give me one second."

The girls wanted their picture taken with him and the one turned, cutting Eve off from any further conversation. She stood there feeling moronic as the three girls snuggled up to her husband. This was part of the reason she had sat there at the table and told Imogen she did not want to marry a driver. This was annoying.

When they finally walked away after seven hundred

hours, Nolan kissed Eve on the cheek. Eve forced a smile because she didn't want her petty jealousy to destroy the mood when he'd won the derby.

"Let me get your picture," Tuesday said, her phone up in the air already. "Get close. Hold the trophy between you. I'll put it on my blog."

"Sure." Eve pinned a smile on her face and leaned in to Nolan.

"You're not really jealous of those girls, are you?" he asked in a low voice.

She turned and stared at him. "Of course not. They just seemed a little trampy, that's all."

"Eve, you turned!"

"Sorry." She faced forward and smiled again.

"Because I'm committed to you. I don't cheat. I don't even flirt when I'm with someone."

"I just wish your ass wasn't out there for everyone to see."

"If you want, I'll tattoo your name on my ass."

Eve laughed. "You would not."

"Hell, yeah, I would."

"Eve, now your eyes are closed from laughing!"

"It's not necessary to brand your ass." Though she was starting to think she wouldn't mind a wedding ring. "And if you're going to tattoo me anywhere on you, I don't really think I want to be where you sit down all day."

"Pay attention!" Tuesday said. "Smile."

They smiled. Nolan's hand cupped her ass. Hers cupped his.

"That one's perfect."

Eve wasn't going to argue with that.

NOLAN came into the condo on Tuesday, taking care to remove his shoes and put them in the closet. Eve didn't like shoes in the house. It was a thing she had about germs. He could hear her on the phone bitching someone out. Something about promising a certain amount of advertising and not delivering. She was good at her job. There was no doubt about it. But there was also no denying she hated it. He wished he could offer her a nine-to-five alternative but he couldn't. He could, however, offer her some fun for working so hard.

He had a couple of surprises he hoped she was going to like. It had been a strange and challenging week, but oddly exciting. Living together was a huge adjustment. Neither of them had ever lived with anyone before and Eve was territorial. She was trying to accommodate him, clearing out dresser drawers and a shelf in the bathroom, but it wasn't easy for either of them. But he figured that would be the case whether they had dated for a few weeks or a few years.

At least once a day she got that look in her eye that said she was wondering if they had made a mistake. He hated to see that look. It made him feel like he wasn't working hard enough to please her. Then he felt the same doubts creep over him. Eventually they had to move past that phase of insecurity, when they got totally comfortable with each other and their living circumstances. He didn't think he'd ever feel good about their uneven finances, but there wasn't a whole lot he could do about it. He just needed to learn to manage his money better, because he wasn't underpaid.

Coming up behind her, Nolan kissed her neck. He loved the way she smelled, just a slight hint of perfume, but mostly Eve. He liked that her skin was soft and that when he wrapped his arms around her, his hands landed on her amazing breasts. She kept talking on her cell, but she did arch her hips so that her bottom bumped against him.

Nolan felt an erection spring to life. Maybe he was about to get lucky.

Eve hung up the phone. "He's an idiot. How hard is it to recheck the schedule? He's in charge of promo for a billion-dollar company. He doesn't know it's hot dog Sunday?"

"Guess not." Nolan nuzzled her neck, biting her ear-lobe. "I have a wedding gift for you."

"What?" She whirled around. "We're doing wedding gifts? Why didn't you tell me? I don't have anything for you. God, I suck at this."

"Shh." Nolan put his finger on her lips. He tucked her hair behind her ears because he thought she looked ador-able like that and because it was an amusing game to see how long it would take her to undo it. She hated having her hair tucked.

She must have been distracted by worry over gifts, be-cause she left her hair the way he put it.

"It's just something I wanted to do for you. It doesn't mean you have to reciprocate." He raised his sweatshirt and the T-shirt underneath it to reveal the tattoo he'd just gotten on his chest.

Her jaw dropped nearly to the floor. "You tattooed my name on your chest?"

"Yeah, you requested it not be on my ass so I thought over my heart was appropriate." God, he was so freaking corny these days. But he couldn't help it. He was in love.

"That's . . . big."

It wasn't really that big. Only about two inches with some scrollwork around it. "Your name is short so the let-ters look bigger. If your name was Stephanie we'd have a big tattoo."

She just kept staring at it. Nolan started to think maybe she didn't like it. Great. She kept putting off wedding ring shopping, and now she looked more horrified than im-pressed by his ink.

"Wow. I'm not sure what to say."

Nolan felt deflated. Sometimes he wasn't sure what it was going to take to get a genuine response from Eve. "You don't have to say anything. And you don't have to get my name tattooed on you. It was just something I wanted to do. I also got you this." He handed her a brochure.

She took it and read it, her lips moving. "A driver's experience?"

"Yep. I know that you don't need a lesson in driving, but it's almost impossible for you to drive a car since they're so expensive. Driving vintage isn't the same as a current car, so I talked to the staff and they're okay with you opening it up without the usual training session."

"Wow."

If she said "wow" one more time, he was going to shake her. "I thought it would be fun. A good stress reliever."

"That's really sweet of you," she said, looking absolutely miserable. "You're too good to me. I don't deserve you. I'm a bitch."

He wished she would stop being so hard on herself. "Shush. I don't want to hear that." Couldn't she see that he loved her? Just the way she was?

"I don't have a gift for you. All I have are these stupid postnuptial papers I need you to sign."

Nolan froze. "Come again?"

She turned and grabbed her purse off the dining room table and pulled an envelope out of it. "It's just a standard agreement that the lawyer drew up for us."

He was floored. "So wait a minute. You haven't wanted to talk about a wedding reception or taking a honeymoon. You haven't had time to go ring shopping or think about if you want to change your name or not, but you've had time to whip up a postnuptial agreement with a lawyer?"

Yep, he was seeing red. It hurt. Something bad. To think that she was only half in this marriage at best, it was painful to admit. But it was as clear as the tattoo on his chest that she wasn't sure she wanted any of this. And he would be damned if he would beg or try to talk her into it.

"My dad did it. It's like a form agreement. We just sign it, no big deal."

"So you think I'm after your money? That I have ulterior motives? I don't want your money. In fact, I'm not even comfortable in this perfect condo with your perfect furniture. I want to eat chips on the couch like the working class stiff that I am."

"What are you talking about? This has nothing to do with you wanting my money. I'm not worried about that. This is just standard. It means that we both leave with everything that we each brought to the marriage. It streamlines the process, makes it less complicated."

He loved the way she spoke about their divorce like it was a foregone conclusion. Yanking the envelope out of her hand, he pulled the papers out and unfolded them. He didn't even bother to read it. He had nothing to lose. She was the one with everything material to lose. All he had to give was his heart and he was pretty sure she had just broken that. "Pen."

"What? Nolan, are you okay with this? You didn't even read it."

"Give me a fucking pen."

Her face went pale. She dug in her purse and handed him a pen.

Slapping it on the dining room table, he flipped to the last page and signed his name.

"Don't be upset."

"I'm not upset." He handed her the papers. "I'm done. You were never in this, Eve. And I'm an idiot for thinking that you were." Feeling like his chest was so tight he might have a heart attack, he went down the hall to her bedroom. Grabbing his duffel bag, he stuffed the few clothes he had brought with him into it.

"What the hell are you doing?"

"I'm giving you what you want. Peace and quiet. An end to this inconvenient and embarrassing marriage." He grabbed a fistful of socks and crammed them into the bag. "I'm sorry that I took you to that chapel in Vegas. I thought you were ready for an adventure, for love, but I think I was wrong. Or maybe you are ready, just not with me."

God, he was going to cry. He was going to cry like his nephew Owen if he didn't get the hell out of there.

"So you're just going to leave?"

He stood and met her gaze. "Isn't that what you want? To push me away until I leave and then you can say I'm a jerk and not have to accept any responsibility?"

Her voice trembled. "Asshole."

He'd struck a chord. "Probably. Or maybe just a fool."

And he'd have the tattoo on his chest to remind him of that fact every day.

EVE stared at Nolan's retreating back as he flung his duffel bag over his shoulder, stepped into his shoes, and walked out. She was fighting back tears. What the hell had just happened?

She had ruined her marriage, that's what.

Nolan showed her a tattoo of her name on his chest and gave her a driver's experience and she gave him postnuptial documents?

What the hell was wrong with her?

God, she didn't blame him for leaving. He should leave. She didn't deserve him.

Why had seeing her name in ink paralyzed her like that?

Because she didn't deserve him.

It was the one thing she kept coming back to and had since the very first time he had asked her out.

Feeling like she was going to throw up, she picked up her phone with shaking hands and called her brother. "Elec?" she managed to choke out. "I need to talk to you." Then she officially burst into tears.

CHAPTER
EIGHTEEN

ELEC sat on Eve's deck with her on a glider she had out there. She was leaning against him, bundled up like they were in Antarctica, her hood up and covering half her face. He couldn't claim to be any sort of expert on relationships, but it was safe to say he'd had his doubts about this one from the beginning.

"Maybe you all just skipped a few steps and then didn't know how to recover," he told her now. He'd been surprised when she'd called him, not because her marriage had fallen apart in record time, but by the fact that it had been Nolan who had walked out.

"I just suck, that's all."

"That's not a very productive line of thinking. What did he say to you?"

"That I was never fully in the marriage."

"Do you think there's truth to that?"

"Yeah. I just couldn't trust it. I kept worrying that it was a mistake. I kept waiting for him to change his mind and for it to disappear."

"That was a self-fulfilling prophecy, wasn't it?"

"Yeah." Her voice was scratchy from crying, and even with nothing more than the porch light on them, Elec could see how red her nose was and how puffy her eyes were from sobbing. He'd honestly never seen his sister so upset. She bitched and moaned and berated, but she didn't cry. Nothing ever touched her heart. It would seem Nolan Ford had touched her heart.

"There's no reason the two of you can't work this out."

"How are we supposed to do that? He hates me." She sighed.

"If he hated you he wouldn't have married you. Don't be melodramatic."

"I was born melodramatic."

"Actually, you were probably born cussing. But seriously, are you a quitter? Is that what Eve Monroe is? A quitter?"

"I quit racing."

Elec wasn't sure what to say to that. He put his right hand in his coat pocket and his left around his sister. She was curled up against him like a wet cat. It was the most pathetic thing he'd ever seen. Eve was not a cuddler. "So start driving again. And call up your husband and make this right."

"In order to fix things, I think I have to fix me. There's something wrong with me, you know."

"Stop making excuses. There's something wrong with everyone." If he had learned anything in his life, that was it.

"I asked him to sign a postnuptial agreement after he showed me that he had my name tattooed on his chest."

Oh, Lord. Elec shook her arm a little. "I'm guessing you realize that was bad timing?"

"Yeah. I'm like Rain Man sometimes. I just blurt shit out."

"Do you feel like you need a postnup?" To his mind, that had their father's mark all over it.

"No. I mean, what do I have? A condo and some money in the bank. Nolan doesn't care about any of that stuff. It was Dad's idea."

"Next time, tell Dad to mind his own business. I say you tear the thing up and give it to Nolan so he knows you know he's not after your money."

"Do you think it will work?"

"I think you'd be foolish not to try." He hugged Eve a little closer to him. He wasn't used to seeing her so vulnerable and he wasn't quite sure what to do with it. "I have some good news. Can I share or is this too bad of a time?"

"You're not renewing your wedding vows, are you? Because I might throw up in my mouth."

"No. Tamara and I are adopting a baby. We've been going through the paperwork for a while, and it turns out a mother chose us and we're getting a baby boy in about six weeks, give or take. We get him two days after he's born." Elec was still amazed that his life had played out the way it had. There had been a time when he'd thought he'd never have children. Now he had two stepkids he loved like his own and a baby that would be his and Tamara's on the way. He was happier than he ever could have imagined. He wanted the same for his sister.

She sat up and looked at him. "Are you serious? Oh Elec, that's awesome. I'm so happy for you." She started crying again. "That's wonderful."

Eve had been the only one Elec had told back in his late teens when he'd found out he couldn't have biological children and she had been there for him. To see her so happy for him even in the midst of her own crisis made him realize how grateful he was to have her as a sister. "Thanks, Eve. That means a lot to me. And you'll work this out with Nolan. He loves you. Anyone can see that."

"Then how come I could never see it?"

"'Cuz you're stubborn."

She gave a watery laugh. "Stupid is more like it."

"Just promise me you won't quit the race before the first lap. Give Nolan a shot."

"I promise." She fumbled in her pocket for a tissue. "And it's too bad you're getting a boy. If it was a girl, you could name her after me."

Elec laughed. "What, Motor Mouth Monroe? That still works for a boy."

She smacked his leg and Elec felt satisfied that he had made her feel at least a little better.

Now hopefully she would see her way to making things right with Nolan.

"YOU'VE got yourself a roommate," Nolan told Rhett as he entered his apartment and dropped his bag on the floor. Ironic that Rhett had just moved in two days earlier and here Nolan was back.

"Are you kidding me?" Rhett was lounging on Nolan's couch, tossing popcorn in his mouth.

"Unfortunately, no, I'm not kidding you." Nolan wanted a beer. He wanted to kick something. He wanted his heart removed from his chest and replaced with one that wasn't broken.

Rhett sat up. "What happened?"

"Eve asked me to sign a postnuptial agreement." It still stung. Did she really think he was such an opportunist?

"So?"

"What do you mean, *so*?" Nolan went to the fridge. There had to be beer still in there.

"I mean, isn't that normal? Don't people do that all the time?"

He gave up rooting around the fridge to stare at his brother. "I don't know. Maybe if you're rich."

"Well, isn't her family kind of rich?"

"Yeah. What's your point?"

"It just makes sense to me, that's all. You're not telling me you left because of that?"

"Not exactly. Not just that. But I don't like being thought of as a gold digger. And the truth is, Eve was never on board with this wedding. She said yes in a moment of impulse and she's regretted it ever since."

"Did she tell you that?"

"No. Not in so many words." Nolan snagged a bottle of beer and contemplated chewing the cap off. "Whose side are you on anyway?"

"I'm on the side of love, man."

Nolan raised an eyebrow. "You're stoned again, aren't you?"

"What do you mean, stoned again? I don't smoke, you know that. Maybe that was a little sarcastic, but I'm serious, bro. You have something good here and you're going to put words in your girl's mouth and throw it away because your ego is a little bruised? If it was worth diving into marriage for, it's worth a little effort trying to fix it."

Desperate to find a bottle opener and ignore the truth of what his brother was saying, Nolan nearly tore a drawer out of the cabinet after he yanked on it. "When did you become such a know-it-all?"

"When did you become a quitter?"

He finally found the opener and popped his beer top off with a satisfying clink. "Little fucker."

"Call me what you want, but you're not living here with me. Go back to your wife and fix your shit. Or move back in with Mom and Dad."

Was Rhett serious? "You won't let me stay here? This is my apartment, twerp!"

"You signed the lease over to me."

Unbelievable. Rhett was pulling some tough love crap with him. "Someday when you fall in love, I'm going to laugh at you."

"I can live with that." Rhett leaned his head back and sank some popcorn into his mouth. "I think I have, actually. She's moving in with me."

"Are you serious?" Well, that explained Rhett's odd behavior.

"Yep."

"Wow. Cool." He was happy for Rhett. He was. But it left Nolan no choice but to either fix his shit or move back in with his parents. He'd go to a hotel if he hadn't maxed out his credit card on Eve's party. Or he could always beg one of his sisters for a room.

He decided that was his best bet. He needed a day or two to get his head on straight before he talked to Eve.

His phone buzzed. It was a text from her.

I'm sorry.

That's all it said.

Yeah, he was sorry, too.

EVE took a deep breath and marched into Evan's office. "Hey, Evan, how's it going?"

"Hey, Eve. I heard you took a spin around the track yesterday. Did you have fun?" He was looking at her like he wanted to ask her more. Like he knew she had sobbed herself into a puddle on Elec's lap.

"Yeah, it was a blast." Eve had used the driver's experience package that Nolan had bought for her the day before, and she'd been amazed at how good it felt to be behind the wheel. The freedom had been immense, the joy almost overwhelming. In the two days since Nolan had walked out of her condo, she hadn't slept at all. She had lain in her bed at night, reflecting on her life, her choices, what she really wanted. What was realistic and what was possible. She knew she needed a change, and hitting the track had only cemented that opinion.

So she'd made some decisions. That was step one. By the time she got to step three, she was going to go to Nolan and try to talk to him about a second chance. But first there were a couple of things she needed to do.

"Cool. So what's up? I don't see any to-do list for me in your hand."

"I want you to accept my resignation. I've already spoken with Elec but I wanted to clear it with you." She was done with PR. She was so done, they needed a new word for it.

"What?" Evan looked concerned but not necessarily surprised.

She wasn't finished though. "And I'm asking you to sponsor a car for me to drive in the local circuit."

Now she had his attention. His eyebrows nearly hit the ceiling and the pen he'd been playing with stilled. He grinned. "Well, well. Now that's an interesting proposition. How do I know it's a sound investment?"

"Because I want this bad. I have the skill, you know I do. I'm dying here in a skirt and blouse every day, Ev. I need to do something else."

"I know. You can have the money. I know you'll kick ass."

Her shoulders relaxed. "Thanks. You know I won't squander it."

"I know. And hell, I was telling Kendall in the next few years I want to shift from driver to owner. This is as good of a time as any to test the waters." He stood up. "Shake on it, big sis. This is awesome."

"I hope so. I'm listing my condo for sale this afternoon."

"What? Why?"

"Too expensive. I can rent for a third of the cost, and without a steady income, I need to trim the fat in my budget." Besides, it had been ringing in her ears ever since Nolan had left that her condo was perfect. It was. Which shouldn't be a problem. Except there was none of her in it. It was a magazine photo shoot, not a home.

"Dang, girl, you don't mess around."

"I'm trying not to."

"Have you talked to Nolan?"

"I sent him a text but he didn't answer."

"A text? Eve, come on. Go talk to the guy. He's walking around this garage looking like someone kicked his dog. Or like he lost his wife. Whatever went down between you two needs to be talked about in person. Not in text. Trust me on this. I almost lost Kendall, remember?"

She remembered. Evan and Kendall had nearly given her a full head of gray hair. They'd taken a roundabout way to getting together. "I know. I'm going to talk to him after I meet with the Realtor this afternoon." Then the tattoo artist. Nolan had told her she was only halfway in and he'd been right. She wanted to prove to him that she was all in. One hundred percent.

IT had been two days of absolute hell wondering if he should call Eve. Wishing she would call him. Nolan had been camped out at his sister's house, sleeping on the couch, and waking up to children using him as a jungle gym. His heart started pounding double time when the phone rang and he saw it was her.

"Hello?" Asher was sitting on his chest, but that wasn't the only reason he felt breathless.

"Hi, it's me. Are you busy? Can you talk?"

"I'm not busy. How are you? I . . ." He wanted to say he missed her, because he did, but he wasn't sure if that was what she wanted to hear.

She gave a shuddering breath. "I've been better. But I've made some changes and I want to talk to you about them. I seem to remember you like barbeque. Want to go to dinner with me tonight? It's on me."

His heart started to beat even faster. That was good, right? That she wanted to talk to him? Or was she serving him with divorce papers? If she did, he was going to try with everything in him to talk her out of it. "Hey, I happen to have won a hundred-dollar gift card to a BBQ joint, so what do we say I pick up the tab and you pay the tip?"

"Sure, that sounds good."

"Six?" He wasn't sure he could wait any longer than that.

"Okay, see you then. Text me the address if you don't mind."

"Of course." He paused then he went for it. "I miss you."

"I miss you, too."

That put him in a much better mood. Nolan hung up the phone and tossed Asher upside down, letting her hair dangle over his chest. She giggled.

"Why are you staying with us? Did your apartment burn down or something?"

"No. Eve and I had a little disagreement and I said some things I shouldn't have." Things that he should have thought about more before he had stormed out on her.

"Oh, so you're in a time-out?"

That was one way to put it. "Exactly. Though she just let me out."

Asher's face was starting to turn red so he righted her. She swiped her hair out of her face, then said, "Then you should say you're sorry."

"I aim to." He was going to apologize, then he was going to tell her everything he felt.

Then if he had to he was going to carry her out over his shoulder back to her place and make love to her all night long.

"You should take flowers. My daddy always brings flowers when he's been a jerk to Momma."

"Good call." Flowers didn't really seem like an Eve thing, but he knew how she felt about chocolates. He would pick some up on the way. He was going to win the suck-up award if nothing else.

"And kiss her. Girls like that."

Nolan laughed. "Well aren't you just the expert? Do you want to come and do it for me?" He tickled her stomach. "Huh? Huh?"

Asher laughed, shoving his hands away.

The lightness of the sound matched his new mood.

EVE saw Nolan immediately in the restaurant. He was sitting in a booth by the jukebox, his head down as he studied the menu. Her palms felt sweaty and her body tingled at the sight of him. It hadn't been that long, but she had been certain she'd lost him forever. Just seeing him there, willing to talk to her, made her realize how badly she wanted to keep her marriage. Keep him.

Armed with a stack of papers, she marched over and slid into the seat across from him. "Hey. Thanks for meeting me."

"Hey." He studied her, not quite smiling, but not frowning either. "You look tired."

"I am." She was weary but she was hopeful.

"I'm sorry for the other day. I'm sorry for just bailing on you like that. I should have stayed and talked about it. But I was just caught off guard . . . it hurt me."

Eve felt a pang of regret. "I know. I'm sorry, too. I never cared about the postnup. That was my father's idea. I know you were never motivated by money." She opened the manila folder she had all her documents in. "So I wanted to do this." She held up the agreement and tore it in half. "Gone. I don't need some legal document to trust you." She was tempted to shove it over the candle burning on the table, but with her luck, she'd set the restaurant on fire.

He nodded. "Thanks. I appreciate that. I would never in a million years take anything from you that was yours."

"I know." Her throat felt tight and tears were threatening to form, but she forged ahead. "So, I wanted you to be the first to see this." She put her resignation letter in front of him.

"What . . ." He scanned the paper then looked up at her in astonishment. "You're quitting your job?"

"Yes. I'm not happy there. You know it, and I know it. I was just afraid before. But you and me . . . it taught me that taking risks sometimes brings the greatest rewards."

His gaze dropped to the paper and she suspected she'd disarmed him. When he looked up, his own eyes were a little damp looking.

"I'm proud of you," he told her, his voice rough and low. "I think this is great. You deserve so much more happiness."

She nodded, touched, but wanting to get this all out before she lost it. "And then there's this." She flipped through the stack to the papers from her real estate agent. "I listed the condo for sale an hour ago. I need to downsize my mortgage now that I won't be taking in a biweekly salary."

"Your condo? Are you sure?"

"Yeah. The market is recovering and I should turn a profit. It's too much for me at this point in my life, and it's a little, well, too perfect."

He shook his head. "No, no, I didn't mean that the way it sounded. That was so rude of me. I was just upset. Please don't sell the condo unless it's what you really want."

"It is. I'm not going to lie, I'm a little terrified that I quit my job, but I want a smaller place, something that I can make homey instead of a designer showcase." She took a big breath. "Which brings me to what I will be doing for a living. Evan is sponsoring a car for me. I'm going to hit the local circuit and see if I can crack into the national level."

His face split into a grin. "No kidding? Eve, that's awesome!"

"Thanks. I may suck and fail miserably, but I'll never know unless I try, right?"

"Exactly. God, that's fantastic. We break up and two days later you have your whole life rearranged. I've just been laying on the couch feeling sorry for myself."

"Did we break up?" she asked before she lost her nerve.

"Can I get you a drink, sweetie?" the waitress asked, her pen over her pad.

Seriously? "Um, just an iced tea, please. Thanks."

"You got it."

Eve refocused on Nolan, trying to read his expression. "Because I'm kind of hoping we didn't break up. I love you. I really, really do, and I don't want to worry anymore. I just want to live my life. With you. Not perfect. Not tidy. But happy."

There. That was it. Her whole speech. She didn't have anything else to say that wouldn't just muddy the waters.

But Nolan wasn't saying anything. He was just staring at her. She swallowed nervously.

"If we did break up and you want it to be that way, I had papers drawn up for you to look at . . ." Eve was sweaty. She felt a little sick. A lot sick. But she wanted him to know that she wanted to respect and honor his wishes. "I wanted to make this easy for you because I know I haven't made anything easy." She pulled the final papers out. A divorce petition. "I don't want . . ." She forced herself to shut up. It didn't matter what she wanted.

Nolan picked up the papers and glanced at them. Then he ripped them in half. Then again in quarters. "I don't want a divorce, Eve. What I want is you. That's what I've always wanted."

Relief had her gripping the edge of the table. "Really? Are you sure?"

"I asked you that on our wedding night and you said yes. Now my answer is the same. Cupcake, I've been in love with you since you took out that target at the fair five times in a row and handed out stuffed animals to kids like it was nothing. A chick who shoots and makes my heart race? I was sold."

The waitress appeared with her drink. Lord, the woman had bad timing.

"I love you, Eve."

The waitress's eyes went wide.

"I love you, too." Now she was crying like the girl that she was.

Nolan stood up and said, "I hope you're not really hungry."

"No." Eve shook her head.

"Grab your papers." He threw a twenty down.

"What . . ." The waitress looked confused.

Eve shoved the papers in her purse. Then shrieked when Nolan picked her up into his arms.

"It might not be the threshold, but it's a BBQ joint, which is even better."

She grabbed his cheeks and kissed him. "Strongman, you are hot."

"Let's go home and do it in your bedroom before it gets sold."

Eve laughed. "I have something to show you. A new tattoo on my thigh."

His eyebrows shot up. "You don't have to ask me twice."

NOLAN stared at Eve's inner thigh and started laughing. "Cupcake, you crack me up. I can't believe you did that."

She went up on her elbows, her hair flowing over her naked chest. "I wanted you to see that I'm not halfway into this relationship. I'm all the way in."

"I appreciate the visual reminder." Her old tattoo had a new companion. It now read: NOLAN'S DINER. OPEN 24 HOURS.

It was a nice little block, like a real diner sign. He bit it, then sucked her warm skin into his mouth. He loved her sense of humor. He loved her.

"I'm about to be all the way in, too," he told her, moving up over her body. He had planned to suckle her clit a bit, but he found he couldn't wait. He wanted inside her.

When he pushed inside her wet and welcoming body, Nolan paused, wanting to study her, capture the perfection of the moment. His wife was beautiful.

Her finger came up and traced her name over his heart. *I love you*, she mouthed silently.

And nothing else mattered.

Turn the page for a special preview of
Erin McCarthy's new contemporary romance
as she returns to Cuttersville, Ohio

Coming in 2013 from Berkley Sensation!

PIPER Tucker heard the footsteps on the hardwood floor of the parlor and smiled. "Lilly or Emily, whichever twin you are, it is bedtime. No more glasses of water, no more back rubs, no more excuses."

She turned, expecting to see one or both of her eight-year-old cousins she was babysitting. Well, they technically weren't her cousins, since they were the children of Piper's father's ex-wife and her second husband, but that was too complicated for a town like Cuttersville, Ohio. They just called each other cousins.

Only it wasn't cousins coming into the room, biological or otherwise.

It was a ghost.

Dang it. Piper had been hoping to spend the whole weekend in the house without seeing a single dead person, and here she'd only been there for three hours and already a spectral woman was staring at her. The entity wore a poke bonnet, a dusky mauve gown with a braided pelisse, and button boots. Young, her shadowy face was free of lines or blemishes, and the eyes set in that pale, ethereal frame were deep, thick black. Funeral black. Filled with sorrow. This ghost was Rachel, a woman who had died nearly a hundred and fifty years before of an opium overdose after bludgeoning her indiscreet fiancé.

Piper knew the story about Rachel from her Aunt Shelby, her father's ex-wife and the owner of the house. Piper knew that's who she was seeing because she'd encountered the murderess a half-dozen times or more since childhood.

"Hi, Rachel. Is there something I can do for you tonight?" Piper fought a sigh. Seeing the pain on the vision's face, sensing her sorrow and confusion, always made Piper feel a little sick to her stomach. Guilty that she was the one ghosts came to, and yet she didn't know what to do to help them.

Rachel didn't move, but the sound of a foot stamping on the floor echoed around the room, ringing loudly in the quiet dark. The one lamp Piper had been using to read a gardening magazine flickered off and back on.

"What's the matter? If you'd tell me how to help you, maybe I could." When she was a kid, ghosts had actually talked to her, unless her memory was playing tricks on her. She could swear she'd had whole conversations with the people who had appeared in front of her randomly and without warning. But now they never said anything, not Rachel, not the other various spirits she saw around town.

In her teens, Piper had taken to begging them to leave her alone, to go away and bug someone else, but now that she was older, she couldn't bring herself to shoo a soul who'd been restless for more than a century. Piper still wanted to be left alone. She still wanted to be normal, to blend into the town and into her family, until no one remembered she had ever lived anywhere but Cuttersville.

Seeing ghosts was her secret. But she didn't yell at them anymore.

Arms stretched out, reaching for her. Eyes beseeched with aching intensity.

"Tell me how to help. I don't understand what you want." Piper gripped the back of the sofa she was sitting on, her throat closing up. She remembered what it was like to feel lonely, vulnerable. Before Piper's father had taken her in when she was eight, she had been unwanted and unloved by her stepfather, and sometimes it didn't take much to drag all those feelings right back up to the surface.

"She did it." The words came from Rachel even though her lips didn't move. Even though the sound seemed to flow and ebb and surround Piper like a cloud, misty and shifting.

A clap of thunder made Piper jump on the couch. It had been threatening to rain all day, and she figured this was appropriate timing. "Who did what?"

This was why she hated being the weirdo who attracted more ghosts than a graveyard on Halloween. Most days she didn't even do all that well with people who were still alive. She certainly had no social skills when it came to the dead. And she couldn't exactly invite Rachel to sit down and have some iced tea and tell her all about it.

"She did it."

Okay. Piper needed a little more to go on than that.

Before Piper could ask for clarification, a knock on the front door had her sitting straight up. "Geez, oh Pete." Would anyone else like to startle the heck out of her? She was not a jumpy sort, but she didn't like being caught unaware.

Clutching her chest, she stood up, patting her pocket to make sure she still had her cell phone. Rachel was already dissipating. The spirit didn't like Shelby's husband, Boston, and made a hobby out of tossing plates at him from time to time, but as far as Piper knew, no one had actually seen the ghost but her. Rachel wouldn't appreciate a visitor.

The clock on the wall glowed ten-oh-three and Piper hesitated as she headed for the door. It was awfully late for anyone to be stopping by, and Boston and Shelby had gone to Cincinnati for the whole weekend.

A quick glance through the peephole showed a man's head, too distorted for Piper to identify him. His head and shoulders looked rain-soaked, which earned some sympathy. But while Piper was compassionate, she wasn't a complete idiot.

"Can I help you?" she called through the door, hand on her cell phone button in case he axed his way through to her and a call to 911 was needed.

"Shel, it's Brady. Let me in, damn it. I'm drowning out here."

Brady. The name brought a rush of pleasure she wasn't all that sure she was entitled to.

"Brady?" she said in astonishment. Glancing down at her pajama shorts and tank top, she grimaced. Not exactly what she wanted to be wearing when encountering the man of her childhood dreams, but she opened the door anyway. "What are you doing here?"

"Standing on the damn porch . . ." Brady Stritmeyer locked eyes with hers, his expression surprised. "Hi, uh, sorry, I thought you were Shelby. Is she or Boston here?"

He didn't recognize her. That was a little deflating even

as Piper reasoned Brady hadn't seen her in twelve years, since she was all of eleven years old and he had been eighteen, preoccupied with getting out of Cuttersville.

"They're in Cincinnati for the weekend and I'm baby-sitting the twins. I don't think they were expecting you." Piper moved to the side. "Come on in out of the rain."

It had been more than a decade since she'd seen him in person, but over the years she'd seen photos of him from visits Shelby and Boston and the kids had with Brady in Chicago. She'd always had a crush on him. Always thought he was good-looking. But in the flesh he had a presence that a picture couldn't express.

A head taller than her, he had short, dark brown hair and a rangy, muscular frame. Droplets of water trailed down his temple and dripped off his stern chin. She couldn't see his eyes in the hazy darkness of the porch, but she knew they were green. Many a pubescent fantasy of hers had been built around those green eyes.

"This is really embarrassing," he said with a half smile. "But you obviously know who I am and I don't recognize you." He stepped into the house, glanced around the hallway, turned back to her, and shrugged. A charming grin flashed at her. "I was thinking about faking it, but you look like you're already onto me."

"That's okay. You've been gone a long time." And never once in twelve years had he come back to visit. Piper wondered why he had now, without even calling his family first.

She tucked her long hair behind her ear and leaned on the door she closed. "I'm Piper Tucker."

His eyebrow shot up. "Little Piper? Danny Tucker's daughter?"

When she nodded, he ran his eyes over her, looking a little more closely than she was comfortable with. He smelled like rain, his shoes squeaking on the hardwood floor, and God, she did not want him to see in her face that she'd once cared about him. Wanted him to sweep her off her feet and make her his wife, with the sort of vagueness toward details that thirteen-year-olds are so good at.

"Damn," he said. "You've done some growing since the last time I saw you." He held his palm out in front of his waist. "You couldn't have been much more than this tall when I left."

Plucking at her tank top, trying to pull it lower over her stomach, Piper gave a nervous laugh. "Well, I was only eleven and I was always kind of short." Puberty had come late for her, which the pediatrician had speculated could have been the result of poor nutrition in her early developmental years.

"It looks like it all worked out for you in the end. You turned out just fine, Piper."

Well. That was probably meant to be a compliment, but it landed on her ears offensively. Like while he wouldn't go so far as to call her pretty, she should be lucky she hadn't turned out plain old ugly either. Piper had never had any illusions about her attractiveness. She'd always been gangly and awkward, with eyes too big for her head. A head that had been bald from age six to nine, with hair long enough to ruffle not appearing until she was nearly eleven.

No, she'd never been beautiful like her stepmother, Amanda, but hearing Brady's offhand remark drew out a vulnerability she hated. It lived in her all the time, those deep-rooted childhood insecurities, but most of the time, she ignored them. Having them rise now made her frustrated.

"Thanks," she said briefly, afraid to say anything more.

Brady popped his head into the parlor. "Damn, this place hasn't changed one bit. A new couch, maybe, but everything else is the same. So, the kids all asleep? Is Zach in his room watching TV? I'll go hang with him for a while."

"He's actually spending the night at a friend's house. At fourteen, the idea of spending the weekend with his little sisters and a babysitter was just too mortifying, I guess. He'll be around during the day tomorrow."

Brady was wandering into the parlor, so Piper followed him. He had pulled a doily off an occasional table and was twirling it around on his finger. "Well, at least this way I won't have to sleep on the floor."

Piper crossed her arms over her chest, distracted by the way his jeans clung to his backside. "What do you mean?"

"I can sleep in Zach's bed tonight."

It took her a second, but when his words filtered through her brain, Piper bit her lip nervously. "You're spending the night?"

"Yep. It's too late to go to my grandmother's. I don't want to wake her up. And I don't get along with my father, so I'm not exactly welcome there. My sister Heather moved to Cincinnati when her husband couldn't find a job here." He held his arms out, doily included, and smiled, a charming, confident smile. "Sorry. You're stuck with me."

Oh, Lord. That's what she was afraid of.

A completely innocent slumber party with Brady Stritmeyer.

That was called a cruel irony.

BRADY set the doily down as Piper gave him a very forced smile. Clearly, she wasn't thrilled about the idea of him spending the night. He wasn't sure why it mattered. He was thirty years old—it wasn't like he needed her to cook for him or anything. Maybe she'd planned on painting her nails or waxing her bikini line and couldn't if he was hanging around.

But even if he had another place to stay, he wasn't sure he wanted to go anywhere. It was fascinating to watch Piper, to study all the changes twelve years had brought to her face and her body.

Jesus, her body. She had just that right combination of curves that told a man this was definitely a woman, without being overblown and distracting. Her little cotton shorts were hugging her round ass, and despite the fact that she kept crossing her arms over her chest, he had seen the outline of her full breasts. Caught a glimpse of her taut nipples.

And when she'd first opened the door, and the light from the hallway had hovered behind her, all that hair had tumbled down over her shoulders and breasts and he'd felt a kick of sexual awareness. An instant attraction.

Now that he knew it was Piper Tucker, the hair amazed him even more. He remembered her as a shy little girl clinging to her father, her bald head covered with a hat all the time. No wonder he hadn't recognized her.

Piper was a sensual, exotic woman now.

"Sit down with me, Piper, and tell me what you've been up to for the last twelve years." Brady dropped onto the couch and patted the seat next to him. He would behave himself now that he knew who she was. He was confused enough about his life without dragging someone else into it, and Piper was too young for him anyways.

Not to mention that her father was bigger than he was.

Yet it annoyed him when she sat in the chair across from him, instead of on the couch. She crossed her legs and hugged them to her chest and shrugged.

"Well, you know, there was middle school and high school. Then college. Now I'm one of the two kindergarten teachers at the grade school."

"Hey, that's cool. You must like kids if you teach school and still babysit on the weekends."

"Well, Boston and Shelby are like family, and I love Emily and Lilly. I like spending time with them. And it's only the first week in September, so school's only been in for two weeks. I've had all summer to rest." She gave him a shy smile that challenged his decision to be nothing more than an affectionate cousinly sort to her.

Women in Chicago didn't smile like that. At least not those he worked with day in and day out at the marketing firm. Professional women were confident, aggressive, independent. He liked that.

But he liked that smile on Piper's face, too. More than he should.

"How are your dad and mom?" he asked. He'd seen Amanda a few years back when she'd been visiting her father in Chicago, but they had talked mostly about the city, what were the good restaurants to hit, and Brady's job. Amanda had only briefly mentioned that Piper was in college, and Brady hadn't given much thought to what was going on back here in Cuttersville.

It felt odd to be back home, in a house that hadn't changed, even as everything around it had. Brady had thought that he would be swamped with emotion when he came back after his self-imposed exile, but really so far he'd felt nothing but a mild sort of pleasure and curiosity.

"Great. My dad's looking at a good crop this year, and Amanda sort of has her hands in everything. She raises pure-bred poodles and is president of the PTA at my brothers' school."

That was kind of a humorous image. When Brady had first met Amanda fifteen years earlier, she had been a bored rich girl. "No kidding? And what about you, Piper? You living in town now? Got a boyfriend or a husband or anything?"

It would be easier if she did. Stop him from thinking thoughts about her naked body he shouldn't be thinking.

But a hint of color rose in her cheeks. "No, no boyfriend or fiancé. And I still live with my parents in the farmhouse. I guess that sounds kind of lame, doesn't it? Especially to someone like you who left home right out of high school."

He'd left home all right, chomping at the bit to get the hell out of Cuttersville. And twelve years later he was starting to wonder what he'd been running from. The success he'd wanted, expected to find in Chicago or New York, hadn't arrived, and he had given up painting altogether a year ago. It hurt to pick up a pencil or brush and know that he couldn't replicate on paper what he saw in his mind.

"If you're happy, then there's nothing lame about it."

She nodded. Then said, "Do you want me to put your shirt in the dryer? The shoulders are soaking wet."

He'd forgotten about the damp cotton clinging to his skin. The house didn't have air-conditioning, and it was still summer temperatures. He wasn't cold. But neither was he going to refuse a perfectly legit chance to take his shirt off in front of her and see her reaction.

"Thanks." Brady peeled it off, and wondered what the hell he was doing. Hadn't he just told himself this girl— seven big long years younger than him—was off-limits? And here he was going for the flirt.

But he supposed every man had a bad habit. Some drank, others smoked, quite a few gambled to excess, and hell, some did all three. His weakness was women. He liked to flirt, liked to make women smile and laugh. He loved to wine and dine and sixty-nine a woman. Nothing wrong with that if both parties knew the score. Brady wasn't the settling-down kind. He had been born restless, and this trip back to nowheres-ville for no good reason was further proof of that.

So he bunched up his shirt and stood, stretching a little so she had a good shot of the pecs and his ripped stomach. All those hours at the gym should be worth something. "The dryer still in the basement? I'll just toss it in."

Piper's eyes had gone wide. He was almost sorry he'd stripped the T-shirt off. She looked horrified, not flirtatious. But then her eyes dropped down, just a little, and she ran her tongue across thick, plump lips. "Oh, I'll get it," she said, her voice a sweet, husky whisper.

Damn, he knew that look, felt that vibe, could practically smell the attraction that had sprung up between them. Good thing the twins were upstairs sleeping, or he'd be severely tempted to taste Piper Tucker from tip to toe.

This was not a woman he could fool around with.

It was a mantra he was going to have to repeat all week long. Along with the friendly little reminder to himself that Shelby would tear his head off, and Danny Tucker would rip something even more important off him if they found out he was fooling around with Piper. And Amanda? Hell, she might be the worst of all. She wouldn't tear something off Brady, she'd string him up by his nuts, spray him with honey, and let the bees at him.

Piper was extra special to them because Danny hadn't known she existed until she was eight years old.

Not a woman he should be messing around with. Repeat ten times twice daily and maybe it would sink in.

Yet he still found himself moving in just a little too close to her when he handed over the shirt. "That's sweet of you. I left my travel bag in the trunk."

"No problem. I . . ." Piper looked over his shoulder.

"What?" Brady half turned, expecting to see one of the kids standing in the doorway. Good thing he hadn't given into his very inappropriate urge to kiss her.

"Nothing." Piper darted her eyes back to him. Then behind him again. Her cheeks flushed. Her head tilted, sending her hair cascading over her forehead and right eye.

"What are you looking at?" She obviously saw something back there. "A mouse?"

"No. Nothing." Step one, step two, she shifted around to his side and stood stiffly, tugging her tank top down again.

Then Brady knew what it was. What he'd forgotten about Piper Tucker from all those years ago, the summer he had been fifteen and she'd arrived in town.

"You still see ghosts, don't you?"

Piper stared at Brady in astonishment. "I . . . I . . . don't have any idea what you're talking about."

Only she wasn't all that great of a liar. She couldn't even look him in the eye as she spoke.

But she wasn't about to admit that a ghost of a man with blond hair was standing right behind Brady, smiling and nodding his head up and down.

"Come on, Piper. I remember. You used to ask me to draw pictures for you. Pictures of the ghosts you saw."

Dang. Why would he remember something like that? And why were they having this conversation while he wasn't wearing a shirt? She had almost whimpered when he'd exposed his chest to her. Brady had filled out a bit in the last twelve years. In all the right places.

"I was just a kid. I had an active imagination." Her parents had forgotten about her imaginary friends and ghost sightings. Or at least, they never mentioned them to her anymore. It wasn't something Piper ever wanted to discuss with anyone, least of all Brady Stritmeyer, a lifelong crush she clearly hadn't quite gotten over.

"Bullshit," he said.